OLYMPIA
THE BIRTH OF THE GAMES

The Illustrated Edition

J.A. Martino & M.P. O'Kane

OLYMPIA
THE BIRTH OF THE GAMES

Foreword by Professor Alexis Lyras
Illustrated by

Addison & Highsmith

Addison & Highsmith Publishers
Las Vegas ◊ Chicago ◊ Palm Beach

Published in the United States of America by
Histria Books
7181 N. Hualapai Way, Ste. 130-86
Las Vegas, NV 89166 USA
HistriaBooks.com

Addison & Highsmith is an imprint of Histria Books. Titles published under the imprints of Histria Books are distributed worldwide.

Library of Congress Control Number: 2024931032

ISBN 978-1-59211-428-3 (softbound)
ISBN 978-1-59211-443-6 (eBook)

FOREWORD

"And as in the Olympic Games it is not the most beautiful and the strongest that are crowned but those who compete (for it is some of these that are victorious), so those who act win, and rightly win, the noble and good things in life."

-Aristotle, *Nicomachean Ethics*

From the philosophers of antiquity, Socrates, Plato, Zeno, and Aristotle, to the visionaries of the modern Games, Evangelos Zappas, Ioannis Fokianos, William Penny Brookes, Demetrios Vikelas, and Pierre De Coubertin, the richness of the Olympic heritage and ancient Hellenic civilization, also known as Olympism, has served as a source of inspiration and a point of reference for imagining a better, more peaceful world. I was fortunate enough to grow up around, learn and serve these ideals throughout my life as an athlete, actor, coach, policy maker and public intellectual, committed to preserving and re-infusing this heritage in order to meet the challenges of the modern world. From my days studying under an IOC scholarship to my early years in academia as a sports management professor committed to 'Olympism in Action' scholarship, to becoming the founder and president of the Olympism for Humanity Alliance, to my many trips to ancient Olympia itself with students and faculty from many continents, eager to learn and be inspired by the significance of the Olympic Games — both ancient and modern — the first and oldest peace-building institution in human history.

I was born and raised in a region with a long history of conflict. I have had the opportunity to experience warfare, hatred, and division — I have witnessed mass displacements firsthand and developed a lifelong commitment to understanding the complexities of peace and conflict. Growing up in Cyprus, in a family environment strongly influenced by the triptych of athleticism, Olympian heritage and giving, these values have shaped the core of my sociological imagination and political philosophy foundations over the thirty years of my academic journey. These foundations have provided me with the tools and the vehicle to design and deliver Olympism-driven inspirational ventures across fragile communities and regions of conflict. The core of this platform was grounded in what I now call Olympism for Humanity *praxis* (or in action). It has been further guided by the richness of ancient Hellenic civilizational ideals, blended with humanism and contemporary bodies of knowledge that embrace peacebuilding, personal and community resilience, human creativity and social innovation, international co-operation, and global cross-cultural dialogue. My scholarship and fieldwork were based on one proposition — that this Olympic ethos and heritage can serve as both a universal platform and a peacebuilding process to address the many challenges of our current century. In other words, I argue (and practice what I preach) that the more we understand and connect with the depth of Olympic ideals and heritage — enriched today with contemporary Sport for Development Theory and Olympism for Humanity praxis — the more we can transform today's 'Olympic divide' into pathways for an 'Olympic divine' that triggers imagination, inspiration and human creativity. This is a proven pathway for regeneration, peace-building, and recovery across continents.

On March 11, 2020, I met John Martino at the birthplace of the Olympic ideal, ancient Olympia itself, during the Tokyo 2020 Games Torch Lighting Ceremony. This date was chosen by the Tokyo 2020 organizing committee to honor the victims of the March 11, 2011, great East Japan earthquake — and helped spread, in this way — a message of hope, resilience, and recovery. The following day, John, my students, and I attended the Lighting Ceremony and the first stages of the Torch Relay while talking about this book you now hold before you and our shared vision. We began exploring synergies for doing more to restore the origins and the hidden treasures of the Olympian heritage — as a vehicle of hope and inspiration — as well as being a form of psychological recovery from man-made and natural disasters. A few hours later, the World Health Organization announced that COVID-19 was characterized as a pandemic; the Torch Relay was canceled, and the world was put into complete lockdown. Looking back, this can be seen as an opportunity and a call for action (guided by our Muses) to reconnect, re-imagine and spread Pelops's message and ideals — from Delphi to Olympia, from Tokyo to Melbourne, from Colorado Springs to Georgetown and beyond — across the globe. This novel is a tribute to this heritage, especially given the current global need for dreaming the ideal and for imagining a better world whose sources of inspiration transcend isolated pockets of humanity to become modern-day heroines and heroes for us all. The sporting stars of this novel operate as active and engaged global citizens who perform generous deeds, overcome life's challenges, and build bridges of hope, resilience, and prosperity. Humanity needs narratives that are rich in the wealth of human learning — with both anthropological and historical soundness — expressed in a language that can be relevant and universal.

All these elements were brilliantly crafted into this novel. As we enter the post-COVID-19 new beginning for our world, this book — filled with the light of Olympia — is needed more than ever. It is a source of inspiration and a platform for the imagination, hope, and global action. Thank you, Mick and John, Drs. O'Kane and Martino, for this outstanding contribution and for giving me the privilege to introduce your great endeavor. As for the readers — the future Olympic dreamers, visionaries, believers, fans, and sportspeople — I wish you all an Olympism-inspired, life-long journey of action towards a better world. Let the hope, imagination and divine essence of Olympia light your way — in theory and through personal application. Enjoy the ride!

Alexis Lyras, PhD
Georgetown University
Olympism for Humanity Alliance

PROLOGUE

Olympia, 1881 C.E.

Under a blazing midday sun, three men emerged from a copse of olive trees. Sweat dripped from their brows as they strode through knee-high grass toward a large patchwork of the countryside. Ahead lay a series of excavation plots of varying depths neatly divided by peg and rope. Equipped with spades, trowels, and prospector hammers, an archaeological field crew bustled around these plots. From within the dig pit of a large, partially exposed stadium, an archaeologist glanced up at the sweat-bedecked newcomers, only to resume his burrowing.

Dressed in fashionable blazers, two of these new arrivals had made no concession to the sweltering heat. They followed an elderly local man who was much more comfortably attired. The deep sun-bronzing of his face highlighted light flecked eyes that twinkled with excitement. Turning toward one of the perspiring, mustachioed men, he declared, 'Yes, Baron, we are here.'

Beaming with pleasure, the baron nodded at the guide, turning then to his weary companion. 'At last — Olympia!' he exclaimed with a pronounced French accent.

His fellow aristocrat, an Englishman, replied, 'Let us hope it was worth the effort, Baron. These Germans…' sweeping his arm around to indicate the archaeological team behind them '…seem to have cleared very little.'

Unable to contain his pride, the Greek guide interrupted, 'Yes, the Germans move slowly and carefully, but the true story of Olympia is not to be found in these old stones they chip away at. It is in the memories of my people — what you educated men would call myths and legends.'

The baron turned back to the guide, 'You promised us that story when we reached this site. We have followed that promise a long way.'

Flashing a grin, the guide ushered them towards some tree-shaded rubble, 'Yes, yes, I did promise. And I am a man of my word. First, though, take my flask — you two look like sardines out of water.'

Gratefully, the Englishman accepted fluid from the guide, although the baron strode through the rubble and settled himself. He was eager for the guide's tale.

Ensuring that the English gent was also seated, the guide then stood before both men, 'My country has known many periods of great misfortune. One of these is now remembered as the Greek Dark Ages. After the fall of legendary Troy, Greek fought against Greek for hundreds of years. The carving on these stones around us was young then, and the sacred site of Olympia stood firm, but all else was in chaos. We had no central government, no unity, no shared national identity, and my ancestors had lost much — even the art of reading and writing had been forgotten. It was a time of great terror and rivers of blood, a time when few good men stood tall, and even patriots like the great poet Homer wandered blind and alone.

From this part of Greece, from Olympia herself, something extraordinary was born. Although the Greek cities around her were forever in combat — Elis and Pisa to the north, Sparta to the south — one young Greek who lived here chose not to go to war. He stood apart from it all. He stood against the conflict. He defied everyone: his father, the Spartans, even the foreigners who then pulled the strings of Sparta, the Phoenicians, rulers of the Mediterranean from their mighty city of Carthage in North Africa. He defied them, but not with violence. It was his idea of peace that triumphed. The name of this almost forgotten hero was Pelops…'

I

A top a densely treed hill, a high-ranking Spartan, evident from the quality of his armor, watched with hooded eyes consuming all below. Every inch of ground was carefully examined; nothing escaped his gaze. Flinging back his travel-stained scarlet cloak, he maneuvered his warhorse towards the looming trees to ensure concealment, while below him, two opposing armies began to form up on a dry, flat plain. Sent by the twin kings of Sparta to descry this battle, the grizzled veteran was himself keen to see how this new style of warfare — said to be the deadliest ever engaged in — would play out between these bitter rivals.

Ψ

Packed within a body of grim-faced men pleading to the gods or cursing their fate, a young man prepared to face his first battle. Like many of his comrades, he was no professional soldier or hardened mercenary. He was just another reluctant target for the spear and sword of the foe. Caught up in endless wars of domination, the Greek royalty, often little more than empowered brutal children, spent the blood of these common men like so much liquid gold. The young combatant-to-be, Koroibos, knew this better than most. As head cook to Iphitos, king of Elis, he had experienced both the generosity and mercurial whims of a monarch first hand. Temperamental by caste and character, Koroibos mused, a king could raise a man above all others while he is in favor and still send him to die in battle on an impulse. In Koroibos's case, one careless remark was all it had taken. Even now, he could not believe his own stupidity.

'If you could fight like you cook, young Koroibos, we would bring Pisa to its knees in a heartbeat,' King Iphitos had slurred to him at the banquet table only scant days before.

'I would welcome an opportunity to impale those Pisatan pigs upon my spit for you, Lord,' Koroibos had boasted in the belief that so long as the king was enjoying his table, he was safe from any actual fighting.

This belief proved in vain when the wine-befuddled regent lurched upright, declaring to his court, 'See what men we grow in Elis — even our cooks thirst for the glory of battle. How can we lose with men like this? Koroibos, you shall carry your king's spear into our next battle and honor us all.'

From there, the nightmare only worsened. After the hellish basic training, with barely time enough for bruises to heal, let alone acquire even any modest martial confidence, Koroibos was convinced that the impending day of battle between Elis and Pisa would be his last. With the king having all but forgotten his decree, he was just another body lost in the press of a formation of hundreds, all of whom were expected to fight and die for their city and its ruler.

Their march called to a halt, Koroibos and his fellow warriors stood jammed together within a rectangular battle array, positioned at one end of the Great Plain of Olympia, itself roughly equidistant between the cities of Elis and Pisa. The ragtag army of Pisa darkened the other end of the field. Tradition, as always, had dictated the choice of site; this field had drunk much ancestral blood: the rival kings would again seek to quench its thirst. The battle formation of Elis stood dutifully frozen, with just the odd man here and there swaying from fear or the first signs of heat exhaustion. Their battered armor and shields refracted the sun's bright rays through the thick swirls of dust that eddied around them. Finally came the cry Koroibos dreaded — King Iphitos screamed, 'Advance!' The Elean warriors shuffled forward, their accompanying panpipe musicians disguising the dry hollowness of the battle paean they began to chant.

As row after row of combatants advanced, huge billowy clouds of dust sprang up to join the dust swirls already aroused by the wind. To a man, the Eleans coughed or spat. Many had drunk deeply from wine flasks to allay their terror; these wine-parched throats soon became their most immediate regret.

Raw fear tinged with sweat and the stench of fresh vomit assailed their nostrils, while the outside world, limited to what they could see through the narrow eye slits of their helmets, became a place of murky dread. Soon the false bravado of their battle chanting sounded more like the bleating of goats, even to their own ears, while that of their enemies reached the crescendo of baying wolves at the climax of the hunt.

Koroibos stumbled along, gripping and re-gripping his long spear while trying to maintain the marching discipline so new to him and so foreign to his nature. Elbowed and shouldered by more seasoned warriors, he struggled not to foul the moving forest of spear shafts that loomed above with his own upright weapon as the two enemy formations drew slowly closer to their moment of impact. Locked within this press of warriors, he wondered what good he was to these hard men or how he could survive the clash without disgracing himself and his family. Never one to put too much faith in the Immortals of Mount Olympos, he found it increasingly difficult to believe that Aries, fearsome Lord of War, would favor a cook over his dedicated warriors. 'O Gods, I need to spill my water,' he moaned, sacrilegiously.

Overheard by the Elean keeping step beside him, the veteran glanced at the outline of a cooking pot painted on Koroibos's battered helmet and chuckled, 'Just nerves, cook. We all need to dampen the ground right about now. Welcome to the pointy end.'

Koroibos began to feel his face burn from embarrassment, knowing the veteran had his measure by the helmet's insignia, the inescapable sign of a press-ganged civilian. Yet such was Elis's need of fighting men that Koroibos found himself in the fires of combat rather than in the heat of the kitchen, where he belonged. This reality of battle was already a far cry from the oft-drunken braggadocio he had heard from the old men crafting their warrior reputations in the taverns back home. He decided there and then that he would not follow their example. If, of course, he was lucky enough to grow old as they had.

The veteran shoved an elbow into his ribs and yelled above the din of stamping, chanting men, 'Get a hold of yourself. Didn't you hear our king? Time to kill, time to maim! Let's show these Pisatan cowards what the men of Elis are made of!'

Dropping his twelve-foot spear to the horizontal plane and tucking its haft beneath his armpit, Koroibos imitated the battle-ready maneuver of those around him. His spear-tip was threaded through the ranks of those before him to help form a wall of staggered, deadly steel, while the buckler he grasped with his other arm protected the man on his immediate left.

Under the harsh Hellenic sun, the armies of Elis and Pisa stood ready to initiate a radical form of close-combat warfare that was dependent upon discipline and blind courage. Unbeknownst to the combatants, who had simply submitted to what they thought was a new training regime implemented by hired Spartan instructors, this battle would mark the dawn of phalanx warfare. The full extent of the changes the Spartan trainers had wrought now become visible to the men of the Elean front line, as neither they nor their Pisatan counterparts were ordered to break formation to prepare for the usual melee of small group and single combat, but continued to advance right into the protruding spears. The all-enveloping clouds of dust helped obscure this brutal reality until the last possible moment. Having trained their charges to believe that this ramming tactic was merely designed to intimidate their foe, the Spartan instructors — delighted with the additional cloaking effect of the dust clouds — failed to arrest these juggernauts with any counter orders, broke ranks, and slunk from the field. Their dust-concealed subterfuge was complete. As the opposing kings were positioned out of harm's way at the extreme right of these tightly-packed, hedgehog-like formations, the frontline warriors were now literally driven by the weight of numbers behind them onto a wall of razor-sharp spearheads.

ΨΨ

Screaming in shock and pain, they fell in their droves. Both formations' front ranks crumpled, with those deadly tips not embedded in flesh far enough into the enemy mass to slay and injure warriors of the second and third ranks. As the horror of this first strike registered, and geysers of blood sprayed those still standing, a few remembered their training or acted from instinct, trying to interlock their shields while disengaging their spears for further thrusts. Warriors now stabbed blindly at what remained of the first three ranks opposing them as they sought to avoid the punctured bodies of fallen comrades and stay upright upon the streams of blood flowing underfoot. The fresh warriors in the following ranks stepped forward or were pressured by those in the file behind to fill the many gaps in the broken front ranks, all the while trying to control their rising panic at the inevitability of harm when they reached the killing zone.

Koroibos still had three men between himself and the spears of the Pisatan phalanx. As a first-time warrior, this was not unusual; all he had to do was maintain his position in the formation and keep the same faces, or recognizable helmets, to either side of him. That was the theory, anyway. Between the exhausting heat, the blinding dust, the hypoxia of fear, and now the lightning strike of first contact with the enemy, Koroibos lost the contents of his bladder and all sight of the veteran who had upbraided him on the way into battle. What stunned him back into awareness was the intense pain of a wooden pole being smashed over his helmet. From behind.

Discipline in that part of the formation was maintained by a middle-aged *decadarchos* — a notorious martinet — and, after a week of drilling, Koroibos was more afraid of him than the enemy. Having screamed himself hoarse trying to get the inexperienced rear ranks to obey, the *decadarchos* had taken to clouting their helmets with a broken spear haft. Koroibos was an early victim. Caught off-guard by these stunning blows, he lurched forward to evade the madman's reach. Slipping on a large puddle of blood, he bounced off two comrades trying to right himself and found himself pushed even further forward. It was the final mistake Koroibos made that day.

Despite his trepidation, when he had earlier felt like a child straining amongst adults for a glimpse of a deadly brawl, he now found himself not needing to clear any obstacles to view the carnage. The meat-grinder of close combat was exposed in all its gruesome detail: blood, severed limbs, spilled intestines, steaming feces, gore-encrusted men bellowing for all the cosmos like they had been struck with madness and, everywhere he glanced, edged weapons snaked out like enraged vipers to deliver bites of death. Wide-eyed with shock, Koroibos had reached the spot where the second rank of his phalanx had only moments earlier fallen *en masse*. Here the battle was at its fiercest amongst those who still held their nerve.

While a veteran could survive several minutes in such intense hand-to-hand fighting, protected, though ultimately enervated, by his heavy bronze armor before he could fall back to restore his strength, a tyro like Koroibos was little more than bone and metal to dull the edge of an enemy weapon. The first spear to strike him dislodged his helmet; the second tore his shield away, dislocating his arm. Screaming in pain, he failed to see the next spear. This one was damaged so that its rear spike, the *sauroter*, or 'lizard-killer,' as the men jokingly called their spear butts, was used to punch him in the lower thigh, knocking Koroibos down onto one knee. As he reeled from this flurry of blows, a shield wielded by a brutish Pisatan first-ranker crashed into his unprotected head, sending him, blessedly, to the lands of Hypnos, Morpheus, and Nyx.

Stunned at what he had witnessed and finally regaining his own senses, Iphitos, the Elean king, fearing victory would come at too great a cost, was the first to cry, 'Retreat!'

Almost simultaneously, his opposing number, the Pisatan King Kleosthenes, saw too the impossibility of anything other than a hollow victory and, rather than sacrifice more brave souls, commanded his men to disengage.

Exactly who was victorious that day will ever be a matter of debate. The Elean king claimed victory, knowing he had lost fewer men while maintaining the private fantasy that Pisa would no longer be able to resist Elean efforts to bring it to heel. If ever, that is, the now sadly-depleted Eleans could mount such a force again.

The Pisatans claimed a victory of sorts, too, as this stalemated battle of attrition meant that they had retained their status as an independent city able to enforce their own taxation and governance. Just. At least in the eyes of their king, they had fought their larger neighbor to a standstill and had refused to bend their knee to the Eleans. Invasion and conquest were a fear for tomorrow. As archers in the rear rank stepped forward to cover the disorderly retreat of both armies, loosing flights of arrows into the bodies of wounded enemies too disabled to crawl to safety, the surviving fighting men on both sides considered that neither army triumphed, given the sickening number of slain and maimed. Demoralizing them even further, they were ordered to leave the fallen where they lay, as neither king would offer respite to collect the dead. This was a stain upon their warrior honor and a crime against the gods that left the city's shrines, many a mourning family, and the Boatman of the Styx all wanting.

Koroibos remained where he had collapsed.

ΨΨΨ

From a nearby hilltop, the spy smirked at the carnage below. What work, he thought, his fellow agents had done amongst the Eleans and Pisatans to convince them that such tactics would achieve a visit from the goddess Nike. He turned his horse towards Sparta and home.

ΨΨΨΨ

Loping along the broken roadway, the relic of a more accomplished age, a youth of nineteen summers kept his breath even and his stride long as he raced towards Olympia, bearing a message for his father, the chief priest, Tantalus. As the sun beat down, leaving him in a sheen of sweat, Pelops sighted what appeared to be a large body of men approaching in the distance — the haze and dust rising from the road made their identity uncertain. With the gap closed, he spotted first the royal banner of Elis flying over a dusty, though regally-attired, figure on horseback in the vanguard, then some distance behind, a great number of foot soldiers, slick with sweat, grime, and what appeared to be the caked gore of a recent battle. 'Another battle,' Pelops cursed. And this one seemed to have gone very poorly for the men of Elis, many of whom he knew as supplicants to the shrines of Olympia, judging by their disheveled state and the near-lifeless carriage of their king. Jogging past the king on the other side of the roadway, he nodded deferentially. King Iphitos failed to acknowledge him. The regent swayed to the gait of his stallion, transfixed by the line of the horizon Pelops had just crossed. Glancing at the Elean warriors behind, Pelops could not only see the ravages of battle-buckled armor, ruined shields, broken spears, as well as broken men amidst those who still struggled to hold their heads high — but he sensed their collective despair. He caught himself stepping up his pace to escape this grim spectacle, rather than slowing, as his conscience cried out he should, to lend what succor he might. Too many bloodshot eyes stared lifelessly at his now-sprinting form, and he raced to escape their gaze.

In the fields surrounding the roadway, farmers had paused in their toil to contemplate Elis's gutted militia. Despite a passing curiosity as to the outcome of the battle, they were largely inured to the ways of kings and armies, even when fathers, brothers, and sons had been press-ganged into the king's force in the past. So meager were this year's crops and so gaunt the men who tended the fields that King Iphitos had spurned their service. Truly the gods had a caustic sense of humor! To starve or to serve — which was worse? For these men and women of the earth — as no farmer survived without the help of his womenfolk — one city, one king, one army was as bad as another. Nothing controlled their lives but the weather. Helios might be their sun god, but rain was their ruler; and the other gods, no matter how much they beseeched them, often withheld it for mystifying reasons. The landscape around them testified to yet another of these Olympian-sent blights. As what remained of Elis's fighting men trudged beyond their sight, with still more than a half day's march to reach their city, the farmer folk turned back to familiar verses; a chorus of quietly chanted pleas to Demeter, goddess of crops and harvest, imploring her aid as they toiled within her bosom.

A silent observer to their misfortune, Pelops counted his blessings as he jogged past these victims of the fields. Like them, he was uninitiated in the ways of war, although he rarely went without the bounty of the earth as a guardian of Poseidon's sacred horses, housed within the precinct of Olympia. His father, Tantalus, had served with Sparta in his youth, before a crippling blow rendered him lame, compelling him to enter the priesthood. Pelops was considered a great disappointment to his paternal line because he had refused the blood-red cloak of Spartan warriordom. Complying instead with the wishes of his beloved mother before the wasting disease snatched her away, he had entered the peace-ful temple life of Olympia, where conflict was forbidden and all who served there were beyond the violent whims of earthly authority. This suited Pelops's temperament and private philosophia. However, many a visitor to Olympia had commented that the young man appeared more a warrior than a messenger boy or keeper of horses.

Pelops broke into a bounding stride that ate up the distance to his tem-ple home. A born athlete, he often found tranquility in movement when he could not resolve the tension between his peaceful nature and the demands of a warlike world. Although raised as god-fearing beneath the spiritual shadow of Olympia, Pelops felt he knew the gods for what they truly were — impossible to understand. As he saw it, the world around him could only be bettered if people invested faith in their humanity, or when they understood that if the gods were actually there, then they were far too preoccupied with their own, imponderable machinations to care anything for the lives they were supposed to rule. While the tiny kingdom of Elis, only a small, dilapidated city, in truth, plus a few poor villages and some barely-arable land, continued devoting so much of its dwindling wealth to the pursuit of grudges and unwinnable wars, commoners increasingly went without. The gods surely laid wagers on their fate and laughed from on high. Shaking his head to clear his thoughts and the building sweat, he recalled the dangers of such spoken heresy in a world where the powerful justified their actions by theatrical appeals to this same godly pantheon. This was the very reason that his home, Olympia, existed; and why there were no shrines or deities dedicated to such a thing as peace when the absence of conflict offered so little to those who craved power. He knew, though, that to question the existence of the divine, like interrogating the actions of those above him socially, could not end well. Neither was renowned for their compassion.

Pelops pulled up sharply. Before him sprawled the ugly ruin of the battlefield — a vista of mindless destruction. Scores of dead were abandoned where they had been slain, their bloody limbs splayed like those of dolls carelessly discarded by children. Where was the glory here? Where was the glory to be spoken of amidst the swarms of flies that settled in a dead man's mouth, or heard above the harsh cawing of crows as they fought over the lifeless eyes of the fallen? It appeared that some of the survivors must have paused long enough to retrieve what little of value was left, as serviceable shields and weaponry were conspicuously absent. Still, no attempt had been made to salvage the bodies of those lost to this sport of Ares. What of the wounded? What hope had they?

Carefully scanning the plain, Pelops caught the angry cawing of a small murder of crows as they dived at a distant object. Plucking up his courage, he left the roadway and walked towards the commotion, cautiously avoiding dead limbs, the sightless gazes where eyes remained, and the countless arrows that peppered both bodies and earth. Pelops could not help but see where a brave or foolhardy man must have made his last stand before his life was ripped from him, or the bodies of those who had clearly broken and run, their wounds taken in the back, their faces planted down as life had left them. What was that? A cry? Was that the call of a voice from where the crows bickered? Weaving quickly now through the corpses, Pelops was sure he could see an arm fluttering weakly above a pile of bodies. A survivor! Screeching angrily, the crows parted before him to reveal the owner of the flailing arm and plaintive voice; a barely-alive warrior with a spectacularly bruised face, seeping leg wound, and a badly twisted left shoulder.

Koroibos had survived, although his fear was evident. Trying to raise himself up, he stammered, 'Away from me, corpse... corpse-robber! I am not dead yet... and the punishment, if you are caught is... execution.'

Smiling at this show of courage, Pelops spread his hands to demonstrate that he was unarmed and informed the prone man, 'You have nothing to fear from me, Elean. You have been through enough.'

'What... what do you want of me, then?' Koroibos replied.

'I am here to help if you will allow it. I am Pelops of Olympia, a neutral, and I mean you no harm.'

Taking a moment to digest this, the tension in Koroibos's frame visibly relaxed, and he sagged back down, 'My thanks, stranger... Pelops. I... I need all the help I can get,' he grimaced.

Pelops returned what he thought was an attempt at humor with a smile and stepped closer to Koroibos. While the Elean's bruised face and twisted shoulder did not appear to be life-threatening, the ragged wound on his left thigh with its steady pump of blood could prove to be. As a horseman of some experience, Pelops suspected that the large vein that ran down a human thigh was as vital to the preservation of human life as it was to equines. He had seen more than one old mare deliberately bled in this fashion when it was judged that time and service had outworn her utility, and such deaths had been rapid. Removing the small water gourd at his hip, he upended some of its contents on the wound to expose its edges and offered the rest to a grateful Koroibos. Turning then to a nearby corpse, he tore a length of cloth from the man's tunic and wrapped it tightly around the wounded thigh.

Koroibos cursed and spat from the pain.

To distract him as he tightened the makeshift bandage, Pelops enquired, 'Who are you, Elean? I know a few from your city but have never seen you before.'

Close to passing out, Koroibos gritted his teeth, sucked in air, and began searching the ground around him. Spotting the object of his interest, he raised his good arm and pointed at it.

'What?' said Pelops, 'What in Hades name are you doing?' Glancing again, Pelops noticed a battered bronze helmet pressed up against the side of another corpse. The helmet possessed a curious insignia painted on its side. A pot? Is that a cooking pot? Turning back to Koroibos, 'Well, you're no nobleman, if I have guessed right. Are you just a cook, Elean?'

Stung back into speech, Koroibos retorted, 'Not just... a... cook. The king's cook.'

Smiling at this recovery of a pride more wounded than its body, Pelops could not help himself, 'That bad a cook, eh, that he sent you out here? Remind me never to eat at your table!'

Koroibos's face purpled with anger before he exploded into pain-wracked laughter.

Pelops grinned. Then, taking advantage of this distraction, raised his right hand with the palm outwards, placed his left behind Koroibos's damaged shoulder blade, and slammed his palm with all the force he could muster into the declivity of the dislocation.

His stunned patient screamed once, tried to swing a punch at Pelops, and then blacked out for the second time that day.

Pelops caught his slumped form and laid it gently to rest. Searching around for a broken spear, he located a haft missing its deadly tip, and using his foot, snapped a short end off, leaving some seven to eight hand lengths at the other. He inserted the shorter end of the haft into the thigh bandage and, twisting it, tightening the cloth as much as he could. Even in his unconscious state, Koroibos moaned in pain. Locating his water gourd, Pelops then poured the remainder of its contents onto the Elean's face to revive him. A few brisk slaps brought the sputtering man back into the realms of the living, although he was less than grateful at the rough handling.

'What... what in the name of Zeus's black beard do you... you think you are bloody well doing to me?' Koroibos sputtered.

'You can thank me later, cook. With one of your better meals.' Grabbing the greater length of the spear haft, Pelops placed a supporting arm under Koroibos's left armpit and helped raise him upright. Tottering when Pelops stepped away, he was immediately offered the remainder of the spear shaft. Still shaken, if not downright surly, Koroibos accepted the prop without comment, leading his rescuer to proclaim, 'That's the only use I ever want to find for such a weapon!'

Despite himself, Koroibos allowed the ghost of a smile to flit across his features.

Moving to Koroibos's right side, Pelops placed an arm under his, and the two young men began slowly moving back through the plain towards the roadway. As he grunted and moaned at the exertion, Koroibos asked, 'Elis or... Olympia?'

'Olympia is closer, Koroibos. We can revive you properly there, and then, with my father's permission, I'll borrow a horse and ride you back to your city.'

Drawing several deep breaths, Koroibos paused, then turned to face his rescuer, 'I cannot thank you... enough, Pelops, my... my friend.'

Pelops simply nodded, and they resumed their awkward hobble. The sun was hot on their skin, the rising wind now felt fresh, as if to balance the heat, and the two young men, though aggrieved at what they had experienced that day, once again felt sufficient vigor to face their troubled world.

II

A weary horseman galloped through the gates that marked the entrance to the city of Sparta. There were no guards present. Night was rapidly descending, but what little natural light was left silhouetted the simple architecture that distinguished this most famed of Doric sites. The austerity was so pronounced that it approached the military in its function-over-form aesthetic. In keeping with this minimalism, pitch-daubed torches were scattered few and far between, adding little by way of light. But this was the way of Sparta. Her sons and daughters were trained almost from birth to rely upon their senses in all things.

Slowing to a trot, the horseman glanced proudly around him, taking in the sight of a multitude of impressive-looking men and women still training on the *agoge* parks that adjoined the various warrior schools. Stripped down to the bare minimum or, in some cases, even less, they uniformly exerted themselves to the utmost. With his gaze lingering upon a number of Spartan women sprinting down a nearby track, he dismounted and indicated for a waiting slave to take the reins. His identity now made visible by the flickering torchlight, the veteran spy who had witnessed the ill-fated battle between Elis and Pisa fixed the slave with a steely glare, 'Messenian, tend this beast. And be mindful. It is worth more than you.'

Harsh enough towards their own, the Messenian slave, one of a huge chattel population of Greeks indentured through conquest, grabbed the reins, counting himself fortunate not to be struck by the surly warrior as well.

The Spartan strode through the portal to the central council chambers of his city. Within the *Gerousia*, a band of seniors heatedly debated. Arrayed on both

sides of the grand chamber, their voices reverberated in all directions. Pausing at the fringes of this noisy assembly, the spy awaited the attention of one of the three agitated-looking men positioned on the floor of the chamber. As he stood to attention, trying to draw a glance of acknowledgment from the trio of fellow Spartans, he noted the two regally-attired figures were staring down at a large sand map, positioned beneath a frieze depicting the demigod Hercules grappling with the Nemean lion. The third aristocrat, a younger version of one of these distinguished Spartans, the resemblance almost uncanny, stared with barely veiled disgust at the exotically clad, dark-hued foreigner. Sneering, the Spartan spy recognized him as the Phoenician princeling, Melqart, envoy of his immensely powerful city-state, Carthage. Despite being less than a generation old, Carthage already ruled much of the Mediterranean basin with an iron fist, and this barbarian reeked of a conqueror's arrogance. It was a demeanor well known to the Spartans, but even they grudgingly deferred to Phoenician naval power and gold.

Melqart lisped out, in heavily accented Greek, 'That's all very well, but we must have more battles. Without your wars we lack quality slaves, and Carthage will not build itself.'

King Prytanis, one of the two regents facing the Carthaginian on the floor of the *Gerousia*, turned to him while also directing his voice to the ranks of Spartan elders, 'Your Phoenician gold is well spent, Lord Melqart. Only today, two more cities sought to destroy themselves. We will soon collect what is left of their manhood.'

Prytanis's fellow king, Arcelaus, glowered at the foreign envoy, then caught sight of the spy still standing to attention. Arcelaus nodded at him to approach.

Stepping forward, he declared, 'My Lords, I have news of the battle.'

Arcelaus swept his arm around to encompass both Melqart and the spy, 'Ah, Menander. The result?'

Bowing his head, 'King Prytanis, King Arcelaus, it went to plan. They tried the new way of war, and both cities left the field littered with bodies. Their fighting spirit is broken. The pickings will be good.'

Both kings smiled at the tidings. His duty performed, Menander grinned wolfishly at his monarchs, twirled on his heel, and marched from the chamber.

Turning back to Melqart, Prytanis crowed, 'A good man. As I told you, they tear themselves apart. They're weak now and can be easily raided.'

Melqart spat out, 'That's still an empty promise. What do I have to show my queen?'

Bristling alongside his father, King Prytanis, Prince Lycurgus could restrain himself no longer, 'We are Spartan warriors, not slave-traders, you gods-forsaken Phoenician! When we crushed the Messenians, only then did they become our rightful spoils of war. We cannot keep dishonoring ourselves just to fill your ships with Greek slaves. What more would you have us do?'

Prytanis boomed, 'Quiet, son. It is a question he is entitled to ask. Lord Melqart, we will help you take some, ah, samples back to Carthage. I will make the arrangements.'

With a final glare at Melqart, Lycurgus stormed from the chamber. The Carthaginian smiled frostily at his retreating back. As the elders of the *Gerousia* rumbled back into their debate, Prytanis took the elbow of Melqart and guided him back to the sand map they had been studying. Less ambitious than his peer, King Arcelaus glanced worriedly at all parties, his heart filled with doubt about the soundness of these plans.

Ψ

The same moonlight that glittered down on Sparta that evening also illuminated another famed Peloponnesian site not more than five day's ride away — Olympia. Resting beneath the shadow of Mount Kronos, a broad, lush plain, nourished by the river Alpheios, which itself flowed down to the sea, contained this most sacred of Greek sanctuaries. Dotted with the dedicatory temples and treasuries of many a Doric and Ionian city, Olympia was the obverse to her warlike neighbor; for here, all was dedicated to the peaceful worship of the gods. Stumbling over the sacred boundary that marked the religious precinct, Pelops shouldered the bulk of Koroibos, who had swooned from fatigue and blood loss. Laying him against the base of a statue of the god Asclepius, Pelops collapsed and drew a series of ragged breaths.

Spotted by Iphicles, manservant to Pelops's father, Tantalus, the elderly former slave hobbled over from a cleansing fountain, 'What's this about? The blood, Pelops, is it yours?'

Wearily, Pelops shook his head, 'Another battle between the Eleans and the Pisatans. Koroibos here is one of the few survivors.'

Bracing against the statue, Iphicles levered himself down to inspect Koroibos's wound, 'Not too bad; he'll fight again. He is blood-polluted, though, boy, as are you. You know the rules. Your father will not be pleased.' Just as Iphicles muttered these words, two men emerged from the rear of the looming temple to Zeus.

Instantly sighting the prostrate Koroibos, Tantalus lurched forward but was restrained by his Spartan companion. Unable to discern what was being spoken into his father's ear, Pelops noticed the passing of a small, though weighty-looking sack into his father's left hand, while the Spartan congenially slapped the priest on his back and then strode off to his tethered horse. With a pronounced limp, Tantalus stamped over to the awaiting trio.

Iphicles stretched himself upwards as a mark of respect. Nervously. Pelops began to rise, 'I can explain...'

Tantalus drove a clawed hand into his son's shoulder, forcing a wince of pain, and bellowed, 'Who in Hades is this?'

Shrugging off the vice-like grip, Pelops rose to his full height, 'Just a wounded man, father. I helped him from a battle-site. He needs our aid.'

Iphicles sought to support his beloved young charge, 'They're both exhausted, Lord. Your son has...'

Almost screeching, Tantalus turned on the manservant, 'Silence! You speak only when I say so! And you, fool, how dare you bring a man of arms, an agent of death, to Olympia in this state. He has the contamination of battle-blood, and this is sacred ground. Have I taught you nothing?'

Locking his father's gaze, Pelops attempted to stand his ground, 'But, father...' A vicious backhand silenced him.

Tantalus ranted, 'Such a disgrace. You deny your Spartan blood and hide away from our warrior traditions here at Olympia, though you now take to haunting battlefields where real men fight. And you rescue weaklings like this. Get rid of this creature before I do.' Spitting in disgust, the priest scowled at his son, then lumbered away to his temple quarters.

Placing a hand on Pelops's shoulder, Iphicles sought to offer him kind words, 'He cannot mean what he says. You are but Spartan on his side and your mother was pleased with this life of peace you've chosen. You have kept your faith, and the horses of Poseidon you care for here will always need you. As will I.'

Pelops avoided the gaze of his mentor and friend, sighed deeply, and rubbed his still-smarting cheek. He said nothing. For what, he thought, was there to say about another such incident involving his father's explosive temper and intolerance for any view but his own?

On their post-dinner walk around the grounds of Olympia, the high priestess Europa, and her daughter, Hippodamia, approached the three men. A distinguished-looking woman in her mid-forties, Europa had a commanding presence and projected a firm, but warm, resolve, 'What has happened here, Iphicles?'

Nodding in greeting to both women, he glanced fondly at Pelops, 'He has done a noble thing, priestess Europa, and rescued this wounded man.'

As her mother ran a calculating eye over Koroibos, Hippodamia smiled at Pelops. He flushed with a blend of pride and bashfulness. Iphicles beamed knowingly as Europa walked across to the cleansing fountain, returning with a small pitcher of water. Kneeling, she gently poured a small amount across Koroibos's brow to revive him. He sputtered and came groggily to his senses.

Pelops grinned at the rude awakening, as his newfound friend muttered, 'Am I... home?'

Turning to his rescuer, Europa enquired, 'Where is home to this one, young priest?'

Pelops said, 'Elis, Lady Europa. The hour is late, but may I borrow a sanctuary horse and return him to his family? They must be fearing for his life.'

Turning to her daughter, she responded decisively, 'Of course. Bring us a steed, Hippodamia. Quickly.' Shooting a concerned glance at Pelops, Hippodamia dashed off to fulfill the request.

As Pelops and Iphicles assisted Koroibos to his feet, the high priestess lowered her voice to ask, 'Has Tantalus spoken to you yet of this matter?'

'Yes,' volunteered Pelops, 'He has, but in a manner I do not wish to repeat.'

Europa glanced sidelong at Iphicles, though he simply shook his head at her to indicate that further questions might be unwise. She pursed her lips and held her tongue. She had long played witness to this struggle between father and son.

Pelops pretended to focus all his attention upon righting the swaying Elean cook while the two sanctuary elders looked with concern upon the young victim of violence.

Hippodamia returned, leading a beautifully-groomed Thracian mare. The dappled beast broke from her grip and affectionately nuzzled Pelops.

Visibly lifting from his funk, he rubbed the mare's snout and grinned at Hippodamia, 'You know your horses. She's ready to go.'

Smiling, she replied, 'What little I know is all your fault.'

As they chuckled, Koroibos prodded Pelops, attempted what he hoped was a winning smile at the young woman, and said, 'Very sorry to interrupt... your romantic moment, but I... I need to go home.'

Again flushing with color, something Pelops found himself doing on an increasing basis around Hippodamia, he retorted, 'Keep that up, Elean, and it'll be you leading the horse as I ride.' Raising him up, Pelops bundled Koroibos over the small of the mare's back and tried to right him in place. As Koroibos grunted and wheezed, trying to settle himself, Pelops asked, 'Have you never ridden before?'

He replied, 'I'm a... cook... not a... cavalry... officer! Just get... me home.'

As Pelops took the mare's bridle and turned her towards the sanctuary entrance, Hippodamia placed a hand upon his arm, 'Ride safely.'

He smiled at her, then caught the grave look on Iphicles's face, 'It is not too far you go, I know, but watch the roads. Especially now that it is dark. There are bandits and raiders everywhere.'

Nodding affirmatively at his sanctuary friends, he assured them, 'I will, Iphicles. Don't worry.'

ΨΨ

Outside the fortified walls of Elis, two guardsmen peered anxiously into the dark. The taller of the two whispered, 'I told you I heard something, damn you. Are you deaf?' Straining his senses even further, he turned back to his swarthy companion and declared, 'There! What's that?'

With more than a hint of mockery, the second guard cocked a hand behind his ear, 'Yes, yes, maybe... no, no, it's nothing. Again. You are just panicked after the battle.'

Snarling at him, the tall guardsman exclaimed, 'We are the first and last defenders here. How many of us do you think survived...?'

Before he could complete the thought, a man leading a horse emerged from the nearby forest line. Both guards snapped into aggressive postures, spears leveled a touch shakily if anyone had observed closely, at the ready.

'Halt! Hold there!' shouted the tall guard.

His companion followed up with, 'Declare yourself, stranger.'

Pelops paused, shook at the exhausted Koroibos, and called back, 'My father is Zeus's priest at Olympia. I am here to return a wounded son of your city.'

Relaxing his stance, the tall guard cried back, 'Which son of our city? Who do you have there? I know of your father, though I know nothing of you.'

As Pelops resumed walking the horse, Koroibos rose up on the mare's back and called out, 'Antikles, it's me... stop being so damn good... at your job.... Let us through.'

Stunned, the tall guard, Antikles, stepped forward to confirm the identity of the rider, 'No, Koroibos! You live? My niece has offered up many prayers for you. Come through, both of you. Come through.' Sweeping his arm wide to indicate the gateway, Antikles led Pelops and Koroibos into Elis.

The second guardsman resumed his position by the gate, nodded respectfully as Pelops and Koroibos passed by him, and gave Antikles a cheeky wink to acknowledge that his hearing had proved, in this instance, surprisingly accurate.

Unfamiliar with the city, Pelops craned around, trying to absorb what he could. Given the battle that Elis had just fought, the substantial loss of life, and the time of night, there was, in truth, little for him to observe. Deserted side streets and the odd stray dog were all that greeted him as they moved slowly up Elis's main thoroughfare, the Sacred Way. His ears, however, caught a very different level of activity, as sounds of grieving were everywhere to be heard. Even over the banter of Koroibos and Antikles, who trailed behind his instinctive guiding of the mare towards a dimly-lit central hall at the street's end, Pelops could hear keening and mourning cries everywhere.

As the men and their mare drew up to the illuminated hall, Antikles stepped forward to assist Pelops lower Koroibos from the horse's back. Visibly weakened but relieved to be within familiar surroundings once again, Koroibos did his best to assist his friends by sliding down the mare's flank. It did not go well. Misjudging the distance, Koroibos startled the horse with his shift in weight, and the mare lurched forward. Pelops and Antikles ended up beneath a flailing Koroibos as they sought to break his fall. The mare sprinted up the Sacred Way, her rear hooves flicking out angrily. Despite his pain, Koroibos could not help but laugh, while Antikles and Pelops sputtered and chuckled at the mess they had made of such a simple task.

Attracted by the commotion, a silhouetted form filled the hall's doorway. It was King Iphitos, weary and unkempt, but trying to exert what strength he had left for the sake of his people. A smile flitted over his features at this moment of levity amidst so much suffering. Then he froze, more than a little stunned. Peering into the dark street at the three men trying to disentangle themselves, the king said, 'Koroibos — is that you?'

Koroibos propped himself onto one knee and, steadied by his two companions, rose up, 'Yes… My King… I've returned.'

All too familiar with the telltale signs of wounded men, the king turned to the bowing Antikles, 'Quick, guardsman — get him a healer.'

Antikles nodded and ducked into the hall to locate assistance.

King Iphitos stepped forward, took one of Koroibos's arms while Pelops held the other, and, as they guided the wounded Elean into the hall, asked of him, 'And you, young man, have you played a part in returning my lucky cook?'

Pelops responded, 'Yes, King Iphitos. I was at the battlefield after your army departed. I helped him away.'

As they assisted Koroibos through the hall, the king hissed, 'That battle — what a disaster for this city. So many lives lost.'

Glancing around, Koroibos saw pallet after pallet of wounded men being tended by healers, family, and friends. He turned back to the king, 'Was it worth it, Lord?'

'No. It never is. But that's the way of it. Unless we defend our territory, the Pisatans will claim it. We fight for our survival.' Finally locating an empty pallet, the king instructed Pelops, 'Here, here — lay him down here.'

With Koroibos swooning again from blood loss, Pelops assisted the king to place him down and asked, 'Is there no other way than these relentless wars?'

Stepping back to let the healer Antikles had returned with examine Koroibos, the king sighed, 'A question worth asking. We have fought this way since long before my father's time. It has become a way of life for us. I would change this if I could.'

Catching the eye of Antikles, who had now stepped forward to bow to his king before resuming his guardpost, Pelops nodded a silent appreciation. He turned back to the monarch, 'And Sparta, why doesn't it intervene to put an end to this bloodshed?'

'Don't speak to me of the Spartans! It was they who helped turn that battle into a slaughterhouse. They care only for power. I was mad to trust them.' Iphitos shook his head to clear his anger, 'Enough of this. I must reward your courage.'

The king walked over to his ceremonial table and removed an olive-leaf wreath that was one of a number suspended on the wall behind it. Returning to Pelops, he placed it in his hands, 'This was meant for a brave warrior. It is considered a great honor in Elis. Better that it goes to the brave man who saved a life. Take it with our gratitude.'

Choked with emotion, Pelops managed the words, 'Thank you, Lord. I... I will prize it.'

The king beamed at him, 'You will always be welcome in our city. Now I must leave you — so many wounded to attend. Oh, your name, young savior?'

'Pelops. Pelops of Olympia,' he uttered quietly, with pride.

The king nodded, consigned the name to memory, and rejoined the wounded.

Pelops paused a moment to reflect upon the battle-injured and their bereaved, turned to check a final time upon Koroibos, who had passed into a fitful slumber, and then departed the hall. His honorary wreath dangled almost forgotten at his side. Sighing, he confronted the tasks before him. He had a spooked horse to catch and a troubled home to return to in the pitch darkness.

III

Pelops tended the sanctuary horses outside the stables of Poseidon, at the side of the temple to Zeus. He worked lovingly on the Thracian mare that had endured the previous night's dash to return the wounded Koroibos. The horse was in fine fettle, despite her exertions, and Pelops removed the last of the roadway grime from her coat with a wooden comb. Individually tethered on a running line draped between two sturdy fir trees, a number of equally pampered equines awaited his attention. In a poor, war-torn land, such animals were greatly prized, and Pelops prided himself upon maintaining these symbolic children of Poseidon at their peak. The sound of rumbling chariot wheels caught Pelops's ear; the Thracian mare whinnied as if to confirm the approaching transport. Glancing towards the sacred entrance to Olympia, Pelops saw the ruler of Pisa, King Kleosthenes, and a retinue of officials aboard dual-horse chariots.

Pulling up before Zeus's temple, they dismounted as Tantalus emerged from within, limping down the stairs towards them. As the regent and his men moved to ritually cleanse themselves in the nearby fountain, Tantalus cried out, 'Greetings, King Kleosthenes. What brings you to Olympia?'

Peering up at him, the king replied, 'Ah, Tantalus, I am here to pray for guidance. We hope that Zeus, almighty father of gods and men, will confirm our desire to make peace with the Eleans.'

Tantalus struggled to maintain a look of respect for the king. 'Peace? After what they just did to you on the battlefield? Best you take that up with the god.' Clambering back up the precipitous stairs, Tantalus was followed by the king and several of his ministers. A small number of the king's retinue remained with the chariots. Tantalus paused and called back down to them, 'Find my son, you men. He will see to your animals.' As the king's entourage reached Tantalus's position, he bowed to them, indicated the temple entrance, and ushered them past. Instead of joining them, though, he walked around the temple's narrow ledge, beneath the ornamental entablature that overhung the outward-facing sections of the supporting columns towards its rear.

Pelops waved at the charioteers to lead their animals towards the bundles of hay and leather water buckets he had arrayed for his own animals. They smiled their thanks, uncoupled the horses from their chariots, and began guiding them over. Turning to Iphicles, he asked, 'Can you take care of these Pisatans? I need to speak with my father.' Iphicles nodded, and Pelops departed for Zeus's temple.

After climbing the temple's rear stairs, Pelops passed into the cool, dim interior of the *adyton*, where entry was forbidden except to the priestly class. The soaring ceiling and towering wooden columns painted to look like stone gave this antechamber space an airy, though poorly ventilated, and dimly-lit ambiance. As his eyes adjusted to the shadowy interior, he spotted his father performing a startling reversal of a one-time divine act; where the goddess Athena was said to have been birthed, fully-formed, from the brow of her father, Tantalus was now inserting himself into the cultic statue of Zeus, whose broad back dominated this portion of the votive *cella*. Blinking hard to adjust to the diffused light, Pelops realized that this was no supernatural feat — the chief deity's wooden statue must not only be hollow but contain an entrance he had not previously seen. Freezing until his father had concealed himself within and sealed the portal, Pelops crept forward to examine this mystery.

As he approached the towering statue, he heard King Kleosthenes cry out from the temple's chamber, 'Father Zeus, lord of lightning, master of storms, ruler of Olympus — I call upon you. All is within your power; all bow to your will. I ask you for a sign, great one. Lift the drought, the famine, the pestilence that afflicts us. Help me to end the wars of state that so reduce your people.'

Peering around the edge of the statue, Pelops could see the Elean suppliants all down upon their knees before the sunken, still-water pool in front of Zeus's towering statue. Heads bowed, they piously awaited a sign from the chief deity.

Surprising all within the temple — none more so than Pelops — the god answered the king's entreaty. Or at least his statue did. 'No, O King. There can be no peace.'

A paroxysm of fear shot across the king's face, and he abased himself before the statue. His ministers prostrated themselves further in terror, with some back-pedaling on all fours at this most unexpected intervention. Pelops maintained his stunned silence.

The statue, or at least its occupying animus, certainly did not, 'No peace until victory. Obey me!'

Like his ministers, King Kleosthenes now scrambled rearwards, appalled at what his prayers had conjured up, 'Yes, Lord, yes... I will obey. This will cost us dearly, though... I... I and my people shall try.'

Recognizing the voice all too well, despite the muffling effect of the statue and reverberations within the temple, Pelops shook his head in disgust. Pressing himself behind a large Doric column positioned at the edge of the *adyton*, Pelops concealed himself as best he could. He need not have bothered. Tantalus was far too pleased with himself to do more than exit the statue, seal the rear hatch and depart the temple. Pelops could have sworn he even heard his father chuckling as he passed his point of concealment. Waiting until he was certain that Tantalus had hobbled down the rear stairs of the temple, Pelops strode across the *adyton*, into the *cella*, and investigated the rear of Zeus's statue. Running his hands over the painted wood, he detected a rectangular seam that exposed the hidden portal. Although no naive believer in the power of the gods, he shook his head at the sacrilege his father was committing by impersonating Zeus himself. If there was one thing Pelops believed of the deities of his native land, it was that they were capricious — and none more so than the all-powerful ruler of the Olympians. As he crept back towards the light at the rear of the temple, he wondered at the punishment Zeus would inflict upon Tantalus for this blasphemy.

Ψ

Pelops stretched and limbered up beside an old running track on the eastern side of the temple to Zeus. Iphicles hobbled over, slapped Pelops's thigh muscles to promote blood flow, and then began rubbing oil into them.

Nearby, a small group of youthful Elean athletes had just completed their own pre-race warmup. They were barefoot and stripped down to just their lightweight summer kilts in readiness for the event. They bantered amongst themselves while shooting calculating glances over at Pelops. He ignored their appraisal.

At the race start line, Hippodamia stood with Pelops's Elean victory wreath in hand, awaiting the runners' assemblage. Tasked with launching the competitors, Hippodamia had accepted this post, not as the sole woman present, something her ingrained sense of equality would never allow, but as the only other representative of Olympia who was not otherwise preoccupied. Pelops competed, Iphicles coached: so she officiated.

At the other end of the start line, Koroibos reclined on the tray of a donkey cart. His right leg was still bandaged, although he was healing well from his wounds. With his head elevated on the rear of the driver's seat, his cloak stretched overhead to provide shade, and his bandaged leg propped on a large amphora, he looked every bit the jaunty veteran he now pretended to be. He radiated this cockiness towards his fellow Eleans, who competed in his stead that day against Pelops. This race was Koroibos's idea; he acted as a trainer to his men, just as Iphicles mentored the young priest of Olympia.

Iphicles leaned in close to Pelops, whispering, 'They may be your friends, but what I tell you holds true. Run your own race and show no mercy, for you compete for the favor of the gods.'

Pelops could not help but smile, 'I hear you, although which gods are so jaded that they would bother looking in on this event?'

The elderly trainer grabbed his arm, 'They are always above, and they hold a great love for physical excellence. Don't let them down. Or me.'

Pelops grinned but nodded his assent.

Unable to resist a jab, Koroibos propped himself up on the donkey cart tray and cried out, 'Come on, Pelops — the pride of Elis is keen to destroy you. Enough with mumbling your prayers.'

Pelops laughed, 'I am ready. I hope you Eleans run better than you fight.'

Koroibos called back, 'I could beat you like this, but the view is much better from here.' Koroibos grinned directly at Hippodamia, who blushed and shot an affectionate smile at Pelops. Koroibos laughed out loud as Pelops muttered a curse at his friend's brashness.

Iphicles nodded at Hippodamia, who assumed her post at the start line, and boomed out, 'Athletes, take your places.' Iphicles then hobbled down towards the track's end to act as the finish adjudicator

The five Elean runners took their places alongside Pelops.

After glancing again at Pelops to ensure that Olympia's champion was prepared, Hippodamia cried out, 'Eleans — are you ready?'

Adopting their standing start positions, the Eleans nodded excitedly. Glancing down towards the end of the one-stade track to ensure that Iphicles was now in place, she raised the victory wreath up high, then dropped it with the shout, 'Make ready… Go!'

Despite not getting the best release, having forgotten to clear sand off the stone starting block, and sacrificing traction, Pelops was third out of the gates. Still, splitting the field from the outset, he overtook the two leaders, raced away from them over the next two-thirds of the track, and trounced his opponents by the time he reached a wildly cheering Iphicles. The old man was winded from his exertions, but he proudly slapped Pelops on the back. Iphicles did not bother adjudicating over the minor places as, in the sporting tradition of the Hellenes, only the winner counted. As the Elean runners caught up with him on the finish line and congratulated him, Pelops took Iphicles's arm and guided him to where Koroibos and Hippodamia awaited.

She was clapping with joy, while the bandaged cook struggled up onto both feet to cry out, 'Bravo, young priest! The gods must have set your feet on fire.' Almost toppling over with excitement, Koroibos abruptly sat down to prevent a fall.

Pelops and Iphicles chuckled at his ungainliness.

The group congregated around Koroibos's cart. Pelops addressed them with a thought he had long harbored, 'You know, it is a great shame that we no longer honor the Olympians this way. It is good for body and mind.' Grinning at his El-

ean friends, he continued, 'Especially when you win.' Then he turned to Iphicles, 'How long has it been since we last held sacred games?'

Iphicles pondered for a moment, 'Since before my time. The games of mighty Heracles are only a memory now. It is a wonder that this old foot track even survives.'

Koroibos feigned seriousness, 'Then that would explain our loss today. It has been too long. We Eleans are badly out of practice.' Grins greeted his remark. Turning to his Elean companions, he said, 'Home, my friends. We've work to do to beat this golden boy.' Koroibos shot one of his winning smiles at Pelops, who smirked at his friend's sarcasm.

As the Elean athletes piled their belongings into the donkey cart, Hippodamia turned to their self-appointed coach, 'If you are returning to your city, Koroibos, may I ride with you all? My mother has asked for supplies from Elis.'

He greeted the request with pleasure, 'Of course, of course! With you leaving golden boy behind, we Eleans don't depart Olympia as complete losers.'

Unable to prevent a blush, Pelops leaped to her defense, 'Watch this cripple, Hippodamia. He can't fight or run, but by all the gods, he can talk.'

A round of good-natured laughter followed the remark, as the Eleans now tied down their belongings on the cart and hitched the donkey back to its halter. Hippodamia walked over to the stables of Poseidon to collect her favorite horse.

ΨΨ

Behind a tangle of bushes less than half a stade away, two men surveyed the Elean athletes, Koroibos, and the donkey cart itself. The forward observer, a swarthy-skinned Carthaginian, turned to Prince Lycurgus, who crouched, aloof, some distance behind him, 'They're unarmed, Prince, just as your father said they would be. Good.'

The prince merely grunted by way of reply.

The Carthaginian turned to signal a large group of his countrymen, who had remained at a distance in order to muffle any noises their borrowed Spartan mounts might make. Acknowledging his signal, the Carthaginians clambered onto their horses; though natural-born sailors, these Levantine men spent little time on land and even less on a horse. Their cavalry skills were wanting, at best, whether on equines or the camels that dominated the terrain of their new home in North Africa. Fortunately, their mission this day required little skill with equine transport — stealth and surprise would produce the results they needed to impress their queen.

As they awaited their leader, Lord Melqart's right-hand man, Bomilcar, scanned his targets a final time, grinned at the prospect of success, and then enthusiastically patted Prince Lycurgus on the back.

The prince reacted as if he had been snake-bitten; he grabbed Bomilcar's hand, twisted his arm, and hissed at him, 'Never do that again, barbarian. I will take your arm off at the shoulder if you even think it!'

Accustomed to the hauteur of his own class in Carthage, but immediately realizing this Greek possessed a deadly intensity, Bomilcar snatched back his arm, 'I apologize for overstepping the bounds, Prince. It will not occur again.'

Lycurgus glared at him, stood, and strode over to the waiting horsemen. Bomilcar shook his anger away and followed the Spartan over to his men. Despite the ugly confrontation, he had too much riding on this mission to be distracted by yet another conceited aristocrat who would soon find himself in a slave-pen if Bomilcar had his way.

ΨΨΨ

At ease on the donkey cart's rough seat, Koroibos allowed the youth beside him to guide the beast at a leisurely pace. The rest of his friends traversed the road back to Elis on foot. Astride her horse, Hippodamia cantered some distance forward, though at a speed matching the Eleans. Admiring her form, Koroibos nudged his friend to trot the donkey-cart closer. As they approached, with wooden wheels clattering over the potholed track while the donkey brayed at the exertion, Hippodamia was jolted out of her reverie. Pushing back the brim of her straw sunhat and smiling at Koroibos, she said, 'I had almost forgotten how barren and damaged this land is — it looks scorched by Zeus's lightning.'

With even the king's kitchen he tended often starved of ingredients, Koroibos was painfully aware of her insight, 'Yes, this land cries out. Only Olympia seems to be different. There is drought and famine everywhere, but your home stays fertile. It is strange that the gods…'

Before he could complete the remark, a strange whirring noise snatched at their attention. Multiple whirligigs of rope and rock flew from both sides of the roadway. Recognizing these stun weapons as bolas, even as they began to wrap themselves around the shoulders, necks, and heads of his walking friends, Koroibos had, before being struck himself, just enough time to scream out, 'Raiders!'

A bola aimed at the Elean seated next to him spun two of its weighted rocks into his temple, immediately knocking him unconscious. He slumped out of the donkey cart and fell in front of Hippodamia's horse, causing it to rear in fright and unseat its rider, and they both hit the ground hard. The donkey lurched the cart forward in panic at the commotion, dislodging Koroibos. As he fell to the side of the roadway, another of the weapons struck him above the torso, sending his awareness plummeting into the deepest recesses of Psyche. With all of the Elean athletes now knocked out, only Hippodamia remained alert, though she feigned lifelessness. Her horse had bolted. The donkey and cart were long gone.

As she lay still, fighting her terror, Hippodamia observed through hooded eyelids a group of cloaked men scramble from the foliage at the sides of the roadway.

Ensuring that their victims were unconscious but alive, the raiders bound their hands with rope. As one of them moved to where she lay partially concealed beneath Koroibos, Hippodamia weighed her chances, sprang to her feet, and made a break for the roadside bushes. Despite her fear-driven speed, one of the raiders was faster, or at least his bola was, and he brought her down with a cast around her legs. Hippodamia fell heavily, with whoops of satisfied laughter from the Carthaginians ringing in her ears. The raider who had snared her moved quickly to pin down and truss her, treating her little better than stray cattle. When Hippodamia broke an arm free, snarled, and then slapped him, the Carthaginian struck her so powerfully that he knocked her, literally, into submission.

Another raider flipped Koroibos's still form onto its back, and a look of sour disappointment painted itself on his features. Calling back to his commander, Bomilcar, 'This one was already wounded; maybe dead now. Useless.'

Bomilcar replied, 'Damn. A waste. You know what to do.'

The raider signified his understanding with a scowl, placed his boot on the edge of Koroibos's torso, and, with a hefty kick, rolled him off the roadway into the drainage ditch, where he lay lifeless.

While it was beneath his dignity to assist the Carthaginians to collect these human trophies, Prince Lycurgus was responsible for the horses loaned to them from Sparta. He now brought them forward for the raiders to carry his fellow Greeks away. Finding his distaste for the venture hard to conceal, the prince had at least protected Sparta's valuable horseflesh from any harm during the very one-sided skirmish. He would also satisfy his father's command by witnessing these new slaves boarded onto the Carthaginian vessel before returning home with the mounts. The irony was not lost on him that it was only through a seemingly endless supply of Carthaginian gold that Sparta could purchase and maintain such fine beasts. Lycurgus sought out the attention of Bomilcar, caught his gaze, and the Carthaginian captain snapped his fingers to indicate that each raider should take the reins of a horse. The raiders threw the limp bodies of their captives over the borrowed horses' backs and leaped up behind them.

The prince yelled to Bomilcar, 'Move, Carthaginians! I must not be seen with you!'

The Carthaginian captain snorted but fell in behind the prince's horse. The rest of the raiders also swiftly followed the prince's lead. For without him, they might never find their way back to the docks of the River Alpheios, where their ship awaited.

ΨΨΨΨ

Pelops was moving his horses from one feeding patch to another over the sprawling grounds of Olympia. Following a white stallion, the other horses jostled to keep abreast of their equine leader and the young man who guided them. Rubbing the stallion's snout as he walked him, Pelops murmured, 'There, Pegasus, there; what a beauty you are!'

Dashing across from the temple to Hera, the priestess Europa intercepted him, 'Pelops, can I ask for some of your time?'

He replied, 'Of course.'

Taking a deep breath to slow her heart rate, she asked, 'I need more oil from Elis than I originally asked Hippodamia for — two more amphorae. Can you catch her?'

Leaping onto Pegasus's back, he called down to her, 'Glad to. Just leave these horses here to graze. If Iphicles asks, tell him I'll be back soon.'

Europa nodded and smiled gratefully at him.

Pelops reached full gallop as he departed the gates of Olympia.

ΨΨΨΨ

Hippodamia's horse had returned to sniff around where she had lost her rider at the ambush site. Ambling around the scene of the ambuscade, nudging and snorting at the detritus left behind by the waylaid humans, the mare moved to the side of the road where she found the body of Koroibos. The Elean cook remained in a deathly state, with only the slow movement of his chest revealing that he still breathed. The horse lowered her head and began nudging his body. After several prods, Koroibos began to respond. The mare's head snapped up-right; ears directed at a distant, though familiar, sound. She whinnied excitedly.

Pelops and his stallion burst onto the scene at full gallop, just as Koroibos began raising himself out of the roadside ditch. He had a livid welt on the side of his head where the bola rocks had struck him, and he was bleeding from his nose and mouth. He had also fallen on his injured shoulder and was now feeling that pain afresh. He groaned loudly as he pushed himself onto his feet, while a startled Pelops snapped his head from left to right trying to make sense of what lay before him: a riderless horse, a multiply-wounded cook, several discarded hats and travel cloaks, what appeared to be a damaged bola and neither the El-ean runners nor Hippodamia in sight. Slave raiders! He leaped from his horse to steady Koroibos.

Wiping blood from the side of his mouth, Koroibos croaked, 'Taken.'

Pelops was horrified, 'All of them? Hippodamia?'

Leaning against Pelops, he moaned, 'Raiders… ambushed… taken. All of them.'

Pelops screeched, 'No! Gods, not that! How long ago did they fall upon you?'

Shaking his head, Koroibos tried to recall, 'Can't be… sure. Can't be long.'

'They must be headed to the docks. That's the only way out for them. Stay here. I'll return for you.' Pelops leaped back upon Pegasus.

Koroibos lurched forward, 'Take me… with you. I… I can help.'

Staring at his friend with concern, then down the direction of the roadway the raiders must have taken, Pelops sighed and then maneuvered his horse closer,

'There, Pegasus, there. Calm, my boy.' Levering Koroibos across the horse's back, he said, 'I seem to be making a habit of this. Hold onto me tightly.' Pelops sunk his heels into Pegasus's belly, and the horse bolted forward, the animal almost as keen to make haste as its riders.

ΨΨΨΨΨ

A lathered Pegasus reached the striking entrance to the dock — two huge rib bones of an ocean-going giant, curving up to form an arch large enough for carts and riders to pass through. His riders scanned the busy compound for any sign of their kidnapped friends. Koroibos had recovered somewhat on the ride, having vomited once or twice while Pegasus was at full gallop. Although he heard his friend retching, Pelops was too concerned about Hippodamia to even contemplate slowing Pegasus. This determination persisted when they reached the dock's boardwalk as, despite the bustle of foreign sailors, merchants and locals, he insisted on riding straight through the crowd, almost knocking several pedestrians aside. Ignoring their curses, he raised himself as high as he could on Pegasus's back for any sight of the waylaid Greeks. Nothing. He could see nothing!

Pointing a finger, Koroibos exclaimed, 'There… over there… That skiff. Carthaginians.'

Directing his gaze to the quiet waters of the Alpheios, Pelops spotted the flat-bottomed rowing boat making pace towards a much larger sail- and oar-powered vessel anchored in the widest part of the river. Though captained by a Greek and with Greek rowers, the skiff was packed with standing Carthaginians and what appeared to be several other seated figures. Staring hard, Pelops was convinced he could detect familiar Elean faces, although Hippodamia was nowhere to be seen. Pelops maneuvered Pegasus back through the crowd, with many a curse being slung his way by those on foot, while Koroibos resolutely clung on. 'What was his friend intending?' thought the Elean cook. 'Did he intend wading out after them on horseback, or something even more suicidal?'

On board the skiff, Bomilcar exploited what little standing room remained by moving amongst the captives to check that their ropes had not worked loose. He knew from bitter experience that as soon as the shock of capture wore off, fantasies of flight soon emerged, and the boarding from skiff to Carthaginian warship would be the last real opportunity for a strong swimmer to attempt escape in the calm river waters. Satisfied that the sullen few who were conscious were still bound, he moved then amongst those who partook of the little death. Having been tricked before by a captive who feigned unconsciousness and then escaped to freedom, Bomilcar was especially cautious of those whose eyes were closed. As he shook the ropes belonging to the sole female captive, she instantly woke up and began screaming. Very pretty, thought Bomilcar, as he reached down and slapped her into silence. Hippodamia whimpered from yet another painful indignity but gave him her best evil eye by way of retaliation. He glanced at the prow of the skiff where he felt the eyes of Lord Melqart upon him, and they exchanged a smirk.

Glancing over his lieutenant's shoulder, Melqart's attention was drawn to a commotion on the shoreline. Bomilcar turned to share in Melqart's interest. They saw a white stallion at the nearest point to them on the shoreline, with two lean riders atop it. One of them had raised himself up on the small of its back and appeared to be crying out in their direction.

'Now, what do you think he says?' asked Melqart.

His tone laden with sarcasm, Bomilcar replied, 'Who cares, my Lord? These Greeks all believe their horses belong to a sea god. Let us see him make that one walk on water.' Melqart sniggered and turned back towards the warship they were closing upon, while Bomilcar gesticulated back at the shoreline to indicate that horse and riders should join them. His fellow Carthaginians glanced back at the forlorn Greeks, then down at their captives and laughed. Hippodamia glowered at them, although she could not see over the boat's waistline to identify the object of their mockery.

Still raised above Pegasus, Pelops bellowed again, 'Damn you! Damn you all! They're free Greeks. Bring them back!'

His friend almost hoarse from screaming at the Carthaginians, Koroibos tugged at the rear of his tunic, 'It is... no use... Pelops. None.'

Pelops shrugged off Koroibos's hand, puffed his lungs to yell again, but his voice broke under the strain of his emotions. Barely a sound emerged. He sunk down onto Pegasus's back, head hanging loosely on his chest. Also near the point of collapse, Koroibos clung to his friend as he quietly sobbed with frustration at Hippodamia's plight.

Koroibos glanced back towards the skiff, just as it disgorged its passengers onto the Carthaginian warship, in time to spot a familiar physique. Hippodamia was visibly struggling with her captors as they hauled her on board. Nudging Pelops, he said, 'There, my friend... it's her.'

Shocked back to alertness, Pelops leaped off Pegasus's back and waded into the waters of the Alpheios. He began screaming, angrily, desperately, almost incoherently, at the vessel.

Koroibos wept.

ΨΨΨΨΨΨ

Perched upon a hilltop, high above this futile confrontation, Prince Lycurgus held the reins of the horses he had recovered from the Carthaginians. He awaited the sight of raiders and freshly-caught slaves to finish their boarding of the warship. A look of sorrow flitted across his face as he glanced down at the distraught young Greeks with the impressive white stallion at the river's edge. They must have had family or friends dragged onto that vessel, he thought. Unable to banish his pangs of guilt, Lycurgus decided instead to depart the river — no

matter his father's decree — and ride for home before he, too, attempted something foolish.

ΨΨΨΨΨΨΨΨ

As Bomilcar and two of his men tried to press Hippodamia up the gangplank to their ship, she retaliated this time by biting the hand of the nearest raider. He shrieked, cursed, and cuffed her in the back of the head. Tired of Prince Melqart grinning at his struggles with this girl and taking advantage of her disorientation after yet another blow, Bomilcar pushed away his men, slung the Greek over his shoulder, grabbed at the guide rope, and scrambled awkwardly up the plank. Reaching the gunwale of the ship, he dumped Hippodamia onto the deck.

She rose up immediately and began struggling again with the crewmen who were trying to maneuver her towards the cargo hold. Then she froze. At the water's edge, she could make out the unmistakable form of Pelops, crying out in her direction. Tears moistened her eyes for the first time throughout the ordeal.

Bomilcar caught up with her and said, 'That's better. Like this, you don't seem too bad. Not too bad at all. You'll look just fine on the slave block.' Hippodamia lunged at him as if to butt his head, but the Carthaginian was ready this time — clamping his hand on her chin and locking her gaze to his, he hissed out, 'We will break you of such habits, harpy. Act like this in Carthage and your pretty little head will be turned into a drinking cup.'

Prince Melqart called out from the prow, 'Leave her be, Captain. And get this damn ship moving. I wish to be away from this cursed backwater.'

Bomilcar grunted his assent. He leaned into Hippodamia's face and, to her disgust, ran his tongue along her cheekbone, then snatched his hand away from his captive's now-bruised chin and left for the wheelhouse.

Before his crewman dragged her below decks, she managed another glance towards the shore, where Pelops stood up to his waist in the waters of the River Alpheios. He cried out no more, she noted. For what more was there to say?

IV

Still mounted on the same weary horse, Pelops and Koroibos hurtled through the city gates of Elis. Frantically searching the crowded *agora* for someone in a position of authority, they spotted King Iphitos and several of his ministers about to board chariots. Not bothering to dismount, Pelops nudged Pegasus forward, pulling up before the king just as he stepped onto a chariot deck. Two of his guardsmen leapt forward with lowered spears. The king waved them aside.

King Iphitos glanced up quizzically at these mounted arrivals, having so rudely broken protocol. The king then noticed a familiar, though blood and grime-smeared, face.

Koroibos nodded deferentially at his monarch, 'My Lord, our friends have been taken by raiders. Athletes of Elis; the young priestess, Hippodamia.'

Pelops chimed in, 'Taken by a Carthaginian ship, Lord. We must do something!'

Scowling, King Iphitos replied, 'Curse it! We trade with them, and they still treat us like cattle.'

Pelops volunteered, 'Send a ship after them, Lord. It may not be too late.'

The king kicked at the ground, 'I cannot. We have a treaty with their ruler and aren't strong enough to challenge them. They would crush us at sea.'

Pelops could not restrain himself, 'We are going to do nothing?'

The king glared at Pelops, then, recalling his recent service to Elis, softened his retort, 'We leave now for your sanctuary of Olympia to consult the oracle, young priest. Join us, and I will consider a response.'

'But we are losing time, O King. Is there not another way?' Pelops said.

Iphitos sighed, 'I've wars, drought, and famine to worry me — and now this. I must protect the many above the few.' Turning away from Pelops and Koroibos, he signaled for his charioteer to advance.

Pelops shook his head in frustration, while Koroibos kneed Pegasus in the belly to move him onwards before his agitated friend lashed out at the king. Pegasus trotted across the agora. Koroibos slid off his back. Looking up at his distraught friend, Koroibos murmured, 'Leave me here. I've got to tell their families. If Iphitos sees reason, make sure you come back for me.'

Pelops replied, 'I appreciate the offer, but you're now doubly wounded. You can't travel any further.'

His eyes moist with emotion, Koroibos stared deeply into those of his friend, 'I lost a cousin this way. He was never ransomed, never recovered. If I have to, I will crawl with you to Carthage.'

Pelops nodded fiercely, 'I will find them and bring them back. No matter what.' Turning Pegasus back towards the city gates, Pelops cantered his steed after the king's chariots.

Ψ

Prince Lycurgus dismounted from his horse outside an austere-looking palace complex and lashed its rope halter to a guidepost. He tied off the several other horses he led to surrounding posts. The sounds of heavy physical exertion echoed around him. As he walked through the deserted council chambers through to the palace's private quarters, the grunts and cries were magnified. Arriving at a shadow-filled antechamber flooded with sand, the prince observed the twin kings of Sparta stripped down to their fighting kilts, grappling heavily with one another. After a series of blindingly fast feints, tackles, and locks, King Prytanis finally pinned his opponent and raised his arms in triumph. Mockingly, the prince cried out, 'Hail Prytanis, king and conqueror!'

The king spun to face his son, ignored the slight, and with characteristic brevity demanded, 'Is it done? You were paid?'

The prince nodded, detached a small cloth bag from his belt and hurled it at his father's feet, 'The blood price — the lives of free Greeks for some gold dust. An honorable bargain.'

Now on his feet, Arcelaus managed to restrain Prytanis as he bristled and lunged towards his son. Ripping himself away from Arcelaus' grip, Prytanis stooped, collected the bag, and glowered, 'This is statecraft, Lycurgus. This is what makes Sparta great.'

Lycurgus glared at his father, 'Not my Sparta.' He stormed from the chambers.

His father screamed after him, 'Boy, get back here! Boy… boy!' Prytanis's cries echoed unanswered throughout the palace.

ΨΨ

The chariot-bound ministry from Elis, led by King Iphitos, pulled up before Olympia's temple to Zeus. Pelops followed them through the sanctuary gates and dismounted at the goddess Hera's more modest temple. He had a difficult duty to perform before he could join Iphitos and his father.

At the top of the temple entrance, and rubbing an ointment into his gammy leg, Tantalus greeted them, 'Welcome, men of Elis.'

The king and his men nodded their respects and alighted. Iphicles shuffled over from the shade of a poplar grove to lead the charioteers and their mounts to water.

Pelops approached Europa as she lay sacrifices upon the huge pyramidal bonfire located outside the goddess's temple.

She turned to him and smiled, 'You caught her?'

Pausing a moment to collect himself, he replied, 'Yes and no, Lady. She… she's been taken… by raiders.'

The blood draining from her face, Europa dropped the sacerdotal implements and cried out, 'No!' Rising to her feet, she raced into the temple.

Pelops hesitantly followed her within.

Europa knelt in front of a brazier of fire positioned before one of two carved images of goddesses. Her shoulders gently heaved as she sobbed out a prayer, 'Gentle Hestia, ancient one, dweller in flame; bringer of peace, of love and family. Hestia, I pray to you... aid my daughter; she is lost to me. Help me to see your work, and I will honor the eternal flame of Mount Olympos for all time.' Still on her knees, Europa slid across the floor to pray now before the mother of the gods, 'Glorious Hera, queen of Olympos, chosen bride of Zeus, guardian of women. I ask your favor... My daughter... my daughter... needs your strength. Aid her, mighty queen, and I will hold women's games in your honor until this life escapes me...' Sobbing dreadfully, Europa was unable to speak further.

Pelops moved forward to comfort her. Placing a hand gently on Europa's shoulder, he said, 'Lady, I'll find her... I will return her to our home.'

Although inconsolable, Europa turned to grab at his knees, 'This isn't your fault, though I beg you, locate her. Even if you cannot bring her back, make sure she is at least alive. Please.'

Pelops looked down at her, nodded grimly, and walked from the temple. He strode over to where a somber-looking Iphicles tended the horses of Elis.

The elderly manservant told his young charge, 'I heard what happened from the Eleans. What will you do?'

Pelops replied, 'There's only one thing to do.'

Iphicles paused, then stared deeply into Pelops's eyes, 'If that is what you feel you must do. Your chances of success are not good. You must seek out your father's blessing.'

Pelops affectionately gripped Iphicles on the shoulder and walked away from his friend towards the rear of Zeus' temple.

Within the temple antechamber, King Iphitos lowered himself onto his knees before the statue of Zeus. His retinue of ministers, positioned respectfully behind him in a crescent formation, held torches and clashed small cymbals. They sought to ward off evil and attract the attention of their chief deity.

Abandoning any sense of caution, Pelops entered the rear of the temple and walked directly up to his father just as he opened the door to the secret niche within the statue of Zeus. Pelops addressed his father, 'Father, I need a moment. It cannot wait.'

Startled, Tantalus reacted aggressively, 'Eh, what... what are you doing here, boy? Only the High Priest enters here.'

Pelops could not conceal his scorn, 'I came to seek your blessing though you clearly have other... priestly business... to conduct.'

Tantalus hissed back at him, 'You dare!' He swung a clenched fist wildly at his son. Pelops ducked beneath the well-anticipated blow. Losing his balance, Tantalus slipped and fell heavily. Striking his head on the statue's podium, he slumped to the floor.

Pelops stooped to check his father's life signs — shallow breathing indicated that his punishment was not fatal. Peering discreetly around the statue out at the main chamber, he noted that the suppliants were still clashing cymbals and humming, while the king incanted a droning prayer. He sighed with the realization of what he would now attempt. Pushing his father's body aside, Pelops swung open the hatch and entered the statue.

After a heightened clattering of cymbals signaled the end of his prayer time, King Iphitos cried out to the statue before him, 'Lord Zeus, I call upon your favor. Grant me your wisdom.'

Pelops sweated nervously within. He peered out through concealed eye slits embedded within the statue's torso at the expectant suppliants before him. Then, with a start of recognition, placed his lips upon a pyramid-shaped cylinder located before him that was designed to both conceal and enhance a human voice. He boomed, 'Games! You must hold games, O King of mortals. Stop the wars. Save your people from hunger.'

One of the Elean ministers dropped his torch in shock, then hit the floor nearly as quickly, groveling and whimpering. Equally shocked, King Iphitos abased himself further, not even daring to look upon the statue. The remainder of the Elean retinue prostrated themselves.

King Iphitos mumbled, 'Lord Zeus...'

Pelops continued, 'Games for all Greeks. And for all peoples touched by Greek civilization. A truce must be declared; safe passage and protection for all athletes. Go to the oracle at Delphi. Hear the Pythia speak. She will guide you.'

King Iphitos stammered, 'Yes, Lord, yes. Games, a treaty of peace, consult the Oracle. We will obey.' He glanced up fearfully at the statue, awaiting further instruction. Only silence greeted him. The king crawled backward on all fours and then stood. He smiled down joyously at his retinue, wonderment filling his eyes. His ministers slowly raised themselves upright, bowing continuously towards the statue. They hurriedly followed their king as he exited the temple.

Still inside the statue, Pelops wiped the cold sweat from his brow. Trepidation filled him as he contemplated what he had just done, but he was resigned to his fate, justifying it to himself as an evil performed for the greater good. Stepping out from Zeus's innards, he glanced down at his father's prostrate, snoring form. Thankful that his father still enjoyed the little death, Pelops knew he would face his fury when next they met. He glanced down, sadly, at his only parent, such a bitter, violent man, then hurried from the *adyton*.

Outside, Iphicles stood holding the reins of Pegasus. Pelops said, 'You heard?'

His elderly friend sighed and said, 'I've heard it all before. Come home to me. Don't let us... me... lose another good Greek.'

Pelops stepped forward and hugged Iphicles. Iphicles wiped away a tear and handed the reins of Pegasus to Pelops, the horse already loaded with supplies to consume or barter. He mounted, glanced up at the temple of Zeus, smiled bravely at Iphicles, and rode off.

ΨΨΨ

Pelops cantered up to the docks by the River Alpheios, dismounted from Pegasus, and lashed him to a guidepost. The docks swarmed with foreign sailors, either loading or unloading their vessels. Live cattle were being herded towards gangplanks, tavern owners advertised their wares, while colorfully-clad women and young men plied fleshy wares of their own. Pelops wove his way through this hive of activity toward a particularly large ship where the crew appeared close to completing their loading. He hailed a Nubian sailor transporting a crate on one shoulder, 'I need to speak to your captain.'

Clearly annoyed at the interruption, the sailor grunted, 'Huh? No... Greek.' The sailor waved to a fellow Nubian, the ship's steward, and they exchanged words in their native tongue.

The steward turned to Pelops, 'I speak your language. What are you looking to trade?'

Pelops replied, 'I'm not here for commerce. I'm after passage to Carthage on a fast ship.'

The steward shook his head, 'You're out of luck. We've just come from there. Try Captain Saul. His ship, The Babel, is just over there. He's often in Carthaginian waters.'

Pelops's eyes followed the steward's pointing hand, nodded his gratitude, and walked across to the large, but weather-worn, vessel.

The Babel appeared even closer to completion of its loading than the previous ship, with crewmen bustling about the deck, lashing weather covers over its mounds of supplies while preparing to unfurl sails. The ship looked set to soon depart.

Two men drew Pelops's attention on the boardwalk, one particularly conspicuous by his gargantuan size. The other — though much shorter and quite swarthy— had an air of authority which he casually radiated. They appeared Levantine or Middle Eastern in appearance. Both stared intently at the bustle of activity consuming the ship's crew.

Pelops approached them, 'Do you speak Greek?'

The giant ignored him, while his companion turned and drawled, 'I speak many languages; even yours. If you're here for the shipping tax, I've already had that conversation.'

Pelops shook his head, 'No, no, not that. I am Pelops of Olympia. Are you Saul, captain of The Babel?'

Suspicion narrowing his eyes, the man replied, 'What's it to you, boy?' Even the giant now paused in his scrutineering to glare down at Pelops.

'I need to get to Carthage. Fast. I heard you sail that way.'

The swarthy seaman leaned in conspiratorially and said, 'Yes, I am Saul. I am too well known in these parts, it seems. I captain this fine vessel. But we're not taking passengers. And we need no more crew. Find someone else.' He turned away from Pelops.

His desperation manifest, Pelops reached out and placed his hand on the captain's shoulder to regain his attention.

Before Saul could react, the giant seaman next to him growled, placed a huge paw on Pelops's hand, and ripped it aside.

Saul turned to his companion with a reassuring smile and said, 'Unhand him, Goliath. I'm sure he means no harm.' Turning back to face Pelops, Saul drawled, 'Do you, boy?'

Flushed with emotion, Pelops replied, 'No, Captain Saul, I mean no ill-will. But I must get to Carthage. I can pay… of course.'

Saul looked him up and down, seemingly unimpressed, 'With what? What does someone like you have to barter?'

Pelops pointed at Pegasus, lashed to the fencing by the port's entrance, 'That horse.'

Squinting to appraise Pelops's mount, Saul nodded and said, 'A fine-looking animal, though not for us. No time. We leave here very soon, and we cannot waste time trading that beast.'

Pelops stepped directly towards the captain, their noses almost touching. He said, 'It is a matter of life and death that I reach Carthage. I will do anything to make that journey.'

Saul scowled, 'You're trying my patience. All right, then. Forget the horse. I can always use another rower. Your muscle — what little you have — for a free trip to the city of the Phoenicians, young Pelops.'

He grinned fiercely, 'I'm your man. I can row.'

Saul smirked at his doggedness and told him, 'You're in, then. Settle your affairs on shore and get on board. You report to Goliath, here. And be quick about it.' Saul walked off briskly, having already wasted too much time on this distraction.

As Pelops nodded enthusiastically, Goliath loomed over him, 'Bit of a rough bargain, kid. The Babel ain't the safest of ships. Your people don't like 'er captain, and she ain't registered at Carthage. That means we sail outside their protection, and these waters are full of pirates and the like. You seem decent enough. I thought you should know.'

Smiling his appreciation at such honesty, Pelops declared, 'It's not like I had many choices, Goliath. I must reach Carthage fast and by any means. The Babel it had to be.'

Goliath rumbled down to him, 'Then, the gods willing, it'll happen for you, Greek. Get rid of your horse and find my deck-master for your berth.'

ΨΨΨΨ

Filled with wonderment and fear, Hippodamia and the captured Elean athletes were being slowly led by Bomilcar in single file off the ship's gangplank onto the shores of a majestic city, albeit one still under construction in many places. Melqart pushed past to alight before them on the dock. Turning to his captives, he sneered, 'Yes, the greatest city in this world should fill you with awe. To me, however, Carthage is simply home.' Turning then to Bomilcar, he said, 'Have the filth washed off this lot if you can be bothered. And then ready them for their fate.' Bomilcar nodded his assent, and Melqart strode off through the milling crowd of domestic and foreign sailors towards the most built-up area of the city.

As Hippodamia and her friends were led away, she could not help but notice the elaborate design of this exotic city. The Phoenician ship they had traveled on had sailed through two massive, sunken gates that opened up to a vast rectangular dock, protected by an imposing wall on its seaward side. Countless merchant vessels were moored along the opposite landward wall of this dock, disgorging or loading crew, passengers and cargo at a frenetic pace. This titanic, man-made dock rested alongside an arrowhead-shaped, fortified peninsula that jutted out hundreds of stades into the sea from the Aethiopian continental mass. As Bomilcar tugged and dragged the chain of slaves through the crowd, Hippodamia also noticed what appeared to be another dock — this one circular — at the city end of the merchant dock, with several military-looking vessels bobbing up and down on its heavily-protected waters. And wrapped around the nautical marvel, the sprawling city itself literally glittered in the sunlight with its many stark white buildings and the bands of bright, multi-colored, kiln-fired mosaic work adorning them. A harsh rope-tug at her throat snapped Hippodamia from her observations to focus angrily upon her captor. This pain and fury also sharpened the awareness of her immediate surroundings.

Bomilcar led the Greeks away from the dock, past what was known as the sailor's cemetery and through the outskirts of the vast, open-air market that dominated this side of the city. The crowd here was even more dense and voluble. Many cried out in the Phoenician tongue, hurling what seemed like abuse to Hippodamia at two large effigies that loomed above them in a roped-off clearing. Peering intently at the objects of their scorn, Hippodamia blanched. Upon a large wooden cross affixed to a stone pedestal, a man hung upside down, writhing in intense pain as both his hands and feet had been pierced with spikes. The noise of the crowd drowned out his screams, abetted by priests playing strange-looking musical instruments in some sort of ritual strain. Directly behind the crucified man stood a towering, bronze, bull-headed man-deity — similar to what Hippodamia had seen of the gods of Aegyptus — with its arms outstretched to both sides. Scales holding large bowls dangled from the statue's clenched fists, and within each of the bowls lay a bound and piteously weeping boy of not more than ten summers apiece. Even more horrifyingly, she could make out through gaps in the crowd that yet more priests were setting fire to pyramidal stacks of wood placed beneath each bowl. Their intention seemed clear — the children would be broiled or asphyxiated to death.

Turning for the first time to her fellow captives, she exclaimed, 'Hestia protect me. What evil is this?'

One of her Elean companions, Simonides, whispered to her, 'The people of Carthage only respect victory. He is a failed general or admiral. Those boys must be his sons.'

Shaking her head in shock and disgust, Hippodamia shot back at him, 'To their own people…?'

Overhearing the conversation, Bomilcar gave the slaver's rope a particularly brutal wrench, then yelled at them, 'Quiet! No talking.'

Hippodamia glared at him but was soon distracted by what she saw past Bomilcar's shoulder — her first glimpse of the infamous slave market of Carthage. Pockets of eager bidders clustered around large elevated platforms, where auctioneers paraded their captives in various stages of undress. The misery and shame of the slaves was written on their faces. In stark contrast, the onlookers and bidders ogled, jeered, and abused the objects of their scrutiny. Hippodamia's heart sank in her chest.

As Bomilcar tugged again at the rope to draw the captives towards the center of the square, Melqart approached from a well-shaded portico; without the burden of guiding captives, he had quickly reached the slave yards and refreshed himself. Bomilcar could smell wine on his breath.

Melqart looked over the captives, 'You didn't stop to wash these…'

Interrupted by blaring trumpets, Melqart and Bomilcar spun to face the source of the commotion. The trumpeters played near an opening in the crowd on the northern edge of the square. Mounted within a turret upon a strikingly-caparisoned albino bull elephant, with its tusks wrapped in gleaming gold, a haughty-looking woman was being led through this opening by a dusky-fleshed mahout on foot. A detachment of the Royal Guard flanked the beast.

Bomilcar growled at his captives, 'On your knees for Queen Dido, Greeks.' He wrenched downwards with the rope connecting them to ensure compliance. Hippodamia and her friends grudgingly lowered themselves. All around them, the citizens and slaves of Carthage performed this act of subservience. Only a few, better-attired Carthaginians remained on their feet, although they bowed their heads. Melqart was one of them.

As her gargantuan elephant swayed across the square, Queen Dido glanced down at her subjects, her gaze rolling over Bomilcar and the Greek captives and then being drawn to the nobleman positioned in front of them. With a visible flicker of recognition, she immediately called down to the mahout, 'Hold!'

The mahout yanked twice on the elaborate tasseled leash he held and bellowed out, 'Hup; hup; hup!' His charge drew itself up, punctuating its arrested advance with a disgruntled bellow.

Melqart smiled knowingly to himself as he bowed deeply from the waist before his ruler.

Queen Dido said, 'You've returned, then.'

Melqart replied, 'Yes, my Lady. I've gifts from the Spartans.'

The queen merely sniffed and affected a look of bored nonchalance. She did, though, shoot a veiled look over the file of captives standing behind Melqart and Bomilcar.

Melqart grabbed the slaver's rope from Bomilcar and tugged the captives forward. Indicating the Eleans, he proclaimed, 'These are yours, Queen Dido. They are young and strong. They would make fine guards.'

Dido stared pointedly at Hippodamia and said, 'What of the girl?'

Melqart shrugged his shoulders, 'She speaks no Phoenician. Not good enough for a handmaid. I thought she might serve me; something menial.'

Chuckling sarcastically, Dido sneered, 'What a stupid thing to say. None speak our language when they first arrive. Keep her with the others.' Pausing to glance over Hippodamia's form, she continued, 'She is suitably decorative.'

Melqart flushed with anger but bowed his head rapidly enough to conceal his emotions. Holding his posture, Melqart waited until the queen had indicated to the mahout to move her mount forward; he even paused long enough to hear the Royal Guards shuffle forward, their awkward gait designed to match the elephant's pace. When he finally raised his head, his eyes were shot through with the red of suppressed rage.

Bomilcar made the mistake of addressing his commander, 'We get nothing for these...?' Now noticing Melqart's bloodshot glare, he recoiled almost as if struck. Bomilcar knew well his lord's often-murderous fits of wrath.

Melqart stepped forward, his nose almost touching Bomilcar's own, and hissed out, 'Nothing? You get one more day of your miserable life. I wouldn't call that nothing.' Hurling the end of the slaver's rope at his cowering lieutenant, the nobleman stormed off.

Despite not knowing the tongue they had spoken, Hippodamia shared a covert grin with Simonides at what had been the public humiliation of the man who captured them. She had also carefully observed the freighted interactions between ruler, commander, and lieutenant. She thought to herself, such tensions might prove useful if she ever had the chance to play one off against another to escape the horrors of Carthaginian slavery.

V

n the docks of the River Alpheios, Pelops removed the riding blanket from Pegasus. The horse nuzzled him affectionately; he smiled wistfully and ran his hands through the mane and across the stallion's broad back. With a final hug around the neck, Pelops gently slapped him on the rump, 'Home, Pegasus; home. You're free. Go home, boy. Go!'

As he affectionately watched Pegasus bolt forward and race out of the dock compound, Pelops heard voices raised in argument. Turning towards the commotion, he realized, uncomfortably, that the altercation came from the direction of The Babel. Peering through the many bodies blocking his view, he thought he could make out Captain Saul wrangling with two men, both of whom wore the distinctive attire of local officials. Shouldering his travel bags and striding over to them, Pelops noticed that Saul appeared remarkably calm, while the Greek officials were tense and agitated. Given the captain's disposition, Pelops thought he had probably staged this caper many times before.

Saul wagged a finger at the officials, 'I've told you, and I will tell you again — I will not pay that tax. It's outright robbery.'

In no mood to continue negotiating with this disrespectful foreigner, one of the two officials turned towards the dock entrance and bellowed, 'Guards! Guards!'

A squad of guardsmen positioned near the imposing whalebone entrance heeded the cry and began marching over to where Pelops had now reached Saul.

Saul grinned at Pelops and, with an alacrity that defied his age rammed past the stunned dock officials and proceeded to sprint straight for The Babel, screaming out, 'Weigh anchor! Haul it, boys! We sail now!'

Still frozen to the spot and with the guards bearing down on him, Pelops saw the giant sub-captain on deck cup his hands to his mouth and bellow directly at him, 'Move, boy! Move or lose it all!'

As Pelops sprang into action, leaping beyond the guards' spears and weaving past the two officials, Goliath turned his attention back to the crew. He cried out in all directions, 'Cut the ropes. Push off from the dock. Oars in the water. Row, damn you! Row!' Cursing excitedly, the crew leaped into action with an efficiency that made a mockery of their unkempt appearance and polyglot composition. They would shame the hardened professionals of a Carthaginian warship, thought Goliath, as he proudly appraised their work, before pivoting back to watch the progress of his wild captain and their newest crewman.

Noticing that the guardsmen were weighed down by their bronze armor and lagging behind the fleeing culprits, three more dock officials moved to block Saul and Pelops from boarding The Babel at the jetty edge. Not even bothering to hesitate, Saul slammed into one of the officials, driving him off the dock and into the river just as he launched himself airborne towards the moving deck of his ship. Catching the rear sail rigging to steady himself, he landed on his feet, accompanied by a roar of approval from his crewmen. Goliath beamed with delight, then turned back to the chaos on the dock and screamed, 'Jump, boy! Jump! Or we leave without you!'

Pelops redoubled his efforts. He caught up to the two officials who were starting to fish their colleague out of the murky waters of the Alpheios, spun past them to avoid their grasp, and threw his bags of belongings onto the ship's deck, just before he propelled himself off the jetty. Both bags hit and skid, as did Pelops: right into three large amphorae filled with water, braced against the ship's central mast. A hearty chorus of cheers erupted from the crew, who set to on the oars with abandon, and a laughing Goliath lumbered over to help Pelops to his feet. Saul had already mounted the forecastle to call navigational cues, but he paused to nod his approval at the still-prone form of his newest crewman.

Pelops glanced back at the rapidly-retreating dock and saw the guardsmen brandishing their weapons and cursing the crew of The Babel. The administrator floundered in the water as his colleagues tried to fish him out with an oar. He, too, cried abuse at the departing ship. Although still shaken by the escapade and his ungainly landing, Pelops scratched his head in bemusement at the tumult his captain had caused. Turning to Goliath, he asked, 'What in Hades was that about? What have I joined up to here?'

Saul overheard and called down from the forecastle, 'Just the way I like to do business, sailor. It keeps me fit.' He laughed and returned to calling directions to the crew as they navigated their way towards the river delta. Many of his rowers glanced up at their captain, grinning with undisguised admiration.

Pelops looked to Goliath to make sense of this behavior. He simply raised an eyebrow at the Greek and tapped the side of his head while nodding towards Saul. Pelops shook his head in acknowledgment of what he had suspected, pushed his bags of belongings to one side, and moved sternward to slot himself into a vacant rowing seat. As he raised the hardwood oar, Saul cried out overhead, 'Move this pile of timber. There's bounty to be had and children to father. Faster, boys, before old age unmans me!'

Pelops chuckled as a booming cry of assent came from the crew. He pulled on the oar in concert with his fellow crewmen, and The Babel glided down the river towards the great sea beyond.

Ψ

As the sun sank towards the horizon, The Babel had long since entered the waters of the inland sea Pelops's people knew as the Thalassa or Mesogeios. So awestruck was the young Greek at its expanse that he almost forgot how bone-weary the day's rowing had made him. He also had time to study The Babel herself, and like her captain, what a unique ship he found it to be. Familiar with the navigable waters of river and sea like most of his countrymen, Pelops also knew many ship designs by sight. But The Babel had mystified him at first. He had certainly identified it as a bireme with its two decks of rowers and a double pentecoster, as the Greeks called the banks of rowers on each side. Instead of being the usual twenty-five per bank, it seated a formidable fifty — but its origins were a mystery until he asked a fellow oarsman who spoke Greek. Phoenician, he was told; converted naval stock. Scrutinizing the ship more intently during a break when he was allowed to stretch his legs, Pelops not only detected the exotic lines of a Semitic ship beneath its gaudy paintwork, side-slung shields, and shade awnings, but The Babel retained its most lethal naval weapon — a prow-mounted wooden ram that split the waves before the stout wooden hull, its deadly tip concealed by foam spray at oar-speed but more prominent when just under sail. Mostly hidden under a heavy cloth on the forward deck, Pelops also noticed what appeared to be a detachable metal snout, shaped to be dropped over the ram if circumstances demanded. Very clever, thought Pelops, as he pulled wearily on his oar to the rhythm of his comrades. The Babel looked like a large merchantman but had the speed and weaponry to defend itself very effectively. In what was widely considered a Greek artistic style, the two large eyes painted on the outer bow also indicated that the captain had left nothing to chance — he had even ensured the protection of various nautical gods with these markings.

Glancing up to where Saul stood on the foredeck, Pelops noticed that the captain was staring right down at him. He smiled wryly at his new recruit, looked out over the darkening horizon, then licked a finger and placed it before his face like a wind gauge. Calling the length of the hull to Goliath, who stood with the twin steersmen on the rear deck, he cried out, 'Wind's up. Rest the rowers. Just sails for a while... I want to find somewhere to hide us.'

The Philistine nodded his assent. The coastline of Greece had the greatest concentration of outcroppings, islets and islands he had ever seen; it made navigation by day a dream with always something familiar in sight to set course by, but sailing at night was deeply perilous. If they coasted gently under sail before the sun fully set, they were bound to find something safe to moor alongside, also ensuring that pursuit vessels or pirates — those foolhardy enough to try navigating in the dark — were just as likely to strike their cover or a reef as The Babel. Goliath leaned forward, beat upon a small drum several times to muster the crew's attention, and bellowed at the deck teams, 'Drop mainsail! Drop fo'sail... Oarsmen rest!'

Stripped down to just his kilt and covered in a sheen of sweat, Pelops dropped his oar with relief. Sliding it inboard and lashing it into its rungs, he stood, stretched, and stepped up onto the main deck. Familiar with one another, the rowing crew moved off to eat, drink and rest in their friendship groups. With over a hundred and twenty men on board, space was tight on deck, with many choosing to sleep on their rowing platforms. Walking forward to the prow, Pelops decided that he would talk first with the captain rather than embarrass himself by asking one of these strangers where he should berth.

Saul noticed his approach, 'Well done, boy. You'll fit in well here.'

'Thank you, Captain.' Pelops moved further forward to the ship's ornate railing and glanced out at the tip of the battering ram slicing its way through the waves. Bursting through the water surface immediately in front of the ram were dozens of large muscular fish. No, not fish, Pelops thought — they too breathed air, so they were more like him. Saul also noticed the activity over the waves and exclaimed with delight, 'Ah, that's always a good sign when those sea dogs lead the way.'

Pelops grinned excitedly, 'We Greeks call them 'dolphins' if I've guessed right at what they are. Delphi, our high oracle, is named after them. We hold them to be sacred.'

Saul grimaced, 'The Carthaginians hunt them, you know. With bow and arrow. They consider it great sport.'

Aghast, Pelops blurted out, 'Barbarians!'

Saul shook his head, 'A strange people, but not barbarians. All peoples seem barbaric when they're unknown to us... Wait until you see Carthage. Still a young city, and already it's one of the greatest I've seen; maybe the greatest. And I've seen plenty.'

Intrigued, Pelops asked, 'Where's your home, Captain?'

'Home? Ha! Twenty-five cycles on this ship and I've almost forgotten. I'm an Israelite.'

Determined to learn as much as he could about the kidnappers of his friends, Pelops probed further, 'And your people know the Carthaginians well?'

Saul mused, 'They began their empire-building next to my homeland, so, yes, we know them. Some things we have in common. We're both a religious people, though the Carthaginian faith is darker than ours. And bloodier. They've a lot of strange customs.'

'What customs?' Pelops enquired.

Saul scratched his head, stared long and hard at Pelops and replied, 'You've a lot of questions, even for a Greek. Well, they let a woman rule them. That's unusual. And they're so obsessed with winning that when they compete the victor is allowed to take any one thing owned by the defeated. Anything. When they lose, they get it in the neck, though. They're publicly humiliated and even executed. Damn hard. And...'

A bellow from the Philistine sub-captain interrupted them, 'Sails ahoy! Lots. Might be a battle.'

Saul followed the line of Goliath's outstretched arm towards the darkening horizon and immediately noticed bobbing topsails spread over a wide expanse, with pinpricks of bright light dancing all around them. Knowing them for what they were, Saul calculated at least thirty vessels were exchanging masses of fire arrows. Several ships already looked alight. More importantly, he thought, they were still many stades away from The Babel, despite his ship being headed directly for them. They should still be able to escape any dragnet of outlying patrol ships the warring fleets may have set up. Snarling at the danger, Saul yelled back to his sub-captain, 'Damn it, Goliath, get the men back onto the oars. Turn us away from that.'

Goliath roared, 'To oars! All rowers to oars!'

Before turning back to his bench, Pelops caught the captain's eye, 'Goliath? And he's a Philistine, isn't he?'

More than a little agitated at the Greek's relentless questions, even in the face of peril, Saul still had the good grace to reply, 'You know the story? That's not a nickname. Blame his parents. Be thankful, at least, that we're both worldly enough to speak your tongue... Now get to your oar before I have you thrown overboard.'

Pelops grinned, nodded, and raced back to his bench, joining in the flurry of activity that now consumed the ship.

Goliath strode forward to join his captain in the forecastle. Both men stared anxiously at the sea battle as The Babel attempted to turn under sail in the high winds, while the waters dividing them became increasingly choppy. Heavily laden with cargo and a full crew compliment, their ship was dangerously slow to maneuver. 'Could be problems, Cap'n.'

Saul grunted at the remark. He added, 'Who do you think?'

Goliath pondered for a moment, 'White sails — might be Carthage. The others could be Sicels. Sicel pirates.'

Saul added, 'Then we need Carthage to win this one.' His attention drawn to some physically gesticulating oarsmen on the port side, Saul cursed, 'Ba'al's spit! Ship approaching.' A formidable-looking white-sailed warship had powered in at full speed, quite expertly, on The Babel's relatively blind, rear three-quarter angle, where the portside rowers were consumed by their physical exertion, and the ship's leaders had been preoccupied with the view ahead from the forecastle.

Goliath could not restrain his admiration, 'Brilliant sailing, the swine!'

Saul shook his head in shock, 'Yes. Swine. Quick, get our secret weapon up here… And drop the mainsail. Let 'em know we're not going to run.'

Goliath lumbered off to obey, crying out orders to the deck sailors in at least three languages before he reached the false deck that had been installed to create a restricted storage area.

Having rested his oar under instructions, Pelops watched with interest as Goliath drew up alongside him. Most of his fellow oarsmen chattered concernedly about the giant warship now looming over them, its bow's peculiar upright snout — almost like an elephant's trunk — drawing their attention, though they knew that death lurked directly beneath it in the form of a heavily-bolstered ram. That ram was pointed mid-hull, at The Babel's weakest penetration point.

Goliath paused to note with concern that his sailors had fouled the mainsail, entangling canvas and rope, then turned to the young Greek, 'Pelops, go below here and bring up our guest for Saul. I need to work that sail.'

Leaping up from his bench, Pelops landed on the deck, then slid beneath the roofing of the false deck. Below-decks was dim, although he could make out some surprisingly fine-looking sea chests, lush draperies hung vertically to divide off the space, and the aroma of exotic incense that all but smothered the smells of ship and sea. His eyes adjusting to the filtered light, he could also make out the silhouette of a man striding to and fro behind a gossamer drape. Not sure what the ship's protocol must be with what was clearly an esteemed guest, Pelops decided not to enter his private quarters, calling out instead, 'You... you're required on deck. Captain Saul asks for you.'

Bursting through the drape was one of the most unusual-looking men Pelops had ever seen. Heavily made-up with kohl around the eyes and what appeared to be berry on his lips, the ship's guest also wore an outlandish headdress that resembled a rearing serpent, while his limbs were liberally covered with gold adornments. His armor and battle kilt were also exotic, with inlays of ivory and gold over the various base materials, while the sword he was strapping to his side was an ornate *khopesh*, the ancient sickle-sword of various Middle Eastern peoples and the ruling classes of Egypt. Ah, Egyptian, thought Pelops — that's what he must be. And probably highborn, too.

'You're... you're required on deck,' Pelops stammered.

The exotic foreigner looked him over with a look of annoyance and demanded, 'What's happening up there?'

'We're near some sort of battle. A war-craft from Carthage has pulled alongside.'

Vigorously tightening the belt holding his scabbard, the ship's guest burst out with a telltale curse, 'By Isis's tears! That's not good. Move, sailor. Get us up there.'

Pelops nodded, silently applauding himself for guessing the Egyptian's provenance, and clambered back up the rough-cut steps to the deck. The aristocrat was directly behind him. Striding across the deck, he glanced once at the looming warship and then confronted Saul, 'This is most irregular, Captain.'

The Israelite had a wounded look that a watchful Pelops thought might even be sincere. He replied, 'My apologies, Prince Rameses. They'll search this ship, and you'll be found. Better you declare yourself now. Of course, if you wanted to speak on our...'

Before Saul could complete his sly request, the prince spoke imperiously over him, 'Leave this to me. No matter what, do not utter a word while I set them straight.'

An anguished-looking Saul nodded his agreement several times, then, as soon as the Egyptian had turned his back to face the Carthaginian threat, shot a wink at Goliath, who cheekily mouthed a kiss back at his captain. Pelops almost chuckled aloud.

All was deadly serious with the warship crew, though. Having already cast multiple grappling hooks over the gunwales of The Babel, they began boarding in earnest. Standing back with the rest of the crew, their hands all conspicuously displayed to signal they were unarmed, Pelops noted the precision and agility of the Carthaginian boarding squad. And their aggression. Leading from the front, a beplumed and resplendent officer barked orders at his men to keep their weapons trained on Saul's men while he glared across the deck, searching for those in charge.

Physically arresting their incursion, Prince Rameses stepped directly in front of the officer, who appeared to recognize him after a moment's shocked hesitation. The Carthaginian officer bowed his head and then listened in earnest as the prince whispered heatedly to him. The officer nodded several times, all the while careful not to meet the prince's gaze, and then stepped back, bowing again. As the prince watched, the naval officer turned back to his men and mutely signaled them back towards their waiting ship. Despite a few looks of confusion, his crewmen obeyed without hesitation. The officer shot a final glare at Saul and Goliath, who were grinning unabashedly at him, and then rapidly disembarked. Within moments the Carthaginian ship had disentangled itself from The Babel and moved off. The discipline of conquerors, thought Pelops, or a submissive fear of the infamous Carthaginian military ethos had won the day. Along with their Egyptian secret weapon, he hastened to add. As an intrigued Pelops walked towards Goliath to query him more about the prince, he noticed that the Egyptian had wrenched at Saul's arm and was bending his ear with some explosive outbursts. Goliath smiled broadly as Pelops approached, obviously relieved to have been so little troubled by representatives of the predatory power that controlled these waters, and looked in a mood to answer one of Pelops's interminable questions. The young Greek did not disappoint, 'Who really is he?'

Goliath boomed back, 'Egyptian royalty. In exile. Rameses, son of Rameses. The Nubians overran his country and stole his throne. We're meant to smuggle him into Carthage.'

Glancing back at the secretive exchange between captain and prince, Pelops noticed several angry gesticulations before the Egyptian stormed back below decks.

Shaking his head bemusedly, Saul walked towards them. 'That didn't go so well,' he muttered. 'We've exposed him now.'

Ever practical, Goliath enquired, 'What's that mean for us?'

'Big change of plans. We'll have to sneak into Egypt and take the land route. He insists that we join him after we blew his identity. He pays too well to argue.' Saul pinched his fingers together to emphasize the clink of good Egyptian gold.

Unable to restrain himself, Pelops exploded, "No! That'll take weeks. I need to be in Carthage now. I can't delay.'

Saul shot a jaundiced look at him, 'This can't be helped, Greek. He's our only paying cargo. And I'll not upset him further.' The captain sauntered off to share his new destination with the steersmen.

Pelops shook his head angrily, gripped the handrail, and stared out to sea. Goliath patted him consolingly on his shoulder and then left him to his gloomy ruminations.

ΨΨ

The Babel was moored at a well-lit harbor city know to the locals as Thonis. A simple, though majestic lighthouse beamed its reflective flames over the still waters. Grand buildings flanked it. The sprawling docks were virtually deserted, with only a few sleepy-looking Nubian guardsmen loitering around the entrances to buildings.

Aboard The Babel, the whole crew was assembled around Saul and Goliath. Pelops had joined them, too, as had the Egyptian prince. The sailors had all donned their darkest clothing, while the prince was wrapping a *keffiyeh* around his lower facial features, leaving only his eyes exposed. Pelops draped a borrowed black cloak over his shoulders. They were all armed.

Captain Saul quietly addressed the gathering, 'Now, through the docks to the other side of the city. If you get separated, head for the southern oasis. You can't miss it. It's the only water around. And if you get caught, you know nothing. And no-one.'

The crew all nodded their understanding. Many of them looked pensive; the rest were resigned. Their unruly captain had often exposed them to such dangers in pursuit of profits or to burnish his reputation.

Prince Rameses pulled the captain aside by his elbow, stared intently into his eyes, and whispered, 'I'll find my men and meet you there. Remember your contact, the desert chief, Askari, is a dangerous one. Even by nomad standards. But he is well paid.'

Saul simply grinned — this was his kind of mission. Overhearing the exchange, the Philistine sub-captain and Pelops exchanged concerned glances. Led by their energized captain, the ship's crew began quietly disembarking down the gangplanks.

ΨΨΨ

High atop Mount Parnassus, King Iphitos, his courtly retinue, and their many guardsmen dismounted from their chariots within the sanctuary of Delphi. They moved then on foot to stand before a large cave opening within the wall of the mountain. Above this cave, itself leading to the most sacred inner sanctum of oracular wisdom, the very navel of the Hellenic spiritual world, the age-old inscription, 'Know Thyself,' glittered in gold-leaf paint. The king and his men solemnly bowed their heads towards the entrance, knowing that the mystical Pythia within sensed their every action and thought. As they raised their heads and rearranged their robes, an ethereally beautiful female acolyte emerged from the entrance. She carefully side-stepped the small stream that flowed into the cave, with the tendrils of odiferous vapor that poured out either side of her — the reaction of water upon the ore-laced rock — only enhancing her dreamlike presence. The king and his men again bowed, this time nervously.

Addressing the king with a faraway look in her eyes, the acolyte murmured in a singsong voice, 'The Pythia of Delphi awaits you. She knows what you seek. I shall translate her words for you, as you are uninitiated. You are not to speak.'

The king nodded his agreement and followed her into the shadowy cave. His fellow Eleans gazed after his retreating back with concern, knowing that Apollo could be a mercurial deity even in his most revered sanctuary, then took themselves to comfortable spots to await their liege's return.

Deep inside the dimly-lit cave, King Iphitos's senses were being assailed. Not only were there dense fumes everywhere and the smell of sulfur heavy on the air, but before him sat an outlandishly-garbed woman. Perched high upon a strange three-legged stool, itself positioned precariously over a large crack in the cave floor, the king also felt the dampness of moisture upon his sandaled feet as he gazed upon this apparition. Glancing down, he realized that he stood at the edge of the stream that flowed within the huge recess, where it then spilled below the Pythia's stool into the crevasse below her. Embarrassed at his ineptness, he leaped back from the water — only to collide with an illuminating brazier. The bronze dish clanged noisily off the cave wall, further humiliating the king. He coughed to conceal his shame, then accidentally filled his lungs with the engulfing fumes and coughed even more desperately. The acolyte turned a cold-eyed stare upon him. The veiled Pythia sat unmoved.

Recovering himself, the king nodded frantically at the unnervingly dignified acolyte to reassure her that he was now ready to hear from the Oracle. Who was royalty here? He thought furiously, though he dare not speak. The acolyte turned slowly back towards the high priestess, first gazing up at the giant round stone located behind her that had an ornate serpent's head projecting out from its center, the tip of which rested above the Pythia's head.

Swaying and incanting, the acolyte spoke an ancient form of Greek barely comprehensible to the king — and then turned her attention to the Pythia. Dropping down onto one knee, the acolyte awaited her utterance. The king shuffled from foot to foot, half asphyxiated from the fumes, damp of foot and deeply confused of mind.

Despite her unstable seating, the Pythia inhaled deeply, groaned, and began to violently spasm. Terrified, the king contemplated lunging forward to arrest

what he thought must be an inevitable fall. Fear — and the prospect of even
further embarrassment — kept him rooted to the spot. Almost miraculously, the
Pythia retained her dignity and cried out a string of incomprehensible words.
They reverberated everywhere. Then the cave fell silent. Visibly exhausted by
her efforts, her head sank onto her chest. The acolyte nodded twice, arose, and
turned back to the king.

'The Seer of Apollo and Gaia has these words for you, Iphitos, King of Elis.
There are two roads, most distant from each other. One leads to the honorable
house of freedom, the other to the house of slavery. It is possible to travel the
one through reason and unity. So lead your people down this path. The other they
reach through hateful war and cowardly destruction. Shun it most of all. Compete
in peace and harmony with your games. You must, though, honor the gods with
the name of these games. They are, as ever, the Olympians on high. Recall this
always. When the sun-god blazes most brilliantly, the athletes should compete
for the glory of his light. There is no higher purpose than pacifying the gods.'

As the acolyte dismissed him by turning again to the Pythia, the king took it
upon himself to simply nod and back out of the cave. His heart might be pump-
ing wildly in his chest and his hands covered in sweat, but he had survived this
strangest of encounters. Something to rejoice later, he thought, when restored
to his drinking hall.

As he emerged into the daylight, his men rose expectantly. However, his
eyes fell immediately upon a regal-looking stranger in their midst. His milky eyes
and prominent walking staff suggested he might be blind.

The king called out to him, 'Stranger, what do you seek? Who are you?'

The stranger replied in a mellifluous voice, 'I am a poet, O King. A seeker
of inspiration. I am known as Homer.'

The king's eyes widened in recognition, 'Truly, this is a day of wonders — I
know of you by reputation, poet. I have always wanted to hear your voice raised
on high.'

Homer smiled gently and said, 'What did you learn within?'

The king barked out a nervous laugh, 'As ever, she spoke in riddles, though two things were clear. The games of peace we seek to hold are to be conducted during the height of summer. And, in honor of our gods and goddesses, they are to be called the Olympics.'

The king's retinue broke out noisily into congratulatory exchanges that the Pythia had responded so favorably. His relief evident, the king smiled broadly back at his men.

Unheard over the commotion, Homer beamed and muttered, 'So is born the greatest of Greece's treasures.'

ΨΨΨΨ

Outside the harbor city where The Babel had moored, Saul, Goliath, and their ship's crew were converging on a mass of black tents sprawled around a large oasis. Pelops lagged somewhat behind, not through fear, but because this was his first covert mission, and Saul had demanded he must not expose his men through inexperience. The fact that Pelops refused to carry weaponry — a product of both his priestly training and personal convictions — did little to increase Saul's evaluation of his worth on this subterfuge. Saul raised his hand to draw his men to a halt, glanced meaningfully at Goliath, and just the two of them continued to advance towards the most prominent tent. Positioned outside the tent's main entrance, a burly Sabean guardsman spotted their silhouettes, drew both his scimitars and cried out, 'Hold there! Hold!'

Both seamen froze. Goliath, who spoke his tongue most fluently, called back, 'Prince Rameses sent us. We're after your chief, Askari.'

As the guard looked them over suspiciously, Pelops edged his way forward. Better to be close to the action, he thought, than labeled cowardly among these hard men. The Sabean guard then pressed his hand outwards at the strangers to signify that they remain where they stood. He ducked inside the tent and re-emerged scant moments later. Still wary, he told them, 'Only three.' He pointed to Saul and Goliath and then, surprising most, Pelops.

Pelops shrugged and stepped forward, convinced that his obvious disregard for weapons and his youth made him appear of little threat.

Saul grinned at Pelops as he drew abreast, then turned to speak to the rest of his crew in their native tongue, 'You know the drill. One cry from in there, and you better come get me. Or else...' A number of his men chuckled at their captain's bravado; they all then drew back from the tent's immediate proximity, into the shadows.

They filed into the tent, and once their eyes adjusted to the illumination within, they were struck by how cavernous it was. It was packed full of nomads. At its center, dominating by both his corpulence and his sheer presence, was a flamboyantly-garbed Sabean. He brandished a huge scimitar, which he waved vigorously as he regaled his transfixed men, 'And then with just one stroke of this beauty I carved him a new...' The burly nomad spotted the new arrivals and turned to face them. The spell broken, his men's heads all pivoted towards the disruptors of their entertainment and glared at Pelops and the two seamen.

Shifting into the common tongue of sailors, merchants, and mercenaries, he said, 'Ah, my guests — welcome, welcome. Take seats. I'm just telling the story of how I slew my thirtieth man in battle. When I was twelve.'

The tent exploded with Sabean laughter. The storyteller's own face wrinkled in pleasure, with his carefully-coiffed beard flicking out an oily scent as he laughed, and his one good eye, the other obscured by a large red patch, glinted with amusement. Struck by the collective mirth, the newest additions to his audience relaxed and awaited the charismatic leader to brush several of his men away from their cushions in order for them to be seated.

As Pelops and his companions moved to take their seats, the guardsman re-entered the tent with a newcomer. As Prince Rameses moved into the light, the tent's Sabean occupants all froze; shooting stares between their chief and the prince, who glared at each other fixedly. They were trying to gauge whether scimitars or silence were required. Pelops, Saul, and Goliath awkwardly froze, uncertain whether to take their seats.

Finally, the Sabean chief dropped his huge blade and performed an ostentatious bow. The prince slowly smiled, almost reluctantly, 'Askari, you fat old desert pirate.' Glancing at his former ship companions, he added, 'Have you robbed them yet?'

Pretending to look hurt, Askari broke into a grin, 'Just getting to that, actually. Maybe later.' His men chuckled as he winked at them. 'Join me, my Prince.'

The tension broken, the prince followed the chief towards a map table, while Pelops took his seat. The two leaders quickly engaged in a hushed conversation.

Turning to his companions, Pelops whispered, 'Why are we wasting such time? Can we trust these people?'

Goliath responded, 'We need their camels and guides. It's a long damn way to Carthage. And a hard one.'

Saul grunted, 'Trust 'em? Never. But they're necessary. The Carthaginians now know our ship, and that we guard this prince. This is the only way to enter their city — he's a hunted man here in Aegyptus and a marked man elsewhere. Think of the fun we'll have!'

Goliath punched Pelops in the ribs good-naturedly, as the Philistine and Saul smirked at each other. Pelops shook his head at the endless dangers these men found so entertaining.

VI

On the grounds of Olympia, Tantalus confronted a distraught Europa outside of Hera's temple. Sneering at her, he coldly stated, 'You neglect your duties, priestess. The gods do not care if your daughter has been kidnapped. They only care that...' Turning in surprise at the sound of chariot wheels, he failed to finish his admonition. Iphitos and his Eleans rumbled into the sanctuary, their horses slick and dust-coated from their exertions. Homer rode in the king's chariot.

Tantalus could barely conceal his look of annoyance as the chariots pulled up before him, 'What is the meaning of this? I was not informed that you wished to make yet more demands upon my time.'

Too delighted to upbraid the priest, the king called down to him, 'Demands? This is a day to rejoice. We return from Delphi to share news of new games to be held in honor of the gods.'

Visibly shocked, Tantalus asked, 'What? What games?'

Iphitos replied, 'Games that will change the face of Greece.'

Tantalus tried to assume his usual pontificating, 'No, Lord — you cannot do that. The people of Greece still suffer dearly, and you remain at war with Pisa.'

The king laughed off the suggestion, 'There is to be no more war with Pisa; that has been decreed. And all the peoples of Greece can only benefit if the gods find these games to their liking. What is wrong with you, High Priest? Do you doubt the commands of Delphi?'

Tantalus almost spat out the words, 'No, Lord.'

Turning partially towards his own men, Iphitos called out, 'Now, the games will be held here at Olympia, and the sanctuary must be prepared. Elis will send envoys across the Greek-speaking world to welcome all peoples to compete.'

Tantalus interrupted, 'But who will come? There is no trust between the peoples of Greece. Or any other peoples, for that matter.'

Iphitos brushed aside the priest's surliness, 'They will come. All of them. We will declare a sacred truce to protect all competitors while they travel and when performing here for the gods.'

The high priest sneered again, 'A truce for all? And what would you call this fragile hope?'

The king had had enough of Tantalus's protestations. Glaring at him, he barked, 'It will be called the Olympic Truce. After the games. Enough with your objections — get organized. I will be sending work crews from Elis. And I will request support from Pisa.'

Tantalus tried once again, 'But I have many other duties…'

Europa cut across him, 'It will be done, King Iphitos.'

Beaming at the priestess, the king said, 'That is the spirit. The heights of summer approach and Olympia must be transformed.'

As the king signaled for his charioteer to turn his vehicle back toward the gates of Olympia, Tantalus shot a murderous look at Europa. She ignored him. The elderly manservant, Iphicles, moved closer to her side to lend his tacit support. He was careful to avoid his master's gaze and smiled excitedly at Europa.

Before the Elean chariots could clear the sanctuary, Homer placed his hand upon the king's shoulder, requesting, 'I would stay here if I may, Lord. Let me aid them.'

Iphitos replied, 'I had hoped to hear you perform in Elis, but, very well. Your wisdom may prove useful. It is a very inspiring place…. Halt, charioteer.'

Homer stepped down from the king's vehicle as Europa moved forward to assist him.

She greeted him, 'Welcome, poet. You are known to us. Your presence is most welcome.'

Homer gave one of his characteristic gentle smiles as he was led slowly away by the high priestess. Tantalus growled audibly and tried to lock Iphicles in a deathly stare. Keeping his head down, the old man hobbled after Europa and Homer as fast as his feet would take him. Trouble was brewing, he knew.

Ψ

By the early morning light, Askari's men and the crew of The Babel had loaded camels with provisions for their journey. Pelops, Askari, Saul, and Goliath all assisted; only Prince Rameses refrained from such menial labor. It was already scorching, and the desert winds blew the hot sand everywhere, inducing many a cough and sputter.

Saul turned to Goliath, 'Have half the crew return to our ship. I want it sailed back to safe harbor in Greece. We'll jump a ship in Carthage when this is done.'

Even Goliath looked stunned at this order, 'What in almighty Dagon's name do you mean — jump a ship in Carthage?'

Saul grinned, a wild look in his eyes, 'You'll see. You're still coming with us, my favorite Philistine.'

Although shaking his head ruefully, Goliath began immediately separating the crew from their tasks and dispatching fresh orders.

Saul turned his attention to Pelops, who was struggling to control his camel, 'Ever ridden a desert ship before, Greek?'

Pelops cried back, his voice struggling to be heard over the wind and the camel's nasal grunts, 'No, never. Only horses.'

'They're a lot more exciting than a horse. The smell is worse, though; worse than even my crew. Unbelievable!' Saul yelled back.

Askari stepped forward, grabbing the beast's reins, 'Hup, hup, girl! Behave yourself. Climb on, young Greek.' With deft skill, Askari had made the unruly dromedary kneel.

Pelops grabbed the riding blanket and dragged himself onto the animal's back. Accidentally kicking the camel in the stomach as he clambered over, the animal reared and snapped violently at him; he tumbled off awkwardly, landing face-first in the sand. The nearby nomads laughed uproariously. Even Askari found it hard to keep a grin off his face. Pelops sprang back to his feet, grateful that the swirling winds and sand concealed most of his blushes.

He cried out, 'Curse this beast! And curse this gods-forsaken journey!'

Saul laughed, 'That doesn't sound like a man who believes in the ways of peace. Calm yourself. And try again.'

Askari piped in, 'Take control. Show it no fear.'

Pelops stepped back towards the camel. Saul and Askari shared a secretive smile as they observed him bracing himself. Now mounted on their own camels, the nomads within visible range watched intently. Carefully approaching his mount again, he swung onto its back with all the aplomb he usually had with his beloved horses. The camel merely grunted this time and allowed its rider to settle.

Swaying a little, Pelops yelled out a challenge, 'Right — what are we waiting for?'

The nomad riders cheered wildly, as did the remaining crew of The Babel, who had also mastered their strange mounts. Goliath bellowed his approval. Askari and Saul smiled again at one another, gracefully mounting their own rides.

Askari pointed towards the mounted Prince Rameses and yelled to one and all, 'And remember to protect his Royal Highness. He owes me!'

Rameses smirked back at the nomad chief and launched his camel towards the open desert. The riders swiftly fell in behind him, their whoops of excitement blown skyward by the swirling winds.

ΨΨ

Tantalus limped through the entrance of the Spartan council chamber, flanked by two armed guardsmen. They dropped their spears across his chest after he passed the threshold, forcing him to halt. A meeting between the twin kings of Sparta was taking place; they sat casually across from one another, although they were in a heated debate. They were ringed by the elders of the *Gerousia*, the Spartan council.

The senior king, Prytanis, picked at his fingernails with a small blade. He paused, surprised at the priest's intrusion, then turned back to Arcelaus, '...and my son has departed for Carthage. He will return with more weapons. And more of their wealth. We must keep the flow of slaves moving.'

His fellow king responded with venom, 'But we grow concerned with Carthaginian arrogance. They make many demands but pay slowly. And their attitude lacks respect.' Many of the elders nodded their heads in agreement.

Prytanis sneered, 'Are we old women, fit only to gossip about imaginary slights? Are we so weak that a barbarian's tone of voice bruises our pride? We need the Carthaginians as they need us. That is all. This conversation is over.' Prytanis rose and strode over to Tantalus.

Although far from content with the proceedings, Arcelaus knew that there was little point in pressing his elder peer any further — his intemperance was legendary. The junior king glanced meaningfully at the Spartan elders, many of whom looked upset, and they dutifully filed out of the governmental inner chamber.

Prytanis growled at Tantalus, 'This had better be good, priest. I am in no mood.'

Tantalus replied, 'No mood? I have grave news, King.'

'What now?' he grumbled back at Tantalus.

Tantalus swallowed and spat out, 'King Iphitos has defied my authority and sought out the voice of Delphi. He intends to hold games that will unite all Greece. And beyond.'

Prytanis exploded, 'What? How could you fail me so badly? You are a poor Spartan and barely half a man! Only a halfwit could have allowed this!'

Tantalus bristled, but King Arcelaus cut off his retort before it could form, 'Hold your tongue! Now is not the time. Where will they be held? How are they named?'

Tantalus turned slowly towards the junior ruler, 'They will be held at Olympia in summer. They go by the name of Zeus's domain.'

Prytanis interjected, 'Such conceit — to call them after the sanctuary of the gods. They must be stopped. Do what you can, and when my son returns from Carthage, Sparta will act.'

Tantalus simpered when he realized the pressure he was now under, 'Lords, I've little chance of upsetting these events. Even the poet Homer has placed his authority behind them.'

King Prytanis glared long and hard at Tantalus. With a final snort of contempt, he stalked from the chamber.

Arcelaus smiled grimly at Tantalus, 'I've seen that look before. Men have disappeared for less than what you said to him today. Best you find some way to stop these games.' The king then tapped the side of his head, 'Start thinking. Fast.' With that, Arcelaus also departed the inner sanctum, leaving the one-time Spartan warrior and now-beleaguered priest to his own devices.

Distraught, Tantalus stared at the unforgiving walls of the silent chamber and wrung his hands.

ΨΨΨ

Disembarking from their moored ship, rendered distinctive in the crowded Carthaginian harbor by its scarlet sail and rearing horse figurehead, Prince Lycurgus led a squad of his fully-armored and armed men down the gangway. The Spartan spy, Menander, accompanied them, ordered to do so by Lycurgus's father, Prytanis. Lycurgus and Menander were friends, having once trained and fought in the same regiment, so the prince thought of the older warrior as more of an advisor than a check on his authority. This was fortunate for Menander, as Lycurgus had his father's temper. Striding arrogantly through the marketplace, which bled almost to the edges of the harborside walkways, Lycurgus did not even attempt to hide his contempt as his men cleared a path through the crowds, 'Look at these people! Where is their pride? Their manliness? There is only the stink of greed.'

Not his first time in Carthage, Menander responded, 'It is their way, Prince. They are a nation of merchants. We need their weaponry and gold, no matter what. Your father was firm on that.'

Lycurgus snorted, 'My father!'

As the Spartan contingent moved onto Carthage's royal walkway, which led directly to the palatial quarters occupied by Queen Dido, Lycurgus halted to observe a large work party erecting seating stands and draping huge sheets of ceremonial white and Tyrian purple cloth over them. The prince spotted a familiar face and approached the construction overseer, who was gesticulating angrily at any who dared fumble or dawdle. Mockingly, Lycurgus drawled out, 'This can't be for us — I didn't think we were expected.'

The Carthaginian royal envoy, Melqart, turned and appraised him coldly, 'Ah, the Greeks. We prepare for games here. Anniversary games to celebrate this city's founding.'

Lycurgus puffed out his chest, 'Then, when we conclude our business, we'll give you an anniversary to remember. No-one competes like a Spartan.'

Melqart laughed, 'You'd compete against us?' Lycurgus grinned wolfishly back at him.

'We do not usually allow foreigners, although I will now petition the queen to relax that ruling. The crowd might even appreciate your brand of... er, entertainment.' Laughing derisively, Melqart turned his back to the Spartans and resumed haranguing his workers, 'The musicians! Do not forget spaces for the damned musicians.'

Equally as offended, Lycurgus and Menander glared at Melqart's broad back, vowing that this upstart's day of reckoning would soon arrive, only reluctantly breaking away to continue their march up to the gates of the Carthaginian royal quarters.

ΨΨΨΨ

Across the grounds of the Olympian sanctuary, multiple construction crews labored at restoring the ancient running tracks, erecting jump and fighting pits, gymnasium facilities, a capacious bathing pool, and a vast hippodrome with a central spine of banked earth running down its length. Pavilions for competitors and officials were also being constructed. Europa and Iphicles were prominent, throwing themselves into the preparations. Both the rulers of Elis and Pisa, King Iphitos and King Kleosthenes, directed the construction crews as a sign that the new games had already achieved one of its loftiest ambitions.

Homer was seated on the steps of Hera's temple. Before him was a lengthy file of envoys, all garbed in the distinctive costumes of their region and people. The first envoy stepped before Homer, 'The peoples of Crete accept the invitation. They will compete.'

Homer replied, 'That is pleasing. Crete, Crete, Crete... Next.'

A second, ornately-costumed Greek stepped forward to replace the Cretan, 'The Athenians accept the invitation of King Iphitos. They will send a team for these Olympics.'

Homer smiled, 'Thank King Alcmaeon. Athens is welcome. That must be remembered. Athens, beloved city of Athena; Athens, Athens.

From the shadowy entrance of the temple of Zeus, Tantalus surveyed the construction work with a grim demeanor. He turned, walked through the length of the temple, and exited at the rear. Entering a simple dwelling behind the temple, he stopped before a wooden trunk that sat at the base of the rear wall. Opening its lid, he reached within and removed a scarlet cloak and a sheathed sword. He glanced over them bitterly then placed them to one side. He reached in again and removed a silver locket. Closing his eyes, he cradled the jewelry while raw emotion swept across his features. Staring down intently, his eyes bloodshot with tears, he focused upon the intaglio resting within the silver. It was a white ivory dove seated within a gold filigree nest that glinted in the dim light — his dead wife's most prized possession. At this moment, Tantalus's intentions warred with his conscience. Sensing both his loss and his inevitable damnation, his face collapsed into sorrow.

ΨΨΨΨΨ

At the base of a densely-wooded hilltop some distance from the sanctuary, the kings of Sparta sat astride their horses. Staring over the grounds of Olympia, Prytanis and Arcelaus appeared deeply troubled. Finally, Prytanis spat in disgust, turned his horse, and rode off. Arcelaus paused a little longer, noting, in particular, the group of envoys that milled excitedly around the seated figure of Homer. Shaking his head with concern, he nudged his horse to follow his peer.

ΨΨΨΨΨΨ

After many weeks of hard, unrelenting riding across terrain that had shifted again and again between arid wasteland and semi-fertile grasslands, Pelops and his companions halted at the edge of a vast escarpment. Below them, across a broad plain, lay the walls of a sea-girt city. The harsh sunlight refracted off the roofs of countless imposing buildings.

Slowly unraveling a stained white cloth from his heavily tanned face, Pelops croaked, 'Carthage?'

Drinking heavily from a flask, Saul caught his eye and nodded emphatically. Even that most effervescent of mercenary-adventurers had reached the point of exhaustion.

Prince Rameses drew up alongside them and spoke in a parched voice, 'Yes, the shining city. It begins.'

Completely unconcerned by the others' reactions, Pelops allowed himself to slump from the camel's back and hit the sand. He lay there, almost unconscious. Many of his fellow riders wished to join him.

ΨΨΨΨΨΨΨ

With their dun-colored tents pitched and the camels being collected by their nomad guides, Pelops and the men of The Babel changed into Berber robes. Most wrapped their facial features in the headdress of the Tuareg peoples to conceal their lighter features; some even went so far as to adorn themselves with simple henna patterns to replicate the facial tattoos many Berbers sported.

Prince Rameses approached a Sabean nomad who wore a bright red head-dress and, catching the halter of the camel he was leading to gain his attention, told him, 'Thank your master for us. Isis willing, we will see him soon.'

The nomad nodded deeply and replied, 'Ma'a salama, Prince. We wish you all well.'

Saul, Goliath, and the men of The Babel all cried out, 'Sahit!'

Leading their camels away, the nomads turned and flashed smiles. Pelops patted the lead nomad on his shoulder and said, 'Sahit, my friend. Ma'a salama.'

Pelops and his companions turned in the opposite direction, headed on foot for the impregnable landward walls of Carthage.

VII

After a lengthy trek across the flat veldt, Pelops and his companions entered the rearing elephant-head gates of Carthage. The guards posted there were aloof and bored, not even bothering to question the purpose of their entry into the city as they joined a stream of desert travelers. Even at its outskirts, Carthage was abuzz with activity, with locals and foreigners active as far as their eyes could see.

Pelops was agog at the number and variety of peoples. Turning to his companions, he whispered, 'Is it always like this?'

Saul replied, 'No. Something's going on.'

Never one to hesitate, Prince Rameses grabbed the arm of a local, who bridled, then immediately recognized his aristocratic hauteur for what it was and paused. Rameses asked him in the native tongue, 'What is happening here, man?'

The Carthaginian replied, 'Games to celebrate the birth of our city. Games for many days.'

Rameses nodded, then freed his arm. Turning then to the captains of The Babel and Pelops, he murmured, 'Anniversary games. Our timing is good. It will be easy to stay concealed in these crowds.'

Saul smiled, replying, 'How long do you need us here, Prince?'

Rameses said, 'A fair question. That will depend on how long it takes me to infiltrate the queen's…' His voice was drowned out by a huge roar from the crowds lining a nearby, and very broad, thoroughfare. As their heads snapped in that direction, the rumbling of many chariot wheels cut across the excited crowd noise. Craning their heads for a better view, Pelops and his companions were jostled roughly by would-be spectators streaming across for superior vantage points.

Rather than resist, Pelops cried out, 'Join them?'

Saul gave one of his wild grins, grabbed Goliath, and pressed him in front as a human shield to make his way towards the excitement. His crew dutifully followed. Swept along, Pelops and Rameses brought up the rear.

As they reached the corner of the roadway, a lightweight racing chariot sped past, its twin horses streaked with lather. With unquestioning confidence written all over his features, Melqart adroitly flicked the reins. The crowd cheered at his showmanship. Several other chariots closely followed. As the cavalcade reached its end, the final two chariots accidentally locked wheels, snapping the axle on one and flinging the other onto its side, where it skidded across the roadway and into a mass of spectators. As the horses screamed in fear and pain, nearly rivaled by the outbursts from injured spectators, the crowds bellowed their bloodlust.

Sickened, Pelops turned his head away. When he turned back to the commotion, he noticed that several royal guardsmen were attending the accident. Staring more intently, Pelops was shocked to recognize a familiar visage — it was Simonides, the Elean friend of Koroibos, and one of the runners that had been captured from Greece. Pelops turned excitedly to his companions and pointed, 'That guardsman, there. A face from home. I must speak with him.'

All eyes turned to Simonides. Saul asked Pelops, 'I thought you were here for a girl?'

Pelops burbled, excitedly, 'He was with her when she was taken. He will know her fate.'

As Pelops stepped in the direction of Simonides, Rameses grabbed his shoulder, 'I would recommend discretion. One mistake here and we're all in danger.'

Goliath moved forward, rumbling, 'Allow me.'

The huge Philistine crossed the roadway, bent his shoulder beneath the crashed chariot, and levered it upright with flamboyant exertion. Two spectators pinned under the chariot, bloody but alive, were dragged free by the guardsmen. The remaining spectators cheered his efforts almost as much as they did the original accident. As several of the royal guardsmen patted him on the shoulder to express their gratitude, Goliath spoke a few words into Simonides's ear and nudged his head in the direction of Pelops. The Elean's eyes flared in recognition. Goliath and Simonides immediately crossed back towards Pelops.

A jubilant Simonides greeted Pelops, 'By Heracles! How did you end up here?'

Pelops said, 'No time for that. Is Hippodamia still with you? Is she well?'

Simonides nodded, 'Yes, but guarded closely. If she escapes, then we men of Elis will be executed. The same happens to her if we escape this place.'

Pelops replied, 'Then we will take you all. I have an idea. Is there an event tomorrow?'

Glancing furtively around himself to ensure he was not under observation by the local guardsmen, Simonides nodded emphatically, 'Yes. But why…'

A wild roar from the crowd further up the street drowned out the conversation, causing all Pelops's companions to turn in that direction. At the end of the street race circuit, Melqart had crossed the line in first place and now stood partially upon one of his chariot wheels to elevate himself even further above the crowd. He glowed with self-satisfaction as he soaked up the crowd's adulation. Queen Dido had also alighted upon the chariot's platform to share her people's approval of Carthage's champion. Waves of applause washed over both of them.

Pelops studied them both intently, pondering what a ruthless team they must make, given what he had heard of the queen's reputation for cruelty. And what he had witnessed only moments earlier of Melqart's skill at matching arrogance with ability.

Ψ

The following day, Captain Saul, Goliath, and Prince Rameses strolled along the seaward boulevard of Carthage's merchant docks, discreetly appraising the moored vessels. The captain stopped to evaluate a red-sailed vessel with particular attention. Leaning in towards him to conceal his words, the prince enquired, 'That one?' Saul nodded, 'Yep, new and fast. Good design.'

Goliath interjected, 'Isn't it Spartan, though?'

Rameses looked between the two seamen, adding, 'There will be consequences, won't there?'

Saul nodded, 'Better than jumping a ship of Carthage — they'd hunt us to the ends of the earth. Wait here. I'll speak to her captain. He won't be Spartan; they don't sail.'

The prince winked conspiratorially to acknowledge his acceptance of Saul's plan. Goliath looked more troubled, though quickly cast his doubts aside. Many times his captain had placed him in situations nearly as precarious, and they had always prevailed with few losses. Well, quite a few, at times — but the two of them had always survived. As Saul wove his way through the various disembarked sea-crews to locate the captain he sought, Goliath turned to Rameses, 'Did you manage to complete your... er, affairs, Prince?'

Rameses glanced around warily, 'Careful with that title. Yes, she granted me an audience last night. Things went well. She will meet me in Greece. She even understood the need for all this...' sweeping his arm around '...secrecy'.

Goliath allowed himself a fleeting smile of relief, 'And your men — they're with us?'

The prince murmured, 'Of course. We'll need every rower we can get if this works. It's all up to your captain now.' The two men went silent as they waited, comfortable in each other's company despite the great differences in status and life experience.

Moving with speed through the throng, Saul re-emerged and smiled emphatically at his two companions. Rameses and Goliath nodded subtly by way of response; the mainsail was now set, thought the giant Philistine, time to fill it with the winds of chance.

ΨΨ

In the southwest corner of the city, Carthage's giant amphitheater was filled to capacity; circular in a manner that replicated their distinctively round merchant and naval docks, all levels of Carthaginian society had filled the seating to capacity, their attention focused on the arena floor where the athletes had assembled. Countless pockets of foreign merchants and traders were also scattered through the seats, the strict rules governing participation in the civic life of the Phoenicians relaxed on this one day when they sought to broadcast their might to all who would bear witness. A tremendous roar was ripped from the throats of this polyglot audience as a horse-mounted athlete galloped forward and launched his javelin in a sweeping trajectory. It struck near dead center on a straw mannequin many body lengths from his release point. The Carthaginian spearman threw his hands up with ecstasy at the cast, eliciting another rumble of approval from the seats. Around the fringes of the arena, archery, wrestling, and horse racing events had also commenced. Each prompted mass cries of approval or groans of disappointment at the results.

Most eyes, though, were drawn to the sight of a lineup of some twenty athletes preparing themselves in front of a vast quadrangle that dominated the floor of the arena — this would be the main event, the fabled race-in-armor. Two huge Nubians, their upper bodies glistening with oil and sweat, had just begun the warmup ceremony at either end of the start line, slowly pounding away on their traditional war drums. The deep bass sound reverberated around the amphitheater, building tension and drawing the attention of the audience. Also prominent amidst a virtual sea of Carthaginian competitors were several of the other runners: two more Nubians, two Egyptians, a Nabatean, and a Celt-Iberian were especially conspicuous, as they donned the distinctive battle garb of their peoples. Carthaginian officials fussed about them, checking and re-checking the fit of their attire to ensure that no advantage could be gained over the local runners because of these exotica.

True to his word, Prince Lycurgus and two of his fellow Spartans had also lined up. They assiduously checked the straps and fittings of each other's armor, brushing away the judges with disdain, having already adopted the grim combat demeanor for which they were famed beneath their scarlet plumed helmets. Another Greek stood alongside them, although he was shunned by his ostensible countrymen. Pelops worked alone to fit and adjust the borrowed armor that Simonides had scavenged for him. His white cloak might be ratty and the strange bronze helmet titled back on his head heavily battered, but he had qualified to compete — that was all that mattered. All the while, the local favorite, Melqart, who had paraded onto the circuit fully armored and to rapturous applause, stood silently with his own men. He alternated between a studious indifference towards and open contempt of the non-Carthaginian athletes.

The head official signaled the Nubian drummers to cease. Gaining the attention of the athletes, he pointed towards a nearby rack. Wordlessly — so that language would prove no barrier — he gesticulated that when the signal was given, the final stage in their preparations would be completed when they each raised their own heavy shields, which were embossed in the heraldic designs they had chosen. They would run with the full weight of the bronze bucklers pressed against their bodies. As the runners all nodded their understanding, Pelops took a moment to shoot a secretive look towards Simonides and three other Greeks who had also been press-ganged into Carthaginian service. They returned his glance with discreet smiles and nods.

A solitary trumpet blared from the centrally-positioned royal box. Queen Dido was assuming her seat, surrounded by her customary retinue and a bevy of female slaves. Hippodamia was amongst them. Once settled, the queen nodded towards her factor, who signaled a full chorus of trumpet blasts. All four musicians sprang to life, drowning out the crowd noise. The crackle of audience energy ceased; almost synchronized, thousands of bodies slid forward in their seats, straining to hear every word the queen would speak. As Hippodamia, having been forewarned by Simonides, searched amongst the athletes for Pelops, the queen rose from her public throne and moved to the front of the stand. In a well-practiced, measured cadence, she boomed, 'Citizens of Carthage and welcome guests, today we have something special. In honor of our Spartan allies, we have allowed foreigners to compete in the warrior race. Today we shall see who has the strength and speed to pursue their enemies… Or to run from them!'

A burst of laughter exploded across the amphitheater. The queen resumed her seat and nodded again at her factor. He raised an arm and then flashed his palm towards the head race official.

The head official cried out, 'Take shields!'

Striding alongside the other runners, Pelops moved to where he saw Simonides had just positioned himself behind the shield rack, thrusting a freshly-painted buckler into a slot.

Simonides grinned at him, 'Just had it done. My family knew of your mother. It was her sign.'

Pelops nodded and looked intently across the concavity of the bronze dish — a simple white dove decorated the shield from one edge to the next. Surprised at the gesture, Pelops could only smile his gratitude. Words escaped him. Not only did the device match the coloring of his tattered cloak, but he could think of no better symbol under which to try to advance his fortunes. He hefted the shield into place on his left arm, tightening its leather straps with his right. Staring up at the royal box as he walked back to his start position, he sought out Hippodamia's face. Their eyes locked for a moment — she looked anxious, he thought. He flickered the ghost of a smile towards her, silently praying he appeared confident.

Alongside him, Melqart called out to Prince Lycurgus and his men, 'Interesting test today, Spartans. What if the legends about your people just aren't true?'

Lycurgus grunted, 'We shall see... Carthaginian.' Turning to his men, Lycurgus cried, 'Shields!' With perfect uniformity, all three shields were raised to chest level and then snapped into place against their cuirasses. The Spartans hadn't missed a beat of their stride back to the start line as they performed the maneuver, then spun perfectly into race position.

Melqart grinned, 'Mmm, pretty.' The dozen or so Carthaginians who surrounded him snickered at his response.

The head race official nodded at the Nubian drummers. They began a slow beat on their drums. The runners all acknowledged this penultimate stage by stepping up to the line, muttering their final prayers to deity and daemon, and crouching in preparation for their release.

Pelops again hefted the substantial weight of his shield and refreshed his plan of race attack; without any secondary or tertiary runner on his team to blunt the inevitable assault of other competitors, he not only needed to achieve an early lead but defend it through agility and constant speed around the four pillars of the enormous square. There were few, if any, rules to this martial exercise of athletic prowess, and his slim hope of prevailing rested almost entirely upon the merits of his race plan.

The head official raised his arm, and the runners froze completely in anticipation. Even the constant audience buzz dwindled into silence, such was the tension. After what seemed like an eternity to Pelops, the official finally cried out, 'Prepare yourselves…! Go!'

The Nubians immediately hammered out a fierce martial beat and, like enraged turtles, the heavily-armored runners broke into motion. The crowd screamed its way back into life as Melqart took an early lead, with Lycurgus and his Spartans but an arm's length behind. Pelops had initially scrambled to gain traction, but his years of training asserted themselves, and he held midfield, with only the Nubians and several Carthaginians trailing. The rest of the field already lagged. With clear space before him, Pelops accelerated. Noting the threat, two of the Carthaginians threw everything they had into catching him, as their race plan centered solely upon defending Melqart's position and were within striking distance in a heartbeat. Pelops felt rather than saw them as they began flinging the edges of their shields against his body and buckler to throw him off balance. Weaving away from them, Pelops redoubled his efforts and carved out a lead of a few more feet. Winded, the Carthaginians fell away. Finding his rhythm now unhindered, Pelops drew several deep breaths and aimed directly between the two Spartans immediately before him. Their battle helmets hindered visibility, and with their concentration fixed upon the rapidly-approaching turn post, the Spartans failed to spot Pelops as he streaked through and beyond them. Slamming the bottom edge of his shield into the ground to increase purchase, Pelops pivoted beautifully around the post. He had both narrowed the margin separating him from the race leaders, Melqart and Lycurgus, and increased his lead over the Spartans.

The crowd had begun to follow with rapt attention the agile white-cloaked runner with the distinctive shield, with some repeatedly screaming out the word for 'bird' in their guttural tongue. 'Phoenix, Phoenix, Phoenix!' echoed around the amphitheater. Enraged that their own countrymen would support a foreigner, many more Carthaginians tried to drown them out with roars for their local heroes. Transfixed, Hippodamia watched from the royal box with faint hope rising in her breast. Scattered around the stands to not draw unwelcome attention, Pelops's companions were already on their feet, screaming out his name.

Oblivious to the excitement he was generating, Pelops stumbled upon a small rock in his path, sacrificing a few vital feet. The Spartans behind him pounced. Closing the gap and driving Pelops between them, they assaulted him with shield on one side and armored shoulder on the other. Their race plan was also evident. Their prince — and thus Sparta — must win at all costs. Pelops had mentally prepared for just such a maneuver, and throwing his weight across to the right, he smothered the shield attack while flinging up his own shield directly into the face of his opponent on the left. Stunned, both Spartans lost their balance and fell back.

The crowd roared at this masterful tactic, with even the most recalcitrant Carthaginians now storming to their feet to applaud the cunning foreigner. After all, many of them thought he was only shaming other foreigners, and there was still a Carthaginian hero in the lead. Hippodamia caught herself crying out Pelops's name in joy. Queen Dido turned to stare at her but resumed her focus on the race. 'A spectacle worthy of my city,' she mused, even if it was outlander talent that was so entertaining the crowd.

Repeating his shield-anchoring stunt at the second turn post, to thunderous applause, Pelops pivoted to within striking distance of Lycurgus. Now running neck-and-neck for several paces, Pelops again drew upon his youthful reserves of energy and broke away from the prince. Desperate to counter this challenge, Lycurgus retaliated by throwing his shield and full body weight forward to strike his fellow Greek from behind. Anticipating this recklessness, Pelops broke left and then right. His luck held. The prince missed him entirely, toppled forward, and rolled to the side of the track. His race was over.

Even Queen Dido was now on her feet, applauding the white-cloaked bird-man as the crowd bayed their approval of Pelops. Hippodamia had abandoned all pretense of reserve and hovered at the front of the box, her hands clasped before her in silent prayer.

Pelops collected himself. As he had glanced behind to confirm the prince's fall, he noticed one of the Nubians putting on an incredible burst of speed. With his shield positioned edgeways to reduce wind resistance, rather than across the body, he was slicing towards Pelops. Pelops imitated the creative shield posture, hunkered down, and raced towards the broad back of Melqart. He caught the Carthaginian just as the Nubian drew level on his unprotected right side. Prepared for another assault, Pelops saw the Nubian bracing for a swing of his shield and responded first, sliding his own buckler off his left arm, he swung it edgeways towards the right, catching the African a mighty blow across his bicep. As much stunned as pained, the Nubian tripped over his own feet and fell face forward before him. Pelops leapt over the tumbling body, restored the shield to his left arm, and reached the third turn post almost immediately. As Melqart had employed a more upright posture to take the final corner and had swung wide, Pelops literally slid in beneath him, again smashing his shield edge into the hard ground to bounce into a tight cornering pivot. He emerged barely half an arm's length in front of the Carthaginian, but ahead he was — the lead was his!

Now the crowd response was at its most voluble. And partisan. As many booed Pelops for stealing the lead from the local champion as did those who cheered his impressive form. Pelops's companions in the audience were whipped into a frenzy at the thought that one of their own might actually win the ultimate glory, while Hippodamia was in danger of toppling from the royal box, so far was she leaning outward to urge Pelops towards victory. Queen Dido sat back down, visibly shocked that an upstart might ruin her vision of these games.

Pushing himself to his absolute limit, Pelops pulled two paces in front of Melqart. The finish line was but several dozen more strides away. So intent was the youthful Greek upon crossing the marker that his attention had faded from a now-furious Melqart — he had slipped his shield entirely off his left forearm and, after flipping it horizontally, hurled it like a giant discus at Pelops's rear. The new crowd favorite felt a terrible weight strike him across the back of his thighs; he stumbled forward, somehow stayed upon his feet, but saw Melqart whip past him.

The pro-Carthaginian sectors of the crowd erupted with joy; booing, cat-calls, and loud hissing exploded from the remainder. Pelops's companions were beside themselves with anger. At fever pitch, Hippodamia broke into tears. Queen Dido frowned heavily.

Angry at his lapse in concentration with such a ruthless opponent, Pelops dug deep to catch the Carthaginian. To no avail. He watched with a sinking heart as the Carthaginian crossed the line before him, wrenched his helmet off, threw it high into the air, and soaked up the adulation of the crowd. As the Nubian drummers beat a victory pattern, Pelops crossed in second place, his head drooping on his chest.

While the crowd screamed wildly, the head race official glanced up at the royal box. The queen sat pondering, grimaced finally, and shook her head at her factor. The factor relayed this response to the race official. He immediately raised his arm for attention — silencing the drummers — and cried out, 'Foul! This man is disqualified. No shield; no victory. Dove-shield wins!'

Melqart howled with anger at the official, then shot a deadly stare up at the royal box. The queen locked frostily onto his gaze and stared him down until he stormed off the field, radiating white-hot anger. The crowd watched in stunned silence before it launched into waves of disbelieving booing and cries of triumph. Pelops's supporters ecstatically embraced each other, while Hippodamia sobbed with joy.

The queen rose from her seat and extended an arm towards Pelops. Still not fully comprehending what had just occurred, Pelops stared quizzically between the queen, her factor, and the race official who had made the announcement in Phoenician. Registering his shock, the official stepped towards Pelops and raised one of his arms in victory. Overwhelmed, he sank to his knees, tore his helmet off, and cried out his rapture to the gods of his homeland.

While the other athletes who had finished removed their helmets and armor in order to rest, Prince Lycurgus stepped up to Pelops and placed a hand on his shoulder, 'You won that fairly. Acknowledge your crowd.' Pelops looked up gratefully and nodded his head in understanding, grateful to hear confirmation of his victory in a familiar tongue.

He rose to his feet, slowly pirouetted while stripping off his armor, then applauded the crowd for their support of a foreign athlete. In turn, acknowledging his humility, the crowd responded with cry after cry of, 'Phoenix!'

Pelops made his way across the floor of the stadium towards the stairs leading up to the royal box as the crowd continued their affirmations; it was, he thought, the proudest day of his life.

Simonides had maneuvered himself towards the base of the stairs and greeted him, 'Magnificent run! That swine Melqart will be praying for his life. Now be ready — the queen will want to reward you.' As they mounted the broad stairs, Simonides added, 'Good news from home.' Word on the last slave ship was that new games will be held at your sanctuary. I'll race you again yet if your plan works.'

Pelops grinned, 'They are confirmed!'

Simonides simply nodded as they had reached the royal box. He nodded respectfully towards the queen's factor and then bowed deeply towards the queen herself. The entire retinue got to their feet and politely applauded Pelops's efforts. Queen Dido then slowly rose up, directing a haughty smile at Simonides and Pelops.

Simonides bowed at her again and said, 'He is a fellow Greek, Majesty. He backed away slowly, head still bowed, leaving Pelops to face the queen.

Pelops had eyes only for Hippodamia, who was beaming at him, but he snapped his gaze back to Queen Dido for fear of causing offense. He took another step towards the queen and bowed deeply.

The queen acknowledged his salutation with a wave of her hand and declared in passable Greek, 'Ah, Carthage's latest champion. I found that your performance had... shall we say, flair. Now name your prize.'

With pride ringing in his voice, Pelops grinned and said, 'Thank you, Your Highness. I am very grateful you allowed me to compete. I wish to call upon the victory custom of your city and request one thing that you own.'

The queen replied, airily, 'Yes, yes — that is the intention here. You have earned the right.'

Spinning towards Hippodamia, Pelops stated, 'Then I wish for that women there to be released into my care.'

Hippodamia audibly gasped but lowered her eyes when the queen turned a surprised stare upon her. Dido chuckled, then said, 'Interesting that you should aim… so low. She is yours.'

Abandoning restraint, Hippodamia ran gleefully into Pelops's arms. He held her tightly, almost in disbelief that his luck had produced such a prize. She, in turn, showered her hero with kisses.

The queen studied them carefully, 'Touching. Anything else, champion?'

Meeting the queen's gaze over Hippodamia's shoulder, Pelops replied, 'Yes, Queen. Can I speak to them?' He swung his arm widely to indicate the crowd.

Queen Dido stared at him icily, then softened, 'Most peculiar, but very well. There should be enough out there familiar with your language to be understood.' The queen muttered to her factor, who then indicated that a solitary trumpeter should regain the crowd's attention with his instrument. He blasted out a long, solitary note.

Many of the crowd were already on their feet preparing to leave the stadium but froze at the queen's signal. Even those leaving the stadium began to shuffle back in, curious at the late announcement.

The queen stepped forward in her box and boomed out, 'Your champion wishes to address you — in his native Greek language!'

Pockets of the crowd cheered sporadically at this unusual commandment. Having loitered to accompany him away from the stands, Pelops's companions were equally as surprised at their friend's boldness but cheered his courage. Nearby to where Saul and the Philistine stood, two local merchants exchanged the winnings of their race wager, with the victor then calling out in the stands, 'Interpreter! I need an interpreter. I'll pay!' Goliath grabbed his arm immediately and nodded, eyeing the Carthaginian's small bag of winnings.

Pelops stepped up to where the queen stood, while she moved rearwards to resume her seat. Pelops took a goblet of water that Hippodamia proffered, cleared his throat, and called out at the top of his lungs, 'Sons and daughters of the shining city. I thank you for your esteem.'

The crowd digested his words, then wildly cheered his humility.

Pelops continued, 'I carry word from Greece. New games, in honor of the gods, are to be held in my homeland. Very soon. I'm here to welcome all to compete. Greece will guard your safety with a treaty of peace. Come to Greece. Honor our gods and your own. Win, and your names will live forever!'

Again, the crowd paused to absorb his words or have interpretations relayed to them. A ragged chorus of cheering rose to a full-blooded roar of approval once they realized that Carthage's newest champion had also delivered them another spectacle to enjoy.

Pelops smiled at their response, raised an arm to acknowledge their approval, and stepped back from the edge of the box. Hippodamia grabbed his hand in joy, while the queen sat seemingly aloof, although her interest had been piqued. She looked Pelops over from head to toe, her appraisal so intense that it made Hippodamia visibly uncomfortable.

The queen rose up and addressed him, 'Then we will be seeing you again in Greece, young champion. You are dismissed. And don't forget your prize.' The queen turned away from them, flicking a hand towards her factor to gather her retinue.

Pelops bowed deeply and ushered Hippodamia from the royal box. Simonides accompanied them down the stairwell, where Saul, Goliath, and a disguised Prince Rameses had hustled through the departing masses to join them. The remaining crew of The Babel and Rameses's Egyptian resistance fighters linked up with them. Greetings and hearty praise were heaped upon Pelops. Hippodamia was welcomed, sharing in the collective support her rescuer had attracted. As they moved away from the stadium floor, they failed to notice an aggrieved Melqart lurking beneath the stands, the shade in which he stood failing to conceal his murderous glower at Pelops. Accompanied by guardsmen and his fellow Carthaginian competitors, he moved from his point of concealment to trail Pelops from a distance.

ΨΨΨ

Prince Lycurgus and his Spartans had followed Pelops's announcement with shock written all over their features. Lycurgus turned to Menander, 'Follow him. He must be stopped. As must these absurd new games.'

Menander replied grimly, 'Your father would expect nothing less. Such arrogance to invite foreigners to our land, not to mention that he dared to take it upon himself to announce such an event.'

Lycurgus ran a finger over his throat and slowly nodded several times. His men understood his intent all too well.

VIII

Having bathed and rested after his exertions, Pelops strolled with Hippodamia along the Carthaginian harbor boulevard. They moved with seeming indifference, making no sign that they had noticed the rest of their sailor companions, Rameses and his men or Simonides and the other recently captured Greek guardsmen emerging through the bustle of ships crews. They were all, seemingly without design, converging on the Spartan vessel moored in the sheltered waters. The ship was unattended.

Bursting through the crowds at the other end of the harbor, Melqart and his elite Carthaginian guard searched for their prey, shouldering and shoving the unwitting away from the wedge they had formed. Melqart's face was a mask of fury, the shame of his defeat and disgrace etched deeply upon it. Almost simultaneously, Prince Lycurgus and his Spartans stepped onto the wharf — only body lengths away from the Carthaginians — and were clearly searching for more than just their ship.

Menander pointed, crying out, 'There! Just over there.'

Prince Lycurgus screamed across the press of bodies, 'Hold there, Greek. Hold, I say!'

Pelops froze, spun back towards Saul and Goliath, and started hauling Hippodamia in their direction.

Saul roared out, 'On board! Everyone! On board that damn ship now!'

The crewmen of The Babel scrambled onboard and grabbed oars; Saul and Goliath hustled Pelops, Hippodamia, Simonides, and his fellow Eleans over the bulwarks. Saul raced to cut the anchor rope. Prince Rameses flung aside his cloak and drew his sword, his men holding ground and following their leader. Goliath moved back to join this rearguard, as the Spartans and Carthaginians hurtled towards them with weapons drawn. Saul anxiously screamed orders to his men to begin rowing. They would have to row for their lives.

The first of the Spartans reached the Egyptian resistance and sparks flew as their blades met. Although the Egyptians greatly outnumbered the Spartans, Lycurgus and Menander struck down one after another of their foes with characteristic Spartan ferocity. Goliath more than evened the odds, though, brandishing a huge club he had concealed beneath his cloak, its superior reach giving him a distinct advantage at close quarters. Then the Carthaginians entered the fray, bolstering the numbers of fearless Spartans. Innocents all along the wharf dived for cover, terrified at the deadly clash. Their panicked movements only added to the chaos and the press of bodies where blood flowed.

Quick to appraise the situation, Melqart realized the real threat of escape would not be decided on the wharf but with the slowly moving ship. He bellowed, 'Archers — all archers! Withdraw and kill them. Kill them all! That ship!' Several of his men immediately unslung their bows, backed away from the fray to sight their weapons and let loose upon the commandeered Spartan ship, while Carthaginian bowmen mounted in the harbor guard towers quickly followed suit, now that an officer had made sense of this melee for them. Shafts rained down upon the ship's deck, burrowing into timber and flesh alike. Not satisfied with these results, he screamed out again, 'All of them. Everywhere!' Barely pausing to reflect their surprise, the bowmen adjusted range and began peppering those still on shore. The cries of Egyptians and Spartans being struck joined the yelps of pain from the Spartan ship.

Pelops, Simonides, and the Eleans had all taken up oars to hasten the escape. Hippodamia assisted Saul with the ship's twin rudders, wrenching them seaward with the strength of desperation. Saul cautioned her not to oversteer, as they had to balance their departure pace against not moving too far away from the wharf — somehow, the Egyptians and Goliath had to break away from their opponents and leap aboard. As the battle of grinding attrition continued to wage onshore, Saul realized that the tipping point had been reached; he screamed at the top of his lungs, 'Break it off! Get onto this ship! Jump!'

Prince Rameses repeatedly confirmed the order in Egyptian to his men and began to inch rearwards. His men followed closely, protecting their ruler at any expense. Still in the van, Goliath was engaging three opponents at once. Crushing the skull of one and clubbing aside the others, he turned to close the gap between himself and the Egyptians. He was immediately struck in the lower back by two arrows. The Spartan next to him took an arrow in the rear of his skull, dropping him heavily across Goliath's legs. Arching in intense pain, he fell to his knees, writhing and squirming. He attempted to find his feet, but the Spartans had almost reached him, having pushed aside their fallen comrades. Rameses made an instantaneous decision and ran forward to try to protect the fallen Philistine. His men surged forward with him but were hampered by the relentless Spartans and the hail of Carthaginian arrows that still struck at them.

Saul witnessed Goliath's fall with horror. He audibly groaned, ran towards the shoreward bulwark, and leapt towards the wharf. Barely hesitating to draw his sword, he wove through the embattled Egyptians to stand over Goliath's prone form.

Stunned, Pelops cried out, 'No! Gods, no! Captain, come back! No!'

Hippodamia and Simonides froze in shock, plaintively crying out towards the heroic Israelite. To no avail. Simonides turned quickly back to the Eleans and called upon them to redouble their efforts. Accustomed to their leader's folly, the crew of The Babel kept at their oars. Hippodamia wrestled with both rudders, now steering the vessel perilously close to the wharf.

Saul swung his blade with a madman's energy, compensating for his relative lack of skill through sheer manic force. Emboldened, Rameses's men pushed forward again, edging the Spartans back. This respite was just enough for Rameses and Saul to grab Goliath by his cloak, attempting to drag him away from further danger. Led by Lycurgus, the Spartans smelt blood and rallied, striking down warriors on either side of the rescue attempt. Daring to lay hands on their master, several of the Egyptian warriors forcibly dragged Rameses back from this lethal threat. As he capitulated and turned to flee shipwards, Rameses caught sight of yet another hail of arrows striking both Spartans and sailors. Goliath was mortally wounded; Saul had now been hit by shafts in torso and limbs. Down on one knee and bleeding out, he still tried to shield the Philistine with his back. They were both struck yet again, just as Rameses and his men leapt from the wharf onto the ship's deck.

Pelops screamed out incoherently at the loss of his two friends. Hippodamia wept openly but clung to her task at the rudders. Simonides stepped alongside to assist her, words of consolation evading him. Even the hardened crew of The Babel broke into gasps of horrified anger, cursing violently the demise of their captains. Pelops surged towards the bulwark, seemingly intent upon sacrificing himself to rescue the dying captains. Prince Rameses strong-armed him before he could leap onto the wharf, while trying to comfort him, 'You must leave them. There is nothing we can do. They gave their lives for this cause — for you and me. For all of us here.' Pelops relented, sobbing.

Lycurgus's men had instinctively advanced but were ordered not to pursue by their prince. Enraged at the loss to friendly fire of so many Spartan warriors, the Spartan prince sought out Melqart amongst the Carthaginians who had finally stepped forward to deliver the *coup de grace* to the fallen warriors. Lycurgus spotted the Carthaginian driving his sword through the back of the wounded madman who had tried so valiantly to rescue the fallen giant. He grinned with satisfaction, booting Saul's corpse aside just as he laid eyes upon Lycurgus storming towards him. Realizing the Spartan nobleman's deadly intent, Melqart thrust his sword towards the advancing fury, crying out, 'It had to be done, Prince. The shame they have brought upon my city is as great as the loss of your ship. A few men had to be sacrificed to try and stop them. Help me avenge us both.'

Lycurgus slowed at these words and batted Melqart's sword aside half-heartedly, 'Damn you, man — I lost five, no, six good men to your fire. Blood demands blood. How will you make reparations for this crime?'

Recovering his nerve, Melqart replied, 'Hold, Prince. I must give the command to stop that ship. I will address your concerns then.' Turning immediately to the looming tower behind him, the Carthaginian screamed up, 'Sound all alarms! All of them! Activate the seawall!'

Watchtower-mounted guardsmen dropped their bows and reached for trumpets, blowing three short blasts in rapid succession. They repeated these blasts until an echo of the same could be heard from the harbor mouth.

Positioned on an elevated platform at the mouth of the harbor, two Carthaginians started slowly turning the spokes on a giant wooden wheel. The wheel
had a vast bronze chain attached to it that stretched beneath the waters of the
harbor mouth, being attached to a large stone tower diametrically across from
their platform. They grunted heavily with exertion as the wheel creaked under
the strain. Although the chain was largely impervious to rust and any related
stiffness, its sheer weight and the amount of sea detritus that clung to it made it
enormously hard to elevate. But they knew the perils of failure all too well, and
the vicious shore fight they had just witnessed emphasized the gravity of their
task. They tightened their grips and continued to heave as the foreign ship closed
upon their position.

Aboard the escaping vessel, Pelops despondently wrenched two shields off
a gunwale and placed himself at the ship's stern, positioning himself to cover
Hippodamia and Simonides as they worked the rudders. Rameses had assumed
overall command of the ship, urging his Egyptians to fill the rowing benches
and supplement the escaped Greeks and crew of The Babel. The mood was
heavy with loss and edged with trepidation, but the rowers bent their backs like
grindstone slaves. Satisfied with progress, the prince moved to the rear of the
ship to ensure that the three young Greeks maintained their pluck. He gave them
a warming smile to bolster their resolve. Pelops turned away; his face still ashen
with shock.

A full stade away in one of the dock guard towers, a Carthaginian archer
slowly aimed and released an arrow at the ship's bow. The marksman's bounty
would be his if that shaft flew true; a kill could be identified by its distinctive
feathers and rewarded by his superiors. He leaned forward, eager to follow its
trajectory and terminus as he slotted another arrow into his powerful bow.

Catching the flash of sunlight upon a speeding iron tip, Pelops threw up one
of his shields at the last possible moment — the arrow embedded itself with a
dull thunk into the oaken bracer. Simonides gave a sigh of relief and a grateful
smile, as the shaft had ended scant feet from his head. Pelops turned grimly
back to his task of monitoring the docks for more deadly missiles, his heart even
heavier than the shields he wielded.

Ψ

As the stolen Spartan ship began to move out of effective arrow range, Melqart and Lycurgus glared after its retreating bow. Incensed, Melqart turned and growled, 'Follow me, Prince. We will take my ship, as you appear to have lost yours.'

The prince snarled at him, 'And who is the bigger fool — the man who loses a ship or the one who loses a queen's slaves?'

Wary again of the Spartan's fury, Melqart did not respond, choosing instead to fling his arms outwards, driving his troops before him towards a moored military vessel. Lycurgus cursed, then nodded at his men to follow.

ΨΨ

At the harbor mouth, the two guardsmen working the harbor-chain wheel had settled into a rhythm with the heavy work. Pausing only to lubricate the mechanism with olive oil, they sweated and heaved away at the wheel arms while monitoring the advance of the escaping ship and the ever-so-slowly rising harbor chain; never meant to be raised this rapidly. They privately implored the gods to send them mortal assistance while praying that they could block the harbor in time. They knew that failure was not an option. It was a death sentence.

ΨΨΨ

Still blinded by grief, Pelops had sought the solace of the ship's deserted prow, to be away from his friends. His guilt and sense of loss threatened to overwhelm him. As the Greeks, Egyptians, and men of The Babel rowed furiously behind him, he peered ahead. He noticed an odd movement at either edge of the harbor walls — a thick chain was beginning to rise from both sides. Startled, he turned and cried out, 'They've got a harbor blocker! They're trying to trap us in!'

Prince Rameses raced forward, following where Pelops pointed and cried out to the rowers, 'Faster! Maximum speed. We can beat that thing.'

Recognizing the heightened danger and galvanized back into action, Pelops sprang to the ship's timing drum and began pounding out a furious beat. The rowers responded with a mighty bellow, wrenching at their oars to match the pace. The ship catapulted forward, reaching ramming speed in only a few heartbeats. Rameses strode up and down the main deck, crying out words of encouragement and spraying water from a large amphora across the rower's heads to keep them cool. Their blood still up from the vicious fight on the docks, the oarsmen threw themselves into their task, realizing that much more than just their liberty rested upon their efforts. Again, the ship surged ahead, now only several lengths away from clearing the harbor mouth.

As Pelops continued to pound out a strident beat, Rameses raced back to the prow, scouring the water again for a sight of the chain. It was virtually under the ship's underwater ram, he noted with horror. He screamed back at the rowers, 'Give it everything you've got! Everything!'

Mass groans of exertion broke out amidst the rower's benches, but the oarsmen countered heroically. As their ship almost flew forward, a loud groaning noise from the hull drowned out the complaints on board; the chain was tearing its way down the length of the ship. As the full weight of the vessel settled upon the chain, it began to sag and produce a horrible screeching noise, followed by an eruption of timber, stone, and bodies from the nearby guard tower. The ship's pace and bulk had ripped the giant wheel and its attendants clear through the side wall of their vantage point, destroying the mechanism and sinking the chain. As their ship continued to clear the harbor under its own momentum, the rowers stormed to their feet, releasing their anxiety in cries of joy. Rameses, Simonides, and Hippodamia leapt about, joining the merriment. Pelops slumped over his drum, less physically exhausted than emotionally, his nerves at a ragged edge. His friends, Saul and Goliath, having perished to achieve this mission, Pelops sought to justify their loss against so many lives rescued. With the pain so fresh, he sought in vain.

ΨΨΨΨ

On the crystal-clear waters of the Mediterranean, strong winds drove the hijacked Spartan ship at a brisk pace. The scarlet sails were stretched taut. The rowers still pulled at their oars, although their pace was light and as much directional as propulsive. Days had passed since their escape from the harbor at Carthage, and a real sense of camaraderie had emerged — Egyptians, Greeks, and the polyglot crewmen of The Babel all now worked as a team. Still shattered by the loss of their captains, The Babel's crew sought solace in teamwork and the shared relief at their escape. Having completed his shift, Pelops moved wearily forward to the stern, a place he had occupied with increasing regularity as he sought to distance himself from those his solemn mood might affect. He settled upon coils of spare ropes and sprawled out, staring morosely across the waves.

Her eyes ever upon him these days, Hippodamia placed her amphora down, as she had been distributing drinking water, and joined Pelops. She reached out and took his hand, murmuring, 'You cannot keep blaming yourself.'

Simonides approached and said, 'We all lost friends, Pelops, but it was the only way. The risks were understood by all.'

Pelops stared mournfully at his friends, then glanced out over the waters. A pod of dolphins cut its way before the prow. He muttered, hoarsely, 'He called them sea-dogs. Meant to be a good omen. He gave his life for a man not of his own people. And for us. Two good men.'

Hippodamia and Simonides exchanged a sympathetic glance. Joining Pelops, they stared seawards.

In the ship's bow, Prince Rameses glanced away from monitoring the helms-man, the crew, and the sails to brood over the wake left behind the rapidly-moving ship. Movement on the horizon caught his eye, 'Is that a sail?'

The helmsman, an experienced member of The Babel's crew, stared behind and exploded, 'What? That we don't need. Yeah, curse it, it looks Carthaginian.'

Rameses asked of him, 'What do we do?'

The helmsman muttered, 'If only the captain was here.' He then yelled forwards, 'Ship in pursuit! Increase rowing speed!'

The crew spun on their benches to peer beyond the bow. A chorus of heated curses erupted. Setting to, they tightened grips on their oars and began rowing in earnest.

Pelops rose to his feet and shot a concerned look at the prince. Rameses acknowledged him with a grimace, then tugged his head rearwards to indicate the pursuit ship. The young Greek nodded briskly, grabbed the hands of his two friends, and said, intensely, 'We must help. No more lives can be lost.' They quickly moved midships, looking to relieve tired rowers. Pelops extended a hand towards an Egyptian rower who appeared exhausted, levering him upwards off the bench; Simonides did the same with an Elean friend on the port side.

Hippodamia stood above another Elean she had come to know in captivity; his brow was lathered with sweat. She asked of him, 'Let me replace you for a time, Agathon.'

Rameses approached and declared, 'You can't be serious? A woman?'

Pelops cried out to him, 'There is no stopping our women, Prince. Best you help Agathon from his bench.'

Hippodamia grinned at Rameses, who shook his head in disbelief. He then did what was requested of him, and a bone-weary Agathon rose up with the assistance of both of the Egyptian royal and the Greek priestess.

He whispered to them, 'Thank you. Just for a short time. I am unused to this form of exercise. And most men dislike women with muscles larger than their own.'

Rameses chuckled, but Hippodamia simply leapt down to the rower's bench and grabbed the oar. She quickly settled into the accelerated rhythm of the other rowers as Rameses looked on in astonishment.

He said, 'Unbelievable. What sort of women do you grow in Greece?'

Hippodamia looked up at him and laughed, 'The sort that aren't afraid. You too good to join us?'

Despite their exertions — and their inability to understand much Greek — the Egyptian rowers glanced up in surprise at their prince being so obviously challenged by the only woman on board. Rameses looked nearly as shocked. After glancing back at the Carthaginian ship shadowing them, he grimaced at Hippodamia, slipped off his ornate upper garb, and stepped down into the rower's pit, clad only in his kilt. His men grinned discreetly and made way for him, keeping a respectful distance. Rameses indicated for one of them to vacate the space altogether, and he slid into the vacant seat. Wrapping his hands around the oar, he heaved, matching the pace of the two Egyptians alongside him. Hippodamia grinned across at him; Rameses gave a sly grin in return, shook his head in amusement, and heaved again.

Above them, the helmsman cried out, 'Finished with the games? Row, damn it! Row!'

ΨΨΨΨΨ

On board the pursuing Carthaginian ship, Prince Lycurgus and Melqart leant over the stern, straining seaward to measure the distance between their ship and the stolen vessel. They had pushed their men to the brink, the escapees having proven infuriatingly effective sailors.

As a heavyset drummer pounded a fierce rowing beat, Lycurgus yelled above the noise to make himself heard, 'You haven't been able to close that gap for days, and now it looks like they've spotted us — they've accelerated. I thought you people were meant to be masters of the sea?'

Melqart yelled back, 'I made no promises. Remember who's the captain here!'

Spittle flying from his mouth in anger, Lycurgus screamed at him, 'Let my men replace yours on those benches. They are weak and spent. We Spartans will finish this... Captain.'

Melqart leaned in close; dangerously close, 'It is the added weight of your men that slows this ship. There are other solutions...'

Staring over the port side, Lycurgus immediately caught his drift and glared at him with unmasked hatred.

Fortunately for Melqart, Lycurgus's second-in-command approached; Menander pointed at an isle that had just come into view, 'That's Zakynthos, Prince. Poseidon favors them. They will beat us home at this rate.'

Lycurgus stared accusingly at Melqart, his glare intense.

Refusing to face the furious Spartan, Melqart spoke loudly into the wind, 'Not my problem. It is you who must face the shame of losing that ship. We did everything we could. What will your father say? I've only to return those slaves.'

Barely able to restrain himself, and knowing he still needed this smug creature to get his men safely to shore, Lycurgus muttered angrily and wrenched himself away from the railing. He stormed towards the bow.

Lysander met Melqart's eye and informed him, 'You are toying with fire, Carthaginian. Royal fire. Your luck will not hold up much longer.'

Melqart remained impassive, saying nothing. He watched coldly as the elder-ly Spartan staggered off to join his younger charge. Staring seaward again, his eyes narrowed as he began formulating fresh plans to ensnare those who had inflicted so much woe upon him.

IX

With the promontory of Katakolo portside and the long clean beaches of Elis starboard, the mouth of the River Alpheios loomed quickly before the bow of the captured Spartan trireme. Streaking over the normally placid waters, colored an unworldly azure, the ship's crew urged each other on for the last few leagues of the journey. This pace was no celebration of ability, nor the product of friendly rivalry between the sailors; rather, it was born of the chase. Every soul on board was aware of the pursuing Carthaginian ship that rose and fell with the swell of the waves some small distance from their stern. The hunting vessel had been a constant in their anxious flight from Carthage as, no matter how hard they had tried, they could not gain the lead they needed to put it beyond their sight.

Driven by desperation, Pelops's kidnapped ship surged towards the docks before retracting its oars on the helmsman's order. After days of unrelenting rowing, Egyptians, Greeks, and the sole woman, Hippodamia, had achieved the kind of synchronicity of motion only gained through constant effort. Like a graceful display of dressage, the oars tipped skyward as the helmsman piloted the ship in a sweeping arc that ended in line with the docks on the port side. With the helmsman again calling out fresh orders, the oars dipped momentarily once again into the water and back-rowed, this time slowing the vessel sufficiently to allow lines to be thrown, caught, and secured as it moored to the dock.

Eminently aware of the danger they were in should they allow the military force on the pursuit vessel to catch them at the docks, Rameses cast a worried look towards Pelops. Awake to the threat, Pelops raised his voice for all to hear, 'To the temples of Olympia. We'll run for it. We are safe there, as no Greek would ever violate its sanctuary.'

The words out of his mouth before he could halt them, Rameses voiced what most of the crew must have been thinking, 'What about the Carthaginians? Surely they are not thus bound?'

Pelops turned worriedly towards the sea. The enemy ship was now so close he could see Melqart smirking in the prow, while Lycurgus's cries were audible, as he urged yet greater effort from his Spartans as their ship careened towards shore. Frozen on the dock by this tableau, local fishermen, stevedores, merchants, and townsfolk alike grew alarmed as they realized that the Carthaginian ship would not slow to execute the same careful approach they had just witnessed. The massive Carthaginian warship appeared likely to arrest its pace by smashing into the jetty. They began to run landwards, away from the likely impact point. Pelops spun back to Rameses, a look of horror on his face, 'We must go now! To Olympia! Follow me! Our lives depend on it.' Leading their group, Pelops took off at full speed, with Rameses and his bodyguards taking up the rear to provide protection.

With a massive groaning of timber and splintering of oars, the Carthaginian ship ricocheted off the jetty. It slid headlong into the dock, just beyond the bow of the Spartan vessel that Pelops and his friends had fled, and it was now deeply embedded in the dock's ancient beams. Melqart and Lycurgus immediately leaped landward, not even bothering to glance at what remained of the once-proud vessel.

Scanning the area, Melqart bellowed, 'They have fled. Where would they go?'

'They can only be headed for the sanctuary,' replied the prince. 'After them! Move!' he screamed at both Carthaginians and Spartans, who, giving voice to days of frustration at sea, poured in the direction he indicated.

Literally running for their lives, Pelops's companions quickly realized they were losing ground to their pursuers. Refusing to leave any of their number to the mercy of their erstwhile captors, they struggled on, moving as fast as they could with those wounded in the battle at Carthage arresting their pace. Driven

by steely determination, they struggled through the gates of Olympia, somehow feeling the breaths of their pursuers hot on their necks.

Throwing his arms up to the heavens, Pelops pleaded, 'Divine Zeus, we call upon your protection. Defend us!'

Unwittingly answering this cry for help, a figure emerged limping from the side of the temple, arms and robe splattered in the blood of the latest animal sacrificed to the gods. Tantalus's gaze swung quickly to his son and the exhausted band of fellow travelers now falling on their knees, spent with exhaustion, in the temple grounds. It then fell upon the group of men arriving behind them, clearly in pursuit and now so close to their quarry.

One of their leaders, a Carthaginian known to Tantalus as a confidant of the Spartan kings, drew his sword upon entering the sanctuary, and, at this, his men also drew their weapons. Prince Lycurgus kept his sword sheathed, not willing to let his bloodlust override his respect for the gods and their holy ground. He signaled his men to stand firm and remain without blade in hand. Lycurgus glared at Melqart but held his tongue. Menace and blood were in the air as Melqart advanced on Pelops, drawing his men with him; Rameses and Simonides moved alongside Pelops in solidarity at the threat.

Outraged at this violation of the sanctity of Olympia, Tantalus bellowed, 'Sheath those weapons! Whatever my fool of a son has done, it is a crime against the gods to do violence in this place.' Retreating at his fury, the Spartans were suitably remonstrated but took comfort that they had not transgressed.

Vaguely impressed by Tantalus's ability to inject fear into his fellow Greeks, Melqart refused to lower his sword and glowered at the priest, 'Your gods are not mine, whoever you are.' Pointing his blade at Pelops, he continued, 'Even if this man is your son, he must pay for the offense he has caused Carthage.' Sweeping the sword in a horizontal arc to encompass the Eleans, the Egyptians, and the crew of The Babel, he declared, 'Carthage will not be denied. They all must pay.'

Pelops exploded, 'Offence? From you? Kidnapper? Slaver? Murderer? This place is free of the stain of Carthage. She does not rule here.'

Melqart hissed at Pelops and stepped closer, his blade now scant feet from the young priest's throat. Tantalus wedged himself between them, pressing his fists into both chests to drive them apart. He cursed them loudly with decidedly unpriestly imprecations.

Drawn by the sound of men shouting, Europa spied her daughter in the group of returned Eleans and raced towards her. Immediately spotting her mother, Hippodamia flew into her arms, and the two women embraced tearfully. Also drawn to this most unusual disturbance in the hallowed sanctuary, King Iphitos strode over to the confrontation. His face lit up with joy as he sighted the kidnapped athletes from his home kingdom. Observing an unsheathed weapon, he barked at Melqart, 'You there, barbarian, what in the name of all that is holy is the meaning of this? Do you even know where you stand?'

To prevent yet another ugly confrontation, one between Iphitos and Melqart, Lycurgus interjected, 'This is between us and the priest's son, King. Are you sure you want to involve yourself in the affairs of both Sparta and Carthage?'

Turning from her mother, Hippodamia spat, 'Yes. Carthage and Sparta. This prince would know, as he was there when we were taken.'

'She lies,' cried the prince, even as his eyes betrayed the truth of the accusation.

Simonides added, 'She speaks the truth. He works against his fellow Greeks with these barbarians.'

Unable to contain his fury at this stain upon his honor, Lycurgus finally reached for his sword. His fellow Spartans bristled; their hands fell collectively upon their sword hilts.

Anger flaring in his eyes, King Iphitos spread his arms to encompass the scene before him and shouted, 'Hold, you fools, before blood is spilled here.' The Greeks all froze, but the Carthaginians refused to stand down. The tension was palpable as even Tantalus reluctantly struggled to keep Melqart away from Pelops.

From amidst the antagonists emerged Homer. The old blind poet, tapping his way with his wooden staff, turned his face towards the sound of King Iphitos's voice, and asked simply, 'Lord, may I?

Relieved at the interruption, and knowing the wisdom of the man before him, Iphitos nodded, 'Very well, poet. Have your say.'

Homer turned towards the direction of the recent clamor of voices and spoke, 'Regardless of the reason behind your fight, you have brought it to the wrong place and at the wrong time. Not only is this a sanctuary always kept safe from violence, but from the moment of the announcement of the games, the truce of the Olympics has been in effect throughout this land. Break it, and you will bring the wrath of both gods and man down upon your heads.'

Thrusting Melqart further away, Tantalus snarled, 'What he says is true. Not here, not now, and...,' he added sternly, '...never in Olympia.'

Before Melqart could intercede, a still-enraged Prince Lycurgus stepped forward to achieve some satisfaction in this matter. Looking first to Homer, then King Iphitos, and finally, Tantalus, as the highest authority at Olympia, he declared, 'How do we settle this matter? My Carthaginian companion is owed the price of his slaves.' Glaring straight at Pelops, he demanded, 'And I am owed justice for the theft of my ship.'

Refusing to be restrained any further, Melqart exploded, 'He has insulted both the honor of Carthage and the honor of Sparta!'

Rameses snorted disdainfully, 'Honor? What honor?'

Slicing through the tension with his calming voice, Homer announced, 'There is a way to resolve this. The games will be held here in three short weeks. Wager upon them, and may the best man prove victorious. Let the gods decide.'

King Iphitos, not a man to leave these kinds of things to chance, stammered, 'I... I'm not comfortable staking the lives of my people on the outcome of these... these games.'

Homer asked, 'You have a better way then, my Lord?'

Hesitantly, Iphitos shook his head. In an anguished tone, he said, 'No, unfortunately, if there is another, better way, I cannot see it.'

Taking this as his cue, Homer announced, 'Then this is how it shall be. Are all parties agreed?'

Melqart barked, 'No, old man. What sort of fool do you take me for? I'll not gamble the queen's property and my reputation on athletes I know nothing about. This is what will happen. That Greek and I will compete in the same events, and if I should not prevail, I will gladly leave this place. But if he should lose — and he will — then those slaves are to be returned to Carthage. Otherwise, we finish this thing here. And now.' He hefted his sword once again in a menacing gesture.

Although deeply troubled by the risks, Pelops felt up to the challenge and, glancing at the Eleans standing alongside him, believed they were too. 'We accept the terms. I will represent my friends and Olympia', he said.

Concerned that his own kingdom might be rendered irrelevant by such tactics, Lycurgus proclaimed, 'By all the gods, Sparta will also compete, if only to show you fools the true meaning of excellence.'

Seizing this moment of accord, Homer declared, 'Then the games will bring resolution to this matter, one way or another.' He tapped the ground in front of him with his staff to clear a path and moved off back to his quarters.

Tantalus snorted and hobbled back to the temple of Zeus. He was anxious to digest the implications of this disturbing development, though affected not to show it. Pelops and Rameses exchanged a glance of resignation and encouraged their friends to help the winded and wounded make their way across to the stables of Poseidon to revive. Hippodamia, Europa, and Iphicles assisted them.

The Spartans and Carthaginians were the last to depart. Instead of enquiring about where his men would be bivouacked, Melqart raged to Lycurgus, 'Who in Baal's name was that blind old fool who dared address his betters that way?'

The prince grabbed him forcefully by the arm, 'You are in my land now, Phoenician. Better for you if you to keep your ignorance to yourself. That man is the finest poet in the Mediterranean and, likely, throughout this world. He is a trusted messenger of the gods. Do him no further dishonor.'

Melqart wrenched his arm away from Lycurgus and stormed off towards the gates of Olympia. Confused, his men followed him in dribs and drabs. Still shaking with anger, Lycurgus indicated that his Spartans should follow the interlopers.

Ψ

On the slopes of Mount Cronus, high above the valley of Olympia, a huge mountain lion silently stalked two goats as they nibbled at the tough grass. As the predator closed upon its prey, which remained oblivious to its rank scent, the lion suddenly froze — his ears had caught the distant sound of laughter and grunts of exertion. With hearing better than their eyesight or sense of smell, the goats, too, picked up the noise of humans and quickly made for even more inaccessible ground further up the mountainside. Not able to follow where only goats and gods could clamber, the lion rumbled with frustration and then slunk off.

Within moments of the animal's departure, Pelops, Hippodamia, Rameses, Koroibos, Agathon, and a group of Elean athletes moved into sight. Still lathered in sweat from the many sprints they had competitively engaged in during their ascent, they now moved slowly up more treacherous ground. At the front of their party, Agathon cried out, 'Hold! Liontari.'

Accustomed since birth to treat the animal as a living symbol of royalty, the entire group froze to gaze upon the retreating animal with reverence. Even Rameses was awestruck; he had heard that this part of the world still possessed the majestic beast, though he never thought he would see one in the flesh.

'So beautiful,' murmured Hippodamia, careful not to spoil the moment with too many words, nor attract the attention of the deadly beast with too much noise.

After her friends had followed the dwindling sight of the lion, their gaze shifted back to the spectacular view of Olympia, which they had climbed so long to witness. The valley below was a scene of idyllic beauty, and they carefully noted that much of the construction work on the new facilities for the games was near completion. Amongst the constant traffic that moved through the grand pavilions, more humble tents, temples, and sculpture parks that dotted the sanctuary, they could also make out the stands of performers, merchants, philosophers, and even courtesans that had been drawn to Olympia by the promise of material reward. All knew the games would be an event like no other.

Tearing his mind back to the friendly contest at hand, Pelops shouted, 'We are not done yet! This race is to the top!'

The entire party resumed the scramble up the mountain, close upon each other's heels. First to the top, Pelops sprawled out on the peak near an old, crumbling shrine. Hippodamia, following closely behind, flung herself down nearby, exhausted by her efforts. Soon, the rest of the group joined them, and they sat down upon the mountaintop, staring down again at Olympia.

His many wounds freshly healed, Koroibos said, 'So many attend these games. I have seen Libyans, Scythians from the East, Celtoi, and Iberians from the West, even the Brettanic of the Isle of Tin.'

'Don't forget the Egyptians,' pointed out Rameses.

'Even some Nubians. Friends of yours?' teased Simonides at Rameses.

The prince scowled, then quickly chuckled, 'We will show them on the track who the true rulers of Egypt are meant to be.'

'Ah, but it's the Greeks you need to watch. We're all natural athletes', countered Koroibos.

Rameses retorted, 'Everything you know you learned from we Egyptians. Feel free to thank me later. If you prove victorious at anything.'

Koroibos laughed heartily, pleased that humor and friendly rivalry could transcend cultural barriers. He rose to his feet.

Sensing a challenge, Pelops glanced meaningfully at Hippodamia and smiled. Pelops said, 'Leave us out of this. We'll follow you down — walking'.

Koroibos turned to the Egyptian prince, 'You want to see what we Greeks have learned while you were busy losing a kingdom? I'll race you back down and show you Olympia's first champion.'

Rameses rolled to his feet in one fluid motion and took off, pell-mell, down the mountain. Koroibos laughed at the prince's speed and took off in pursuit. His fellow Eleans launched themselves behind, keen to see who would prevail.

Once the runners were out of sight, Hippodamia's mood turned serious, 'I've seen Lydians today. Your mother's people.'

Pelops nodded, 'I saw them, too.'

Hippodamia then asked, 'Why is there so much trouble with your father? He wasn't this way while your mother lived.'

Although hampered by the shyness of youth, Pelops found that their growing friendship, strengthened through adversity, meant that he could broach these topics with Hippodamia.

'He misses her, I think. She was a gentle, peaceful woman. You remind me of her.'

Hippodamia blushed, then chuckled, 'Greek men and their mothers. You'll not romance me that way, champion of Carthage.'

Pelops rose from where he lay and walked over to sit beside Hippodamia. Leaning in to kiss her while looking deep into her eyes, he whispered, 'Well, if flattery is useless, maybe this will work.' And it did.

ΨΨ

Tantalus stood outside Zeus's temple, waiting as Iphicles walked towards him, leading a saddled horse. Gazing up at the nearby mountain, he frowned. Upon its slopes, he could just make out a thin trail of dust rising into the clear midday air behind what appeared to be three men running at full speed down towards Olympia. Imbeciles, he thought; only idiots would risk their lives so freely in such a childish race. The sight only seemed to increase his agitation as he struggled to cling to the sense of honor that made Olympia inviolate in the eyes of his people. The sound of a voice brought him out of his ruminating, and, snapping his head around to its source, he saw the desert nomad Askari leading a group of his men through the thronging crowds.

'Ho, priest. Yes, you! We need directions', the big man bellowed, pointing a meaty finger at Tantalus.

'Do I strike you as the type who conducts tours here? Find your help elsewhere,' he snapped.

Noticing the curious stares of onlookers as well as the amusement of his men, Askari did not shy away from an altercation with this pompous, self-serving cleric. He swaggered right up to Tantalus until they were nose to nose. 'I've heard of Greek hospitality. You do it no justice, servant of Zeus. Now make yourself useful and tell me where I might find the youth they call Pelops.'

Signaling his boundless disapproval by sighing deeply, Tantalus barked, 'My son? Again! By Hephaestus's limp, what has he done now?'

Taken aback, the nomad exclaimed, 'You're his father? There is no... resemblance.'

Realizing that little could be gained by challenging this annoying man, he turned to the Greek work crew laboring nearby, 'Where is Pelops to be found, boys? We've crossed a desert of water to stand with him.'

Before they could reply, Tantalus hissed, his eyes brimming with contempt, 'He's in Elis. Or Hades, for all I know. Leave him and I be.' He turned immediately to his manservant and demanded, 'Iphicles, my horse!'

Iphicles handed him the reins, and Tantalus swung into the saddle; Askari watched him canter off with a look of amused disdain on his face.

The old manservant, having been mercifully, albeit briefly, freed from his master's tyranny, asked the huge stranger, 'You seek the young master?'

Looking down upon the old man, the giant said, 'Only if he hasn't become as foul-tempered as his father!'

Iphicles grinned briefly, then begged the stranger's understanding, 'Apologies for such poor friendship toward a guest. He is a... troubled man. Pelops trains in the city of Elis, a short ride from here.'

Askari replied, 'We will find him. We should have no trouble purchasing mounts among this gathering. Our thanks. You seem less much a slave to your temperament than your master.'

With nods of gratitude from his fellow tribesmen, Askari and his companions strolled off to locate horse merchants with which to haggle a cut-throat deal or two.

Leading Homer, Europa approached Iphicles and asked, 'More competitors?'

Iphicles nodded, 'Desert people. Berbers, I think.'

'Did they bring any female athletes with them?' probed Europa.

'No, my Lady,' answered Iphicles, still incredulous that Pelops's call to the games had reached such exotic people as these.

Her mind on the women, rather than the men, Europa turned to Homer, 'Then the numbers are now fixed.'

The poet asked in turn, 'It will be women of the Greeks in preponderance?'

'Yes,' replied Europa, 'but from every corner of the Greek world. Even in judging the competition, I will be aided by women from both Elis and Pisa.'

Homer smiled, 'And the victory prize?'

Proudly, Europa announced, 'The women of Pisa have made a robe in honor of Hera. Elean women will purify the victor. It is just. Goddess Hera will be pleased, as I promised her.'

Iphicles politely interjected, 'Can we men watch the event, Lady?'

Smiling, Europa answered, 'Yes, though it will not be the same for your events. Only unmarried and virginal women may attend. Tantalus and the Spartans object to all others.'

Shocked, Homer demanded, 'What is their justification? Surely this is not so?'

'It is fear and xenophobia. They worry that foreign men will lust after their wives,' Europa replied heatedly. 'I have fought them on this, but they will not desist.'

The poet raised his hands and spoke gently, 'Careful, priestess. Anger is the beginning of all evil.'

Her blood cooling, Europa declared, 'That should be told to Tantalus.'

Both Iphicles and Homer nodded in silent agreement.

ΨΨΨ

Stades away, at the training camp in Elis, athletes from across the known world trained alongside each other in preparation for the coming Games. There were but scant days to go before they would all be tested in earnest. Pelops's message of athletic glory had spread like wildfire throughout the Mediterranean world and beyond, and the finest athletes ever assembled in one place now trained shoulder to shoulder. Everywhere the eye searched, all manner of exotic foreigners were limbering up, exercising, and training. Greeks of all stripes were numerically dominant but far from alone, each people casting an appraising eye upon unfamiliar athletes and training routines to better gauge their own prospects. While a Carthaginian strongman power-lifted crude weights, surrounded by his countrymen, their team leader, Melqart, enjoyed a slave's oil rub-down; he sneered as he glanced over the competition. One Greek nearby held unusual hand weights while he practiced the long jump, using the ballast to propel himself further into a sandy pit when he launched off the ground. Others cast javelins or practiced their archery with large, oaken bows. Elean officials, dressed in purple-bordered robes and carrying forked switches, moved amongst them, crying out both results and rebukes. While Melqart admitted to himself that many of them had skill, his cultural arrogance was so ingrained that he could only contemplate how effectively his Carthaginians would shame them all on track and field.

Some distance away on the practice running track, mercifully beyond the sight and scorn of Melqart, Hippodamia led a field of all-female runners in a half-stade sprint. She flew gracefully over the finish line and flashed a smile of triumph at her onlookers, at which Pelops and their Elean friends cheered wildly. As Greeks from every corner of the diaspora milled around the runners, congratulating one and all, Pelops approached Hippodamia and embraced her with joy. Despite the sheen of perspiration that coated her, she returned the clasp unselfconsciously and with great affection. They laughed as they disengaged, their clothing still stuck to one another. Koroibos mused that, despite his affection for Hippodamia, they made a radiant couple.

Having observed Hippodamia's victory very closely, Prince Lycurgus was far less excited to see the daughter of Europa cross the line in first place. A considerable judge of physical ability, Lycurgus sought reassurances from the female athletes in his squad. Turning to a striking young woman with the lithe physique of a natural athlete and the hawklike features of a born competitor, he enquired, 'You can beat that, Cynisca?'

'She runs well, but her technique lacks refinement. She'll not hold a victory wreath on the day,' replied Cynisca.

Lycurgus's advisor and friend, Menander, addressed her sternly, 'That is good. For you know the Spartan motto — either carrying your shield at the end or laying still upon it. Victory or death, woman. If you do not beat her, do not bother coming home.'

With a confidence born of many victories, Cynisca looked him over from head to foot and hissed sarcastically, 'Do you compete here, Menander? No. Like all of Sparta, I certainly heard of the glory you heaped upon us in the games of Carthage. So, leave the running, and the result, to me.'

Menander bristled, moving forward as if to strike her. Prince Lycurgus blocked him and said, 'Leave her be. She speaks poorly, but with truth.' He pushed Menander away.

The veteran Spartan diffidently accepted the reproach and stood down. Cynisca glowered at him.

As the Spartans argued amongst themselves, they failed to notice Melqart's approach. Swaggering up to the group with a muscle-bound Carthaginian strongman trailing him, he hailed them, 'Bickering Spartans — what a sight!'

As one, they turned towards the two men approaching. Lycurgus spoke disdainfully, 'Now what do you want of us?'

Oblivious to the arrogance of others, Melqart chuckled, 'We need to speak. Away from here.'

Lycurgus sighed and nodded to Menander. They followed the Carthaginian nobleman away from the Spartan tents towards a copse of trees. Melqart had pressed a finger over his lips to motion them to silence until they reached suitable privacy. They passed the tents of the Cretan contingent. They were all distracted by the leaping and twirling of the female athletes as they warmed up for one of the many qualifying heats. Their team leader was Atalanta, an Amazonian-looking competitor, who had been the talk of the camp over the last few days. As she oiled her limbs, Atalanta boldly returned their admiring stares. Noting the self-assurance of the Cretan beauty, Lycurgus smiled and addressed her by name.

'Lycurgus,' she nodded and replied, addressing him in the familiar rather than by his royal title.

The prince was pleased she knew of him. Famed not just for their bull-leaping skills but their aesthetic charms throughout the Greek world, Lycurgus made a mental note to drop by the Cretan compound very soon again. As he glanced away, he caught Melqart glaring at him to hasten; he scowled and caught up with the demanding Carthaginian. As they reached the copse of trees Melqart had indicated, Lycurgus turned to him, 'What is so damn important?'

'Guaranteed results,' Melqart replied, cryptically. 'Hamilcar here is unbeatable. I like his odds', he continued, as the Carthaginian strongman grinned and flexed his biceps.

Lycurgus frowned and said, 'And you're not so certain of your own?"

In a harsh whisper, Melqart retorted, 'Let me just say that all measures must be taken to ensure my victory. You have your ship back. I must return with those slaves.'

Suspicion now dawning over him, Lycurgus chuckled, 'You fear one Greek youth so much?'

Taken aback at this mocking challenge, Melqart snapped, 'I fear only uncertainty. Everything that can be done to ensure victory must be done.'

Contemptuous of the implications of what the Carthaginian had dared utter aloud, Lycurgus raged at him, 'We Spartans live by a code, and will not willingly anger the Gods! We will not be a part of what you plot!'

Menander placed a calming hand upon the prince's shoulder and whispered to him, 'My Lord, you remember the words of your father — we must aid these barbarians in their endeavors.'

Knowing that his friend spoke truthfully, although in the direction of dishonor, Lycurgus grudgingly conceded, 'Speak to the boy's father, Tantalus, High Priest of Olympia. He may know of some weakness.'

Sneering triumphantly, Melqart asserted, 'Your code is of no consequence to me, Spartan. I will seek out the father, or yours if needs be. He must be stopped.' He strode away with the muscular colossus stomping behind him.

As he wrestled to control his temper, the prince watched them depart with the distinct feeling that he would live to regret this exchange.

ΨΨΨΨ

Within Sparta's *Gerousia*, King Arcelaus and King Prytanis stood at the chamber's epicenter, surveying the angered councilors. There was outrage among the elders as the forthcoming games of Olympia were busily discussed. All grizzled veterans of many campaigns, one of their number, a man in his late fifties who bore the scars of past battles, stood and addressed the diarchy, 'Sparta has been undermined! Why in Heracles's great name have these games been allowed to proceed?'

Encouraged by this defiance, another elder rose and cried out to the kings, 'You have even sent a team to compete! Headed by your own son, of all people. Has that priest of yours no temporal authority there at all?'

This outburst was greeted by further angry murmurs as the disapproval of the elders threatened to burst into outright rebellion. For battle-hardened and intensely disciplined Spartans, such an irruption would be almost unheralded within their ranks.

Realizing that matters were delicately poised, Prytanis tried to restore calm. He glared first at the two standing councilors, pressing them back into their seats through sheer force of personality, then stepped forward to command all of their attention, 'Your objections are noted, but plans are in motion. If you will just...'

Before he could complete his address, a Spartan guard in full armor clattered into the chamber. He bowed quickly and waited nervously for further acknowledgment, aware that he had just broken protocol.

Angered by the interruption, King Arcelaus commanded, 'What is the meaning of this? You know better than to disturb a full session of this council.'

Deeply embarrassed, the guard again bowed his head and proclaimed, 'Lords, a delegation from Carthage. They are here now.'

Unannounced, Queen Dido swept into the room, a full retinue of councilors and bodyguards in her train. She strode majestically, right up to Prytanis and Arcelaus, and looked them over, unflinching in her appraisal.

Even as they secretly admired the splendor of the queen and her exotic cortege, the Spartan elders were shocked at her conceit. To a man, the elders rose to their feet and stonily glared their disapproval; the chamber was filled with silent tension.

Ignoring both men and mood, the queen took control of the room with a simple command, 'Be seated, men of Sparta. I have business with your kings!'

Stunned at her effrontery again, the elders were left with the stark choice of either petitioning the kings to expel Sparta's most powerful benefactor or follow her order. Having no other viable option, they chose the latter and grudgingly took their seats.

Sensing the dramatic power shift and wishing, at least in part, to restore it, Prytanis declared, 'Queen, you come unannounced. This is most improper.'

'Yes,' she countered. 'This sort of incompetence demands it.'

Loath to let this insult shame him before the assembled elders, Arcelaus barked, 'Remember where you are. We are kings of Sparta, this world's finest fighting men, and your staunchest ally. We will not be spoken to in this manner!'

A smile played over the queen's lips, and with more than a hint of malice in her voice, she drawled, 'Really? As nearly everything in Sparta rests now upon the strength of Carthaginian gold, I believe I may speak to you as I will. Unless, of course, you would rather seek a change in our relationship, maybe a touch more financial independence?'

At this challenge, the Spartan elders verbally erupted, their outrage sweeping through the chamber. The kings sought to restore order, gesticulating to signal calm and glaring down the most conspicuously unruly of the elders.

Oblivious to the bruised pride of the Spartans, Dido raised her voice over the hubbub, 'Silence! You have failed me as vassals, and now you choose to enter the very games you could not prevent? If these Olympics bring unity to this part of the world, then the value of our alliance must be recalculated. Many peoples gather here, yet it is Carthage which dictates their fate. It is Carthage that is the center of this world. And I rule Carthage. I will be observing very closely.' Not bothering to gauge the damage her words had wrought, Dido sauntered out of the council chamber.

Agog, the councilors sat mute as they watched the huge ostrich feathers carried by the queen's bearers and the sound of hobnailed military sandals fade from the inner sanctum of Spartan power. Prytanis and Arcelaus glanced at each other concernedly, knowing they had now to weather a political storm to rival their concerns with the games. While they knew that during their tenure as co-regents they had outwitted every prior foe, both on the field of battle and in the equally vicious political arena, the queen's declaration was of a starkly different magnitude. Even the audacious King Prytanis could not help but flinch when an elder found his feet, the very same veteran who had first voiced opposition to the Games, wagged a finger at him and exclaimed, 'Should things go badly for Sparta at these games, it will be you and your son we hold to account!'

ΨΨΨΨΨ

In the High Priest's quarters behind the temple of Zeus, Pelops and Tantalus sat at a dining table. Although Pelops had requested time with his father and Tantalus had suggested he should join him for a late evening repast, both were uneasy with one another. Few words were exchanged as they awaited their meal, and they spent more time staring at and sipping from their goblets than enjoying common ground—the flickering light of the oil burner cast long shadows in the room as they contemplated their thoughts. Tantalus's cook, Oenomaus, a round-shouldered man with darting eyes, bustled noisily over his meal preparation in the adjoining room.

Always trying to heal the rift between them, even though he had frequently struggled to understand its cause, Pelops addressed his father in tones of respect, 'Thank you for seeing me. I know this is a busy time for you, and your leisure is always brief.'

Tantalus nodded once, perfunctorily, and raised his cup.

'Cook, bring us wine,' he barked at Oenomaus. Long since used to his employer's habitual rudeness, Oenomaus rolled his eyes heavenwards before carrying a small amphora into the main room. Once the cook had filled his cup, Tantalus drained it and held it out once again. As Oenomaus poured the wine, Tantalus looked at his son and, nodding at the cup, asked, 'You?'

Pelops answered promptly, 'No, Father — it is forbidden.'

Looking mildly surprised, Tantalus waved Oenomaus away, and the cook returned to the kitchen.

Pelops sought to explain, 'I am lucky to be here. There are many limits on the athletes — one of which is that no alcohol may be consumed while training for the games.'

Tantalus grunted in a manner that Pelops thought to be disapproving and took another long draught of his wine. 'So, does that also mean that you are riding back to Elis tonight?'

'Yes,' Pelops replied, 'I've come to seek your blessing before the Games, Father. Will you grant it?'

Tantalus locked his gaze onto his son's eyes. The young athlete noted that those eyes were bloodshot, and the face was strangely drawn. Something felt wrong here, thought Pelops, although his father often shocked him with his mercurial temperament and drinking. And his health had often been poor since the passing of his wife, Pelops recalled.

Tantalus declared, 'Eat first, and we'll talk later.'

Oenomaus re-entered the room and placed two large bowls of a simple stew and greens before the men. A loaf of barley bread was also left for the diners. As he walked back over to the kitchen space, Pelops could have sworn the cook stared briefly at him, pity and curiosity warring in his shifty eyes. Tantalus swirled his bowl as Pelops picked up a chunk of bread, 'This smells good, but don't you miss Iphicles serving your meals, Father?'

'You're welcome to him. Oenomaus here makes a stew fit for Olympians', he told his son. 'Now eat,' he commanded. With the appetite of an athlete, Pelops saw no need to debate further and tore off a chunk of bread, dunking it first into his stew bowl before consuming it. Tantalus, drinking heavily now, did not eat himself but watched silently as Pelops gorged his meal. Standing to one side, almost forgotten, Oenomaus perspired. When Pelops had finished his meal, Oenomaus cleared away the table, taking Tantalus's untouched repast with him.

Once the dishes were cleared, Tantalus said, 'I could say many things tonight, but I am wearier than you will ever know. I will waste no more of our time together squabbling with you, my son — you have my blessing, for what it is worth. Go now and let there be peace between us.'

With sincere relief, Pelops stood and beamed, 'Thank you, Father, it will bring me luck. I know it.'

Glancing away from his son's delighted face, Tantalus growled, 'In the eyes of the gods, your fate has already been decided. What will be, will be.'

Still smiling at receiving the blessing of his stern patriarch, Pelops took his leave of the priestly quarters.

Long into the night, Tantalus stared into his hearth fire, drinking heavily and, occasionally, dampening his face with an unfamiliar sensation.

ΨΨΨΨΨΨ

Within the athlete's barracks at Elis the following morning, Pelops tossed and turned fitfully upon his sleeping pallet. Having returned late in the night from his visit to Olympia, he had thrown himself down to catch what sleep he could before the following day's trials and heats. He had slept poorly and was now half-awake. Most of his fellow athletes had roused themselves some time earlier; the pallets surrounding that of Pelops were now empty. Although he wore only a loincloth, Pelops was slick with sweat. Rolling onto his knees, he lunged at a water bucket and vomited into it.

Concerned when he did not see Pelops joining their group of companions to break his night's fast, Koroibos entered the sleeping quarters. He took one look at his retching, spasming friend and cried out, 'Pelops, what in the name of the gods is wrong?'

Pelops slowly gazed up at Koroibos, and the Elean could see that the situation was even more dire than he first thought. There was no color in the face of the young priest who knelt before him, and he looked like he was burning from a deep fever within. Koroibos strode over and put a comforting hand on his shoulder, 'Is it the water? Are you injured?'

Not wishing to admit to any weakness that might keep him from the games, Pelops managed to croak out, 'It is just... a passing... thing. Let me... rise.' He tried, unsuccessfully, to lift himself to his feet. The effort proved more than he could stomach; he lay back down, in danger of losing consciousness.

Koroibos cursed and said, 'This is not natural; something pollutes you. You were in peak condition yesterday, and now your chest rattles like a sistrum.' Koroibos quickly reached for the bucket as Pelops groaned and began to spasm again. He was not fast enough, and he threw up on the floor next to his pallet bed.

As he lay there in a puddle of his own bodily fluids and coated in sweat, Pelops groaned out, 'Punished... I'm being punished... by Zeus.... A lie... the games... my lies.' He slipped into unconsciousness before a horrified Koroibos.

X

The grounds of Olympia had exploded into color and life. Vast crowds, made up of countless different peoples, streamed into the open sanctuary spaces, prepared excitedly for the spectacles they had anticipated for so long. Most had heard the rumor — this was to be the greatest sporting carnival in the cosmos.

While for many of the exotic nationalities, with their flags and banners indicating foreign climes, the gods of Greece were a mystery, the real significance of these games was not lost upon the Hellenes. This was only reinforced when a troop of musicians began playing a stentorian tune, attracting attention to the temple of the goddess Hera. The pandemonium of the crowds died down to a gentle buzz as all heads pivoted towards the imposing structure. The head priestess, Europa, emerged from the entrance of the temple and descended the stairs. Standing at the base of the stairs, she raised her arms heavenward as sixteen priestesses move down to flank her, each selected from neighboring kingdoms: eight garbed in black to her left, the remainder garbed in white to her right. A representative of each of these two groups of priestesses stepped further forward and knelt before Europa, raising high the paraphernalia of their faith. One group held a scepter and a pomegranate, the other a golden diadem, a cluster of peacock feathers, and a beautifully-woven scarlet robe. The ceremonial music ceased. The crowd was immediately hushed by the solemnity of the occasion, and a large group of female athletes, all dressed in crisp white chitons, emerged from their ranks to stand before this congregation of the devoted. Cynisca and Atalanta were amongst them; Hippodamia smiled up excitedly at her mother.

Europa called out in a clear, crisp voice, 'Before Zeus and his mother, Rhea, I announce this contest in honor of the goddess-queen, Hera of Olympos!'

Taking their cue from the clapping female athletes, the crowd roared their approval.

The head priestess smiled at the gathering, then adopted a sterner expression, 'There is an oath, a sacred oath, that I ask these maidens to swear before they compete. Do you all so pledge?'

The athletes all murmured and nodded their agreement.

Europa continued, 'Do you so pledge that you are pure of heart and have trained in good faith? Do you pledge that you have not employed foul means, nor the ways of the witch, the *pharmakois*, to gain victory? Swear this before Hera and Zeus Oath Breaker!'

The athletes responded with a hearty round of assents, all pledging their fealty to the deities named, whose retribution — they knew from lessons instilled in them since birth — could be fierce if they transgressed. Hippodamia stared deeply into her mother's eyes and said, 'I so pledge.'

The crowd cheered with gusto.

Europa lowered her arms and waited for the noise of the crowd to subside, then said, 'Then go forth and compete in honor. Hera observes your skill.' She turned and retreated back up the stairs, her priestesses following in train.

The maiden-athletes strolled off towards the running track to begin their preparations, greeting and waving at members of the crowd as they passed. The crowd dispersed, breaking away for the prized viewing spots they had previously earmarked, knowing that the games were soon to begin.

Hippodamia took the time to first approach Homer, who had been sitting beneath a large poplar and listening intently to the proceedings. She touched him gently on the shoulder and said, 'Homer, it is I, Hippodamia. Can I ask your indulgence?'

The poet smiled up, beatifically, 'Of course. What is on your mind?'

She replied, 'My father passed many years ago. Would you give me your blessing before I compete?'

Homer smiled and stood, 'Of course. Place my hand upon your head.' Hippodamia dropped to one knee and rested his palm upon her tightly-bound hair.

He slowly incanted, 'Remember, O daughter of Hera, that so long as a mortal lives there will be no greater glory than that which is won by hand or foot in these games. Compete with dignity and help bring unity to this land.'

She kissed his palm and said, 'I will. Your words will ring in my ears as I run.'

Homer grinned, his rheumy eyes even more clouded than the sky above, 'Just the words of an old man. Now go — you have a race to lead!'

Rising up, Hippodamia touched him gently on the shoulder again to express her gratitude and ran towards the racetrack, darting left and right to warm her leg muscles. Homer paused, listened to her footfalls until they disappeared, then moved back into the shade, his mind already inspired by the results that would follow.

Ψ

Assembled on an open field later that day, male athletes from across the Mediterranean world prepared to compete. They clustered together in their ethnic groups: while Greeks from all across the diaspora dominated, there were healthy numbers of Phoenicians, Celtiberians, Egyptians, Baltic Sea peoples, Nubians, Italics, Philistines, Israelites, Mesopotamians, Sabians, Bedouin, Gauls, Picts, Germanic tribesmen and many other frequent travelers of the inland sea. Some had even traveled from as far away as the Carpathian Mountains, the Indus Valley, and the lands of the Zhou dynasty. Trade routes had carried word of these games with great speed; the promise of a temporary suspension of all hostilities for athletes and spectators to travel safely in a way they had never known before had intrigued and lured so many.

Melqart and his fellow Carthaginians lounged about their compound, having demanded a space to be segregated from the others. Casting a disapproving eye over them, Lycurgus and his men were positioned nearby, the prince having given a grudging promise to his father that he would ensure the safety of Sparta's wealthy providers. Alongside Prince Rameses and his Egyptian rebels, the flamboyant desert chieftain, Askari, his mission to find Greece for the first time obtained when he moored The Babel in nearby waters, stood proudly with his nomadic tribesmen. With rapt attention, they surveyed the unprecedented spectacle of so many foreign peoples — and often, enemies — in such close proximity. Ogling them back were many others, quietly stunned that the truce of these Olympics had heralded a peace previously unknown to their fractious world.

King Iphitos and his courtly Elean retinue kept watch upon the polyglot gathering, having pressed many of their kingdom into service as guards. While not armed with metal, they carried wooden staves to punish those whose rivalries or grudges might spill over from the competitive arenas. The recently-rescued Elean runners were also in the service of their people; with their strength fully restored, they would now compete for the glory of Elis. Most beamed with pride that their tiny kingdom had achieved such prominence.

Officials from Elis circulated among the athletes, carrying switches and brands; the purpose of the punitive equipment was obvious to all, but the brands were being employed to daub the competitors in colors specific to the sports they would engage in. As the Messenian slaves, on loan from Sparta, juggled multiple leather buckets, with various liquid hues contained within, the head Elean official cried out, 'Boxers! Boxers to present before me!'

His colleagues called, in turn, for pentathletes, riders, runners, and the most daring sportsmen of all, the pankrationists. Lean and taut men, and those more heavily muscled all moved in the direction of those responsible for the color daubing. Some were still training, placing aside skipping ropes or dropping exercise weights before moving towards their designated officials. Many of the Greeks were being oiled — a traditional preparation that was part sun bronzer, part cleanser, and part massage — while uniquely, the Spartans braided their hair before the competition, just as they did before a battle.

From the sidelines, Koroibos and Simonides assisted a grievously-ill Pelops to cross the field to the officials. They moved very slowly. Pelops stumbled more than once; his jaundiced complexion twisted in agony.

Melqart turned his head toward the unusually slow-moving trio; he broke into a wide grin. Lycurgus also spotted the object of Melqart's joy, then turned towards the royal officiator, King Iphitos.

The king was already on his feet, 'Head judge — attend! We've something here.'

The official began shuffling over and cried out, 'Yes, Lord.'

Melqart broke from his team to watch the proceedings more closely; Lycurgus followed him, wary that the Carthaginian would again prove disrespectful.

As they awaited the head official, the king spoke to the trio, 'One of your culinary mistakes, Koroibos?'

Koroibos attempted a smile and failed, 'No, Lord, no. He is terribly sick. I don't think he can compete like this.'

Melqart broke in, his voice triumphant, 'Then this is over. He forfeits. Those slaves are mine.' He pointed over at the Elean runners, who were in the process of being daubed with a distinctive hue.

Raising a querulous eyebrow, the king demanded of the official, who had just reached them, 'Is this true? Is this a forfeiture?'

The head official bowed and said, 'Actually, no, Lord. Our rules hold that a substitute can be appointed in his place.'

Pelops stammered out, 'I... must... compete.'

Melqart sneered at him, 'You must be quiet. These games are for men, not weaklings.'

Koroibos glared at the Carthaginian, then turned to his liege, 'Lord, can I nominate for him?'

The king pivoted to all in the small group, 'Are there objections?'

Lycurgus immediately spoke up, 'Not from Sparta.'

Flaring into anger, Melqart spat out, 'What! You Greeks play by no rules that Carthage recognizes. This sickly one is a coward and that... that's a peasant!'

King Iphitos did not bother to reply, glancing meaningfully at the official instead. The head official shrugged back at his king, 'No rules against it. Games for all.'

Pelops tried to speak again, 'I can't... run, but I... can ride. Just the footrace...'

Simonides turned to him, 'Pelops, you can barely stand.'

He retorted through clenched teeth, 'I will... ride.'

The king snapped his fingers to signal the conversation was at an end, his patience having been tried enough, 'Then it is decided. Pelops rides; Koroibos runs for him.' The king placed a hand on the official's back and steered him towards his royal pavilion, as this disruption had consumed enough time.

With open contempt, Melqart glared at the Greeks. Koroibos could barely restrain himself from spitting at his feet, his tongue rolling over his lips. Even Pelops managed to raise his head enough to stare directly at his opponent, doing his best to ignite his eyes with amusement at the Carthaginian's fury.

Melqart snorted and strode off.

With a sardonic undertone to his voice, Prince Lycurgus said to them, 'Now you two are just begging for trouble.'

Simonides and Koroibos grinned at him, then walked Pelops towards his beloved horses.

ΨΨ

On the running track alongside the temple to Hera, the female athletes completed their warmups. Some of their coaches remained with them, whispering urgent words of encouragement as they limbered up. Hippodamia had drawn a straw to position herself near the center of the field; Atalanta was two positions away, with the Spartan Cynisca to her immediate left. Even a few non-Greeks had been admitted to the race lineup. It was a formidable field of gifted runners, numbering in the dozens.

Hippodamia was highly energized, having longed for this day. She had dispensed with a coach early in her training, as she had chosen to train with Pelops and Iphicles instead. She focused her attention on the track. Half a stade long, with a turn post stationed at its end, the runners would have to sprint its length, then reverse direction upon reaching the half-stade marker. To enliven the race for its audience, pan-pipers and flute players stood all down its central alley, instruments already raised to their mouths and prepared to play a stirring tune.

She also took the time to glance across at the line official as she slowly wiggled her feet into place on the stone starting block; he was testing his string for tautness, ready to kick over the ingenious mechanism that dropped its entire length before the runners at the exact same moment. As she glanced across at him, Cynisca caught her attention, staring coldly back at her. Hippodamia attempted an encouraging smile. The Spartan ignored the gesture and turned back to her preparations. The young priestess mused that she would make few friends today.

A vast crowd had assembled to watch the novel event. It was unique that such a race between all women had never before been held in their experience. To those of more conservative temperaments or cultures, it seemed scandalous that these athletes were so scantily clad, with some deciding to subsequently boycott the event to focus instead upon the many men's events. For the greater majority, though, the Herean Games would be a truly memorable highlight. Sprawled over every possible vantage point, the crowd buzzed with excitement. Europa stood outside her temple portico, having raised up the sacred scarlet robe to Hera in both arms while she muttered prayers heavenwards. Equally as conspicuous was Homer, who had now placed himself at the race adjudicator's desk, ready to help distribute red participation ribbons and a victory wreath for the winner.

The start official stepped away from the desk where Homer stood and signaled first with his hand, following it up with a booming call, 'Places!'

The crowd cheered wildly and began craning forward to drink in the all-important start. The last of the female athletes settled into their launch positions.

Cynisca leaned across and hissed at Hippodamia, 'This had better prove fair, priestess's daughter!' Several other runners glanced at Hippodamia, then followed Cynisca's gaze as she glared at Europa atop Hera's temple.

Atalanta barked out a laugh, 'Only a Spartan who reeked of fear would threaten now.'

Most of the other athletes grinned and relaxed at this remark. Hippodamia smiled her gratitude at Atalanta. Cynisca scowled and stared down at her feet.

The start official slowly raised his arm to signal readiness; he also placed his foot on the starting device, ready to boot the lever that dropped the taut string. The trumpeter positioned alongside him pressed the instrument to his lips. The other musicians situated within the racetrack followed his cue. Now hushed by anticipation, the crowd collectively held its breath. Hippodamia could feel her heart pounding, almost threatening to burst out of her chest, so great was her eagerness to rush headlong down the circuit.

The official finally cried out, 'You are ready, be set and...'

Before the trumpeter could signal, Cynisca burst the line. Several other athletes followed her premature release. They quickly slowed and looked around sheepishly, as they had surged through the start string. Most had remained where Atalanta and Hippodamia still perched on the starting stone.

The trumpeter blew a series of strident notes to indicate a false start. The crowd booed noisily as the line official exploded into anger, having stepped forward to whip Cynisca repeatedly around her calves with his switch. She bore the punishment through gritted teeth, although a flushed complexion betrayed her shame.

As Cynisca settled back into her start position, Atalanta chuckled at her, 'One more false, and your race is over, Spartan.'

Cynisca simply grunted and spat onto the ground, ignoring her fellow runners. The rest of the false starters nervously resumed their positions.

Again, the official and trumpeter repeated the start procedure, 'Make ready. Be set. Release!'

The trumpet screeched as the runners raced over the falling string line. Two athletes tumbled over one another's feet, although the rest of the field either swerved or leaped over them. The crowd ignited into boisterous partisanship, particularly delighted by this spectacle so early into the event. The track musicians struggled to be heard over the noise of the crowd.

As the runners sprinted down the track, Hippodamia and Atalanta fought through to the lead. Cynisca had jostled her way to place directly behind them. The other runners fanned out raggedly behind the lead trio. As the turn post approached, the runners began to shorten their strides and jam up; Cynisca now strained alongside Atalanta while, aware of the threat, Hippodamia surged ahead. She was running joyously, showing little strain. Grimacing with intensity, Cynisca pressed past Atalanta and had Hippodamia firmly in range. The Spartan inched alongside her as they reached the halfway mark of the track's second length. The entire crowd had found its feet by this stage and screamed with wild abandon for their favorites. As most of the runners, now so close to the finish line, were hit by this aural blow to their senses, they became slightly disoriented. As inexperienced with a huge crowd as her peers, Hippodamia also lost focus, stumbling for a few strides. That was all Cynisca needed. With a deadly intensity, she drew up next to Hippodamia, then braced herself to physically assault the race leader. Bouncing off Hippodamia's shoulder and flying sideways, she completely lost her balance and fell to the side of the track. Atalanta leapt gracefully over her tumbling form, barely breaking stride. Still holding a comfortable lead, Hippodamia glanced back at her and began to slow. The crowd went from rapturous screams to cries of surprise; even as her fellow runners flew past her, they shot her mystified glances.

Hippodamia had slowed to a walk and soon stood over a disheveled Cynisca, who remained prone. She extended a hand to her fallen opponent. With undisguised shock. the Spartan slowly rolled over and reached up to her, saying, 'Why?'

Recovering quickly from this latest shock after the first runner crossed the finishing line, the crowd began chanting, 'Atalanta, Atalanta, Atalanta.' The remainder of the field dribbled in behind her, all but forgotten; as in keeping with the customs of Greece, only the victor was rewarded: the best the others could hope for was a commemorative ribbon. Guided by an official, Homer passed Atalanta the robe sacred to Hera. Pressing it first to her face, she raised it on high in triumph. The crowd roared their approval. Many of them descended from their viewing spots to gather closer to the finish line, where Homer was also placing the victory wreath upon Atalanta's brow, who had bowed her head and guided his hand to assist. Hippodamia, followed at a distance by Cynisca, strolled back to where the celebrations were taking place, seemingly ignored. Only her mother, Europa, awaited her, beaming with pleasure at her daughter's display of honor.

Atalanta broke away from her congratulatory fans and approached mother and daughter. Removing the wreath from her head, she said, 'This is for you, Hippodamia. For speed and grace. Even with that Spartan for a foe.'

Hippodamia was shocked, 'What? You won that fairly.'

As Europa smiled even more broadly, Atalanta shrugged, 'You are more deserving. I insist.'

Hippodamia smiled her thanks and slowly bent her head; Atalanta settled the wreath on her brow.

The members of the crowd who witnessed this noble gesture erupted, crying out both victor's names.

Europa said to both women, 'Truly Hera now blesses you both and these games.'

Cynisca walked away from the gathering and approached the table where Homer once again stood. Taking up two of the commemorative ribbons, she returned to Hippodamia and began tying them to her upper arms. Leaning in closely, Cynisca whispered hoarsely, 'Your friend, Pelops, is in great danger. He needs your help.'

With shock etched upon her face, Hippodamia said, 'What? By Eris, cursed harbinger of strife. What danger?'

ΨΨΨ

Outside the tent of a healer, Koroibos, Simonides and Askari sat before an evening fire. The mood was tense as they warmed themselves in the chill air of the Olympian sanctuary. All around them were the sounds of merriment and revelry, magnified by the still air and great numbers of squatting visitors, although their little camp was deathly quiet. Pelops lay within the tent, flickering in and out of consciousness, as the healer labored to save him.

Tantalus limped up to them and demanded, 'Why was I called?'

All three men glared up at him, their disrespect obvious as they refused to stand. Simonides said, 'Your son. He is very ill.'

Koroibos spat out, 'It is a great bloody mystery how it happened.'

Tantalus said nothing, his face flickering with emotion. Finally, he said, 'Where is he?'

Askari snorted and simply pointed at the entrance to the healer's tent. Although his grasp of the Greek tongue was limited, he knew from the anger crackling around him precisely what they were discussing.

Tantalus nodded and stepped into the tent. The smell within was not pleasant; Pelops had repeatedly lost control of his bowels. He lay on a pallet bed, ashen-faced, sweating profusely, and was clearly delirious. He wheezed heavily as he rolled from side to side. Alongside him, a healer glanced up, annoyed at the intrusion. He said, 'You are not welcome here. I told those outside that I must not be disturbed.'

Tantalus could barely tear his gaze from Pelops. He eventually stammered out, 'He... he is... my son. How... bad?'

He sighed, 'Whatever has invaded him is beyond my skills.'

Tantalus flared, 'You are a healer. Heal him.'

The healer stood his ground, 'I have done all I can. I can only repair what I understand. He is in the hands of Apollo, now. He believes he is being punished; he keeps muttering as such.'

As Tantalus absorbed the sight of his son's suffering, the healer turned back to his patient, administering what little aid he could by wiping down Pelops's brow with a cloth and chilled water. The priest finally hardened his face and stepped back through the tent flaps. Without a glance or word to Pelops's friends, who stared accusingly at him, he limped back into the night. Askari looked mournfully at the tent.

Koroibos blurted out, louder than he intended, 'It must have been him!'

A more restrained Simonides replied, 'If treachery was done, we must hope that some love still exists from father to son.'

Koroibos spat into the flames, 'From that! Ha!' He shook his head, angrily, 'As if.'

Impossible not to have overheard them, Tantalus paused beyond the illu-mination of the small campfire. He froze for several moments, lost in thought. Wincing, he moved off again, his limp even more pronounced, just as his whole persona appeared diminished.

ΨΨΨΨ

Within Queen Dido's tent, sprawled between two of Olympia's major temples, the sole occupant was admiring herself in a full length, polished bronze mirror. Her image rippled across the surface, dimly refracting back onto the calico walls. Although the candle illumination was dim, the queen clearly liked what she saw; she pressed her bosom upwards and pursed her lips.

Unannounced, Melqart parted the tent flaps and stood holding one tasseled end. He leered, 'Am I here for that?'

The queen slowly broke away from the object of her interest, 'Never again…. Enter.'

He strode in and said, 'To what do we owe the pleasure of seeing you in this barbarous land?'

Dido replied, coldly, 'My amusement. And curiosity. I am here to see wheth-er I will soon dispense with our Spartan allies. Not to mention the captain of my guards. You've much to lose.'

Melqart laughed, 'Not as much as you might think, Majesty. You'll have those slaves returned if you stay for these games.'

She sniffed, 'Oh, I wouldn't miss them. I hear that many of these Greeks wish to compete naked; such a vain people.'

Melqart returned the contemptuous tone, 'Greeks? They're not a people. They bicker like children. Their divisions remain strong.'

For the first time since he entered her private quarters, the queen met his stare. With deadly intensity, she hissed, 'Not as strong as they once were. Anyone with eyes can see that. We shall have to see what comes of these Olympics.'

Before Melqart could respond, a Carthaginian guard entered the tent and prostrated himself.

The queen said, 'Rise. What is it?'

'There is a Greek priest outside who requests an audience with Lord Melqart, Majesty,' he mumbled, a little overawed at his city-state's two most powerful figures in such close proximity.

Dido simply waved her hand and directed, 'Bring him in. I have heard of this one.'

Tantalus sidled into the tent, bowed low before the queen, and asked, 'Queen Dido, I must have words with this man. In private.'

After the queen had finished inspecting him, she said, 'Speak. He has no secrets.'

Melqart chimed in, 'Speak, priest.'

Tantalus paused to draw breath deeply, then blurted out, 'I will return your gold. I will not see our compact through.'

Melqart sneered, 'You've already administered the poison. The deal is struck.'

Tantalus simpered, 'There are antidotes. I was blind; stupid. I poisoned flesh of my flesh. He's... my son.'

The normally impassive Dido exploded, 'What have you done, by Baal! This man is in the service of the gods.'

Melqart barely hesitated, 'His son is our enemy and rival. He has done us a service.'

'And this is how you compete for the glory of Carthage — by poisoning opponents? Coward!' she screamed. Turning to Tantalus, who had shrunk away from her rage, she declared, 'Priest, revive your son. And never let me set eyes upon you again. You disgust me.'

Tantalus bowed again, shot a nervous glance at Melqart, and scuttled from the tent, grateful that he still had his life.

As Melqart trembled with fury, the queen rounded on him, 'There will be a crucifix with your name on it in Carthage if I hear of such things again. Leave me. Now!'

Melqart remained rooted to the spot, spasmodically clenching and unclench-ing his fists, locked in a stare with his ruler. Dido slowly elevated one eyebrow. Melqart broke, turned away, and punched his way through the tent flaps.

The queen glared stonily after him until the gentle strains of lyre music caught her attention. Her face softened. She pivoted and walked through a series of gossamer-thin curtains veiling the pavilion's inner sanctum. Entering the rear partition, she smiled at the sight. Prince Rameses languished on a divan, picking at honeyed dates. A lyre player stood playing behind him, a cloth stretched over his eyes, effectively blinding him.

Dido asked him, 'You heard?'

Rameses grinned, 'Hard not to.'

The queen nodded, 'Something must be done with him.'

'I've told you that before,' Rameses drawled.

'Yes, yes. I know. You've told me — at least ten times. Today.' she chuckled.

The prince simply grinned again and stretched out languorously, almost cat-like, on the divan, extending every muscle beneath his thin robe. The queen's eyes widened with desire; she began slipping off her robe and drew close to him. Naked, she asked, 'He is such a dull topic. Have you something else to engage me…?'

XI

The following morning, the training camp at Elis was a hive of activity. Countless Greek and non-Greek athletes, coaches, and officials, as well as devoted fans, milled about as the competitors used every spare moment and training resource to hone their skills while their spectators swapped opinions, banter, and gambling odds. Elean officials kept a close eye on all proceedings, their switches flickering around as an ever-present warning against unseemly behavior. They monitored, in particular, a large group of heated fans that had ringed a pankration bout. As the 'anything goes' practice session proceeded, the combatants had laid successively heavier blows on one another, aware that their competitive blood was up. Some of the spectators had engaged in bloodthirsty baying to egg on their favorites. Two of the officials patrolled the circumference of the gathering, thrashing their switches across buttocks and legs to control the more unruly fans. Much to their amusement, Askari and his men watched the Elean officials punishing the boisterous fans while carefully appraising the pankrationists; Askari fancied his chances in the event and his men gave him their unalloyed support. As they continued to observe, a weary-looking Prince Rameses approached.

Askari cried out to him, 'He wakes!'

The prince gave a grin, 'A long night. Of training.'

Askari shook his head and smiled back at him but snapped his head back in the direction of the pankration bout as the crowd roared with delight. One of the heavily-muscled combatants had pinned his opponent, swung him upwards into a standing position, thrust a foot on his upper chest, and was bending his arm into an impossible position. Despite the downed opponent slamming his free arm into the dirt to signal quarter, the standing pankrationist wrenched the arm back even further. An audible snap could be heard. The defeated combatant howled in pain; his victor threw up his own arms in exultation. His fans erupted into screams of delight, even as the officials frantically battered at them in a vain attempt to calm the ruckus. Askari's men also exploded into loud whoops of excitement.

Their chief grinned ruthlessly, 'Excellent. That's one less.'

Intrigued — as he had never seen a sport quite so brutal — Rameses asked his desert friend, 'You next?'

Askari replied, 'Not yet.'

The prince nodded and said, 'Then I have news for you. It seems that Pelops's ruined health has much to do with his father; some arrangement with that Carthaginian, Melqart. A little bird whispered to me last night.'

Askari pounded a fist into his palm, 'We thought as much. What manner of father could do such a thing!'

Nodding in agreement, the prince said, 'This may still be remedied. I have sent word to friends at Olympia. Pelops must finish his trials today, though; he may not last much longer.'

Askari grimaced and looked away.

Ψ

Pelops leaned wearily across the neck of his horse, Pegasus. Koroibos held the reins as Iphicles made last-minute adjustments to the riding blanket, fussing over the tiniest wrinkle. His concern was evident. They awaited the signal for the first heat of the horseracing.

Melqart rode up alongside them on a large black charger. He looked delightedly over his enervated foe, then proclaimed, 'This is how it's done, boy. Count yourself lucky you are not pitted against me. Watch how I ride. From the sidelines.' He wrenched at the reins, causing his steed to rear up and pirouette.

Pelops and Iphicles practiced indifference although, in truth, Pelops had precious little energy to spare, so deeply had the illness seeped into his being. Koroibos threw a deadly stare at the haughty Carthaginian, wishing for the life of him that it was he, rather than his aggrieved friend, who would bear the strain of this ride. Unfortunately, horsemanship was not one of his skills; that was the domain of the fortunate few, aristocrats, wealthy mercenaries, or equine guardians like Pelops, not peasant cooks who could barely afford the lightweight sandals of a runner.

Melqart ignored the reaction and trotted his steed up to the trial start line. Several other equestrians were already poised on the line, reining in their horses. Multiple Elean officials worked to keep horses and riders in check.

The head Elean official slowly raised his switch and called out, 'You know the rules. First three to qualify. Be set... go!' The riders catapulted away from the line, their horses excited by the nearness of so many of their breed and the thrill of exertion. Melqart led from the outset, his horse having been brought in from his personal stables in Carthage onboard Queen Dido's ship, and the race-trained beast and rider won convincingly. The next two riders — one Greek, one Celtiberian — that followed him at some distance over the line counted their blessings that this was not a customary victor-only trial, as they knew they had little chance against such a superior combination. One Elean official pointed at Melqart, declaring him the winner; another indicated the second and third riders to cross the line as fit to run in the main event. The remainder rode off or dejectedly paused to congratulate the place-getters and rest their horses. Conspicuous to all was that not a single other competitor hailed the race winner; Melqart feigned indifference and trotted his steed over to a watering tray. Turning his attention back to Pelops, he imperiously pointed a finger first at the ailing priest, then at the start line.

Pelops caught the gesture and struggled upright on Pegasus's broad back. Koroibos kept the horse's reins firmly in hand as a twitchy Pegasus was accustomed to a gentler authority from his rider. Iphicles stared up at his beloved protégé and said, 'This is madness. You will be lucky to survive this ride, let alone win a place.'

A cold sweat consuming him, Pelops chattered out through gritted teeth, 'It... it... must... be... be... done.'

Koroibos tried to smile reassuringly, 'You'll be fine, my friend. Show him Pegasus's wings.'

Pelops attempted a grin, which was more of a grimace, gasping, 'Come on... my beauty.'

He cantered his ride up to the line, the last rider to join the ten other competitors, his complexion betraying his state of health. Even a few of the other equestrians cast concerned glances his way. The officials ensured that the horses toed the line. From a distance, Melqart was enjoying the sight of Pelops's travails as he sat atop his stallion, beaming with undisguised pleasure.

The head official stepped up to his starter's position. As the riders fell silent and leaned forward over the necks of their horses in anticipation of the release, the official raised his switch and called out, 'You know the system. First three over the line compete... Set... Go!'

Unleashed by their riders, the horses bolted down the track. Exceedingly well trained, Pegasus kept Pelops in the race, having placed near the lead from the outset. Grimacing with pain, Pelops swayed awkwardly on his riding blanket but desperately clung on. As the finish line approached, two other riders placed before Pelops. Scant feet behind the second rider, Pelops breathed a huge sigh of relief that he had somehow won through. With the last of his energy, he nudged Pegasus to one side where the other riders were gathering and slid off his back, slumping to the ground; he was more winded and exhausted than he could ever remember.

The official linesman cried out, 'You, you and... you. You all win through. Someone get that third rider on his feet!'

Koroibos sprinted over to assist Pelops. Melqart chuckled unabashedly at the sight of Pelops, who had begun vomiting, while Prince Lycurgus shot a look of distaste at the merciless Carthaginian. Koroibos had reached Pelops, who was now heaving uncontrollably, and vainly tried to raise him up. They were carefully watched by the head Elean official, who shook his head in resignation after mentally calculating Pelops's odds.

ΨΨ

Hippodamia raced up the stairs of Zeus's temple at Olympia and entered its dim interior, not even bothering to glance, let alone pay homage, to the giant wooden cult statue of the chief god. Then she froze. As her eyes adjusted to the hazy light, she spotted a figure prostrated before the statue. She whispered, 'Head priest? Tantalus?'

The prostrate form slowly pivoted and stared at Hippodamia. She was shocked to see the bleary, bloodshot eyes, raw from weeping — it was Tantalus, though as she had never seen him before. Too anxious to allow his state to concern her, Hippodamia blurted out, 'Lord High Priest, your son is in peril. I have heard of a plot with poison. What... what must I do?'

Tantalus slowly stood, rubbed at his eyes, and stared dazedly at her. She persisted, 'Lord?'

Tantalus finally collected himself, 'He is... fortunate... to have you. That is a sad tiding. I may have something here to help.'

Hippodamia nodded earnestly, gratefully; then, suspicion dawned upon her, 'How could you already have something for him? You knew?'

He shook his head, mumbling, 'No, no, I remain prepared... for such things. That's all. Evil are the ways of weak men.' As she continued to glare at him, he stumbled over his own cloak and moved to a storage box at one side of the *cella*. He withdrew a small leather flask and eagerly thrust it at her. He smiled nervously, brandishing it as if it were a cornucopia of healing beneficence.

A mellifluous voice boomed throughout the temple, reverberating off the *cella* walls, 'Do not trust that man. He is not to be believed!'

Hippodamia's head snapped towards the entrance. Homer was framed in the light, his long beard and tall wooden staff betraying his identity. His staff was pointed directly at Tantalus, the accusation clear.

Tantalus stumbled several paces forward then shouted out, 'You know nothing!'

Standing his ground, the poet bellowed back, 'It is you, a holy priest of Zeus, who has committed this crime. Sacrilege!'

Hippodamia could not keep the look of horror from her face. She backed away from Tantalus towards Homer, all the while watching his every move. Who knew what this impious madman was capable of, she thought. When she reached Homer, she touched his shoulder. He thrust her protectively behind him.

Tantalus cried out, almost weeping again, 'It's a mistake… it is all a mistake.'

Homer ignored him and turned to Hippodamia, 'Let us leave this defiler.'

Tantalus raced forward; the flask extended in his hand. He clawed wildly at Hippodamia, trying to force the remedy on her. He moaned, 'Take it; you must take it!'

Homer lashed out with his staff. It glanced off Tantalus's shoulder and onto his forehead. He fell heavily on the temple floor, weeping piteously.

Homer screamed at him, 'Away, monster!'

Lying on the ground, he bleated up at Homer and Hippodamia, 'Please, please, I beg you. Take it to him.'

Hippodamia turned to the poet and said gently, 'Homer, he holds a cure.'

Homer paused, then snarled down at Tantalus, 'If this is a cure, then demonstrate it. You first.'

Tantalus scrambled to uncork the flask. His shaking hands finally pulled the stopper out, and he swigged at its contents, spilling some across his chin and beard and down his neck. His feverish attempts to prove himself made an ugly sight. Hippodamia cringed at the spectacle, though she tried to remain focused on Pelops's desperate need.

Tantalus screeched out, 'There, there, no ill effects. Plenty left. You must give it to him. You must!'

Hippodamia turned again to Homer, 'I can see no harm.' She reached down and gingerly took the flask from Tantalus, then shrank back. Turning from the priest in disgust, she guided Homer down the temple stairs. She could hear Tantalus sobbing in self-revulsion behind her but ignored him.

Homer snorted in fury as he navigated the steps. He stopped, turned back to the temple entrance, and bellowed out, 'May time torment you eternally for what you have done!'

The sobbing increased from the temple entrance.

Homer resumed his walk down the steps with Hippodamia. At the base, she asked of him, 'You knew?'

He replied, 'Word just reached me. From Elis.'

Shaking her head in disbelief, Hippodamia said, 'I'll ride there now. I only pray that I'm not too late.'

Homer gripped her forearms and spoke intensely, 'Meet him halfway and save time. If he still lives, the athletes must march from Elis to Olympia. It is a two-day journey. The village of Letrini is the mid-march stop.'

Hippodamia nodded resignedly, 'Letrini it is, then. I will get a horse. Thank you from the bottom of my heart, Homer. I would have been lost without you today.'

Homer simply kissed her hand and waved her on. He was still shaking off the last of his rage at Tantalus's egregious conduct.

The young priestess raced over to a picket line of horses, selected a favorite, and raced out of the gates of Olympia.

ΨΨΨ

Within Zeus's temple, Tantalus staggered to his feet. He stumbled through the *cella*, still wracked with tears, passed through the *adyton* and out the rear exit. Storming through the entrance of the priest's quarters located behind the temple, he glared around him, a wild-eyed, manic look competing with a mask of wrath. Detecting the sound of clattering pots and pans, he lurched towards the kitchen where Oenomaus worked.

Not bothering to glance up from his food preparation, Oenomaus drawled out, 'Lord Tantalus, your black broth has been prepared.'

Tantalus lunged at the cook, scattering implements across the small space. Oenomaus had just enough time to register shock at the crazed look on his master's face before Tantalus grabbed him by his long hair and drove his entire head deep into a boiling pot, the super-heated oil lining its sides and bottom immediately contacted the cook's face and set his hair on fire. Oenomaus screamed just once before his entire head was consumed in flames, while his face remained smeared against the oiled pot sides, such was the madman strength that Tantalus exerted. Even as his own hand grew increasingly singed, while the smell of melting human flesh invaded the air, the priest refused to break his hold. Simultaneously weeping and venting his rage, the head priest croaked, 'You! You! It was you who poisoned my son. Not me. You!'

With the last of his dying energy, the cook tried to break Tantalus's iron grip on the back of his head. He scrabbled madly, futilely, for a few brief heartbeats, then his whole body went limp, his dead weight slumping to the floor, dragging the pot and the priest down with him. Tantalus lay there, covered in strips of blackened human skin, burning oil, and the contents of the pot. His robes smoldered as he wept uncontrollably.

ΨΨΨΨ

Within the athlete's mess hall at Elis, the rescued runners from Carthage congregated at a table, a quiet pool of young men amidst the general excitement of their peers. The laughter, boasting, and posturing of the athletes filled the hall, with circulating Elean officials paying scant attention to their boisterousness. They were all to begin the ceremonial march to Olympia that day, with even the sternest of Olympic guardians reluctant to quell the high spirits before this unprecedented event. Koroibos and Simonides entered the hall, carrying Pelops between them. The looks on his friends' faces reflected Pelops's state; he was shockingly, gravely ill. As Koroibos shouldered past the revelers and Simonides protected Pelops's rear, Agathon cleared space at the Elean runners' table.

As they sat him down, a pensive Agathon, the runner Hippodamia had replaced on the rowing benches of their escape ship, asked, 'He still hasn't recovered?'

Simonides murmured, 'No. He appears… no better.'

With an arm around Pelops's shoulders, Koroibos dropped his own head and shook it slowly, 'I… I fear for him.'

Agathon spoke with characteristic Greek frankness, 'Pelops, we grieve for you. What chance do you have in this state?'

Before Pelops could try to reassure his friends, a senior Elean official entered the hall. He added to his commanding presence, highlighted by the stark white robe he wore, by stepping first upon a vacant stool, then onto a table that was surrounded by youthful athletes. Towering over them all, he declared to a now-hushed space, 'Your attention, men of the first Olympiad. You have all proven your worth to the gods of Greece in the trials. Today we march for Olympia!'

The athletes erupted into wild cheers.

The official continued, 'Know this, athletes of the first Olympiad. Elis will release you only if you have exercised in a manner worthy of these games. Then you may proceed to Olympia. If you're not guilty of slothful or foul deeds, then you may proceed to Olympia. But for those of you who are not so prepared, take yourselves elsewhere. Now!'

Again, the hall erupted in loud cries of endorsement.

Pelops's table was more subdued; the young priest rested with his head drooping on his shoulder, with barely the strength to raise it. Koroibos was ever-present, physically propping him up and pressing a goblet of water to his lips.

Agathon turned to Simonides, as the entire table of friends now rose to its feet, 'It is a two-day journey. Can he make it?'

Koroibos interjected, 'He must. Your freedom, if not your lives, depend upon it.'

As Pelops struggled to stand, they all looked upon him with great concern.

ΨΨΨΨ

The Spartan athlete, Cynisca, stood at attention before the diarchy of her home city within their tent at Olympia. Both kings stared at her with disdain. She was blank-faced, stoical — a true Spartan in expression and deportment.

King Prytanis snarled, 'You not only failed us in a race you should have won, but you betray your own people and decorate a false victor?'

Cynisca hesitated, then said, 'Yes. She was deserving.'

King Arcelaus growled at her, 'Deserving! And Sparta is not?'

Before she could reply, his fellow king declared, 'I cannot punish you as I would a man, although you are deserving. You are an unworthy daughter of Sparta.'

Her composure finally shredded, she glared at both kings, 'Unworthy? All you bring is war, death, treachery, and now threats against your own. I acted with honor.' She turned on her heel and marched proudly out of the tent.

Prytanis spat out, 'She is unbearable. Curse her. I know decorated warriors with less arrogance.'

Arcelaus nodded and snorted his agreement. He cried out, 'Guard, guard — bring in the next failure!'

As they awaited their next guest, Prytanis moved across to a low table, pushed his red cloak aside, and exposed his sword. He then reached across and took up a goblet of water and sipped at its contents. He kept his back to the tent's entrance.

Tantalus was escorted through the tent flaps by a Spartan guard, who bowed low and then departed. The High Priest dispensed with such formalities and simply stood there, his face downcast. When he glanced up, his eyes were bloodshot; his attire was disheveled, and he appeared to sway on his feet.

Arcelaus closed the distance to him, 'What is wrong with you? You dare present yourself this way to us?'

Tantalus slurred, 'Welcome, kings… to my Olympia.'

Arcelaus leaned in even closer, inhaling the priest's breath, 'You have been drinking! At this time of day. What manner of man are you?'

The High Priest snapped into a rage, 'I am Spartan by birth, as you well know, and you have always commanded my loyalty. But my time as your creature is at an end. I will no longer pronounce false omens. Or perform acts of treachery.'

Stunned at the outburst, Arcelaus stepped away from him and glowered.

Prytanis roared with anger, spun towards Tantalus, and buried his sword up to its hilt in his stomach.

Tantalus grunted with pain. He swayed even more and stared directly into the king's eyes as they stood nose to nose. The blade remained wedged in his stomach. The king's face was twisted by fury; he bellowed only one word, 'Traitor!'

A horrified look on his face, Arcelaus leaped forward, shouldered Prytanis aside, and ripped the blade from Tantalus's wound. He shouted at his fellow monarch as the priest hit the floor, bleeding profusely and weeping, 'Have you lost your mind! He is still a priest, and this is sacred ground. We face disgrace and ruination!'

Prytanis coughed out a laugh, 'No matter. It will not be discovered. Dispose of him.'

Arcelaus shook his head, 'You have gone too far. You will spend more time in Hades than him if you do this thing.'

Taking up his sword from the tent floor and returning it to the table, Prytanis took another sip of water and said, 'For harming that? I think not. I have other matters to attend; take care of it.' Stepping over Tantalus's body, he nonchalantly walked through the tent flaps.

Sighing heavily, Arcelaus dropped down to his knees and slapped Tantalus lightly on the face to revive him — the priest groaned and slowly stirred back into consciousness. The king told him, 'Plug your wound and leave here. Now. Find somewhere to hide… Guard!'

The guard re-entered the tent and bowed more deeply than usual, trying to disguise his shock at what he saw before him.

Arcelaus commanded him, 'Get him to his quarters. And try to go undetected.' Rising to his feet, Arcelaus grabbed at Prytanis's scarlet cloak and thrust it at the guard. Tearing off a length from the bottom, he thrust it onto Tantalus's abdomen, placing the priest's hand on top to apply pressure to the wound. He threw the remainder of the cloak over the wounded man's head and shoulders in an attempt to conceal his identity. He added, 'If anyone asks, he's just a comrade who had too much to drink. Now get him away from here.'

The guard nodded anxiously but began raising the wounded man up, settling the cloak over his features; Tantalus sputtered with the pain but, possibly aided by his inebriation, started moving towards the exit.

Arcelaus stood there long after they had left, transfixed by the blood on the tent floor.

He finally stepped over to a bronze water dish mounted on a tripod and began washing his hands. He wrung them, again and again, almost compulsively, in the water while muttering a prayer to Zeus. A look of white-eyed fear crept over his face as he stared down at Prytanis's sword.

ΨΨΨΨΨΨ

A bright, balmy day under a glittering Greek sun saw a procession of peak athletes that was unparalleled in its magnificence emerging from the city of Elis. Not only were Greeks from every corner of the diaspora present, their itinerant nature reflected in the many banners they sported that had been transferred from traditional battle shield designs, but peoples from across the known world also marched under their foreign flags and signs. It was a symbol of unity and amity that only Homer could only have dreamt of. Leading the parade in their chariots, King Iphitos and his fellow Eleans — Koroibos, Simonides, and Agathon amongst them —marveled at what they had helped create. Garlanded white bulls, sacrificial gifts to Zeus, were driven before the chariots by a religious order, while marching Elean musicians positioned directly behind the lead contingent stirred the air with rousing tunes.

Farmers in the fields alongside the route paused long in their labors to gaze in wonder at the spectacle. While most of these hard-pressed farmer folks were genuinely awestruck and delighted at their kingdom's stellar rise to prominence, a few grumbles of discontent could be heard from the more cynical. Uttered more than once were the complaints that how could their warrior king have so suddenly lapsed into the ways of peace, while precious resources were diverted away from their dwindling subsistence towards the indulgence of vanity sports such as these? Rebuked by their peers, they were reminded that the young men of Elis also competed for their collective glory, while the games had a purifying role to play in their lives, lifting the blight they suffered through divine catharsis. Ignoring the malcontents, countless peasant-farmers raised their sun hats and cheered the parade, calling out the names of local heroes with immense pride. Koroibos, in particular, took pleasure in receiving their salutations, crying back to many of them by name.

With the Carthaginians, Egyptians, Askari's desert nomads, and the Spartans all before him, Pelops brought up the very rear on a dray horse. Resting Pegasus for the big race, he barely held himself in place on the workhorse as it moved slowly up the dusty road. While his sun hat provided some shade, his complexion remained deathly pale. Many other equestrians trotted in front of him, either mounted on spare horses or carefully guiding their primary animal along the roadway to ensure that no large stones entered their unshod hooves. Pelops managed to keep pace, though only just; he owed his continued forward progress more to his horse, which had traversed the route many times before. He spoke not a word, nor flashed his customary smile, despite the merriment around him, such was his utter exhaustion and pain.

At the head of the column, Koroibos spotted a small dust zephyr, and then a lone rider emerged. He nudged Simonides and Agathon to contest which of them could first make out the distant figure. Long-visioned Agathon exclaimed with joy that it was no male rider but their friend Hippodamia. Koroibos quickly dusted down his linen chiton and smoothed over his hair — while he mourned the plight of his dear friend Pelops, he thought that Hippodamia would surely need someone to comfort her should he not pull through his terrible sickness.

Simonides smirked at his friend's obvious callousness and nudged him in the ribs. Koroibos feigned pain but turned his sunniest smile on Hippodamia as she pulled up before them, 'Greetings, priestess. Have you come to watch me march?'

Although consumed with anxiety for Pelops, Hippodamia had not forgotten her good graces, nor that these were well-meaning friends who had shared many of her own dangers, 'No, Koroibos. As exciting as that would be, I am here for slightly more important things.'

Agathon asked of her, 'Did you race?'

Searching down the column for a sight of Pelops, she distractedly answered, 'I did.'

Simonides chimed in, 'Did you win?'

She turned a fleeting smile on her three friends and said, 'No. Much better. Perhaps we could talk later; I must reach Pelops. Where is he?'

Koroibos replied, 'At the rear. On a big dray horse. He is in a bad way. Do you want me to ride up there and show you...?'

Not pausing to reply, Hippodamia took off at a trot, rising quickly to a gallop as she scanned the lengthy procession for a sign of Pelops.

A miffed Koroibos turned to his friends, 'A bit rude! How did she know that Pelops was in harm's way?'

Simonides good-naturedly cuffed Koroibos on the back of the head, 'Idiot. She must know more than we do.'

Koroibos brushed at his tousled hair and said, 'Mmm, maybe. By the way, what's better than winning? She's obviously very confused.'

Again, Simonides went to cuff him, but Koroibos ducked under the blow and grinned.

Agathon smacked him from the other side, to the amusement of all three Eleans.

Passing the familiar faces of Ramses and Askari along the way, as well as those far from welcome — a leering Melqart — Hippodamia finally reached the very end of the parade. Her heart lit up with joy. Although his appearance shocked her, and he swayed all over the back of the dray, her beloved was still alive. She cried out to him, 'Pelops!'

He looked up at her wearily, although before she could trot the final few feet across to him, an Elean official interposed himself. He glared up at her and waved his switch, 'What are you doing here? This is for athletes and officials only. This is a sacred march. Away with you!'

Hippodamia pleaded with him, 'He is very sick. Can you not see with your own eyes? I have an antidote here for what he suffers.' She reached into her shoulder bag, bringing forth the flask Tantalus had thrust upon her and brandished it before the official.

He barked, 'I don't care if you have Zeus's thunderbolt. Remove yourself!'

Hippodamia refused to budge, 'He is grievously ill. He won't last the day out. You must let…'

Not even bothering to hear her out, the Elean official turned to several of his rearguard companions and yelled over Hippodamia's plea, 'Here, comrades. Help me beat this one away.'

Rearing her horse to ensure clearance over the threatening official's raised switch, Hippodamia cried out, 'Catch, Pelops. Catch this!'

She threw the flask in an arc over the official's head. Using almost the last of his depleted strength, Pelops lifted himself high on the dray's back and plucked it from the air. He barely had the energy to nod his thanks.

Hippodamia cleared the swipes of the official's switch by back-pedaling her horse and called to him, 'Drink it; you must. Now! I will meet you at Letrini.'

As the officials cursed Hippodamia in the wake of the dust her galloping horse threw back at them, Pelops gingerly opened the flask. What do I have to lose, he thought, as he drank deeply.

ΨΨΨΨΨΨ

As dusk descended, the weary athletes and officials entered the village of Letri-ni. They were greeted by the sight of two priests sacrificing a garlanded bull, its bright blood spattering a shrine to Hermes to sanctify the Olympic travelers on the final leg of their trek the following day. The ritual barley that hid the sacrifi-cial knife from the animal was then used to cleanse the blade, and the coagulated grain was also cast onto the shrine to propitiate the god of transitions and jour-neys. The enervated travelers would also find the bull's meat a welcome supple-ment to their diet, as the priests quickly set to carving up the beast. Surrounding the spectacle with torch-brands, the villagers of Letrini incanted a prayer to the gods as they greeted the tired journeymen. There was but one woman among them; Hippodamia sat upon her horse in the shadows of the village fence, await-ing the arrival of Pelops. As the dust and road-grime-covered athletes passed her by, first her Elean friends, then Ramses and his Egyptians, and finally Askari and the nomads peeled off to stand with her. They all waited silently, pensively, for their first glimpse of the sick Olympian priest.

The Elean official who had accosted Hippodamia on the roadway moved into view, leading Pelops's horse by the reins. Pelops was slumped across the animal, clinging to its neck to stay in place. To his shocked friends, the official quietly said, 'Take this horse. And care for this youth. He is well on the way to the Underworld.'

Koroibos grabbed the reins and nodded thanks to his fellow Elean. Hippo-damia leaped off her own animal to run up to Pelops's mount. The rest of their group gathered close to the ailing rider. Hippodamia instantly asked Koroibos, who was trying to raise up Pelops's head, 'Still no better? Still!'

Koroibos sought to reassure her, 'He is strong. Always has been. We just need to find somewhere to rest him properly.'

Princes Ramses said, 'Right. Men — find the best lodgings in this town. Tell them it is for me. I have ample gold dust.'

The rest of the group scattered to find suitable accommodation, as Koroi-bos, Hippodamia, and Rameses slowly led Pelops's dray forward into the village. They were all acutely aware that Pelops had uttered not a single word throughout the encounter.

Observing all from the fireside of their temporary campsite, Melqart turned to Prince Lycurgus and hissed, 'By Eshmun's healing powers, that boy might revive! We must do something.'

Lycurgus recoiled from him and barked, 'We? If you're so afraid, why don't you break his arms and legs as well!'

Melqart bristled with anger and turned to storm away from the camp-fire.

Lycurgus was not done with him; he grabbed him by the arm and declared, 'I am tired of your pathetic scheming. You have no honor. None! Learn how to compete like a Greek or leave my land.' He took advantage of Melqart's shock to walk away, his Spartans following him. They all looked distinctly pleased with their prince having stamped on the haughty barbarian Solon's lofty code of Spartan principles.

Melqart stood rubbing his bruised arm, glaring after them and feeling alone in more ways than one.

XII

I n an explosion of vibrant colors and movement, visitors and dignitaries from across the Mediterranean and beyond clustered at the gates to Olympia, awaiting the parade of athletes. Close by were the stalls of merchants and the temporary stages of multiple performers, from dancers and acrobats to musicians and poets; all sought the attention of the huge crowds. Here, too, were priests representing nearly the whole pantheon of gods, selling blessings and advice on every imaginable subject. King Kleosthenes stood at the gates of Olympia, with kings Prytanis and Arcelaus, the dyarchy of Sparta, and Queen Dido of Carthage close by. In their company was the official welcoming party of senior priests and priestesses who would act as judges throughout the coming days of competition.

King Iphitos, mounted in a chariot as befitted his station, appeared at the head of the column of athletes headed for the gates. Behind him walked still more priests, as well as a full contingent of Elean officials. The waiting crowd burst into life upon sighting them, sending such a resounding cheer into the air that those within earshot could have been forgiven for thinking that it would ring out forever. As Iphitos's chariot rolled through the gates, he nodded at Kleosthenes. The king of Pisa ostentatiously returned the gesture as the athletes walked proudly through the gates. Everywhere spectators clambered madly for a glimpse of their own peoples' favorites.

Now leading his horse on the final approach to Olympia, Pelops appeared much restored. Waiting at the gates alongside the head priestess, Europa, the elderly manservant, Iphicles, beamed his pleasure upon spotting Pelops. Both residents of Olympia were also struck with awe at seeing such a vast gathering

— more people than they had ever seen together in one place, and in peace, in their lifetimes. Koroibos, Simonides, Askari, and Prince Rameses also passed through the gates; Hippodamia had joined them and walked hand-in-hand with her friends. All of the young athletes welcomed the smile of King Kleosthenes as they passed through into the sanctuary.

Once the full column had been absorbed into the grounds of Olympia, King Kleosthenes's voice boomed out over spectator and participant alike, 'To the temple of Zeus, athletes! To the temple!'

The column obediently wended its way across the sanctuary to the temple. Europa had preceded them, scaled the stairs to Zeus's temple, and stood at its entrance, having just been handed a ceremonial torch from one of her assistants. It blazed brightly in the shadows of the entrance as the athletes assembled before her. 'Welcome to the games of the first Olympiad!' she announced to all. 'Trainers and team leaders are to step within!' she commanded before striding authoritatively down from her place in the temple to a jubilant Hippodamia, running to embrace her.

The tightly-grouped crowd issued another mighty, rolling cheer as the designated officials passed through the ranks of their teams and scaled the stairs towards Europa.

As they made their solemn way into the temple, the first thing they noticed were several acolytes laying strips of raw boar's flesh before one of the three statues of Zeus. Centrally placed, the largest of these loomed many hands above them, its fierce visage barely softened by a crown of flowers. This frightening apparition also held silver-plated thunderbolts in each upraised hand, a mute warning of the dangers they faced should they offend the chief deity of the Greeks. Homer stood on a dais before the statue. Even the foreign officials stared up at him in silent wonder. Pelops stood expectantly with Prince Rameses, Askari, and Koroibos alongside. At the rear of the gathering, Melqart glared about him, cynicism awash on his features; Prince Lycurgus warily scrutinized the assembly.

As soon as he sensed full silence, Homer raised his arms and called out, 'Olympians! I ask you all to so swear, before Zeus Horkios, the God of Oaths, that you and your teams have engaged in fair training as demanded by our judges. Do you swear?'

The athletes and trainers responded with a Greek refrain they had all learned, '*Yposhosmaste!*'

Homer intoned again, 'Olympians! I ask you all to so swear that you or your team-mates will use no foul play to prove your worth in these sacred games. Do you swear?'

'*Yposhosmaste!*' replied the assembly.

'Finally,' he continued, 'Olympians, if you have sworn false on behalf of your people before our highest god, then may he rightfully fire your bones to ash for perjury!'

Those present glanced at each other, mildly confused at his words. Most accepted this fearsome imprecation without comment, although a few voices were raised in agreement. Homer turned his back to them and faced the cult statue, mumbling words of entreaty. The assembly waited expectantly.

Unable to contain himself, Askari leaned in to Rameses, nodded towards the statue, and whispered, 'You think he might be a good shot with those shiny bolts?' Not trusting himself to reply without laughing, Rameses simply grinned.

Homer turned back to face the assembly. 'There is nothing more unfathomable than the heart of a god, but Zeus gives his blessings. Go your way and compete for glory.'

Granted this signal, the athletes and trainers moved as one toward the exit. Within the press of bodies, Koroibos jostled past Lycurgus to reach Melqart. 'You would do well to honor this oath, foreign Lord. Our gods do not forgive easily.'

Not deigning to give an answer, Melqart snorted derisively, pivoted, and pushed his way through the crowd to the clear light of day.

As they all began to emerge, the participants and their mentors were greeted by another outpouring of appreciation from the crowd. They waved back heartily, glad to have escaped the oppressive confines of the temple.

Hippodamia pressed her way through the crush to reach Pelops. She leaned towards him and whispered into his ear.

His voice shaking, he asked her, 'My father? Where is he?'

She took him by the arm and led him around the side of Zeus's temple as the festivities rumbled into life around them.

Ψ

In the priest's quarters behind the temple of Zeus, Tantalus was lying on a pallet bed in a darkened cubicle. His torso was heavily bandaged, yet bloodstains seeped through the layers of tightly-bound cloth. He lay morose, ashen-faced, mortally wounded. The fabric at the doorway to the cubicle entrance was thrust aside, and Pelops entered, lowering himself down to the pallet bed. Hippodamia entered immediately after and stood warily to the side.

'I've just heard. Are you badly wounded, Father?' asked Pelops. Still in shock, he had seen enough of what men could do to each other in anger to already know the answer to that question.

Tantalus's face contorted and his eyes misted with tears, 'It doesn't... matter... all my fault,' he told his son.

Mystified, Pelops glanced up at Hippodamia. Torn between grief and anger, she looked away. 'I'll avenge you,' he said with passion, 'Who did this?' For the first time in many years, Tantalus saw the man his son had become. With great difficulty, he began to lever himself upright. Pelops assisted his efforts.

Tantalus placed a hand on his son's shoulder. 'No, you won't,' he said, 'That is the act of... a man of violence... You're not... such a one... I need, I need... to ask your forgiveness.'

Pelops queried, 'For what, Father?'

Tantalus began to weep, 'I have schemed… with others… against you.'

Unable to comprehend his father's treachery, Pelops looked to Hippodamia for reassurance; she could not meet his look and began to sob. Her demeanor told Pelops all he needed to know. With his face now hovering between disgust and soul-deep anguish, Pelops could just utter a solitary word, as much a question to himself as to his father. 'Forgiveness?' He stood and dazedly brushed past Hippodamia on his way out of the cubicle.

Intent on following him, Hippodamia also rose to her feet and began moving towards the entrance. Her heart was breaking for Pelops at his father's revelation.

With the full weight of his sins now bearing down upon him, Tantalus mumbled plaintively, 'Girl... Hippodamia.'

She paused at the doorway but refused to turn her face towards him, 'What do you want of me? Have you not harmed enough!'

'Tell him... that he made his mother... me proud... help him... forgive me,' he begged.

'I will help him always,' she told the pitiful figure that lay with the animus of death hovering over him, 'but I can never forgive you, old man.' She walked out from the dark, back into the light.

ΨΨ

Pelops, Koroibos, Simonides, and Rameses stood watching with a crowd of raucous spectators as two compactly-built boxers hammered away at each other with leather-strapped fists. Short in stature, like many Greeks, they were superbly muscled and able to resist a welter of blows. Far less restrained than other forms of the gentle art that would follow it in later ages, there were no rounds or even breaks in this style of local pugilism. Combatants stood nose-to-nose and rained punches until one of the participants was either knocked unconscious or surrendered. Fighting for the glory of their people and their gods, surrender was rare and frowned upon by all. Blows landed and blood flew as the bout edged towards its inevitable conclusion. An Elean official stood in the ring with the boxers, flicking his switch at their legs when they attempted to foul each other. Ringside, the crowd was now baying for blood and howling with excitement.

'And it's only day one,' Pelops said with a kind of stunned wonder.

Koroibos chuckled, 'Yes, the gentle sports.'

Simonides turned to his Elean friend, 'Are you running tomorrow?' Koroibos grinned and nodded.

Rameses raised an arm and pointed, 'There he is!' They looked over and saw Askari being oiled up by one of his men at an adjoining pankration ring. His fellow nomads stood around their leader, excitedly offering advice and joking about the rewards they would earn when their wagers paid off. Spotting his friends, Askari grinned fiercely before again focusing on the challenge to come. Pelops and his companions pressed through the crowd to lend Askari their full support; they awaited the commencement of his bout as the giant nomad had his protective coat of oil finalized; if he was fortunate, the odd blow or grip would slide away from the surface of his skin, allowing a more rapid counterattack. It was the only introduced advantage the pankrationists were permitted.

At the other end of the ring, a massive Celt was being warmed up by his trainer — he was being slapped vigorously on thighs and arms to promote blood circulation. He snarled savagely as the trainer began to slap his face. Deeming his charge sufficiently enlivened, the trainer stepped away, and the Celt turned his attention to Askari, his features twisted into a ferocious visage. His entourage of Celtic tribesmen erupted into a war chant, soon working themselves into a coordinated frenzy so alarming that the rest of the crowd began distancing themselves from these intimidating madmen.

Flamboyantly fearless, Askari laughed dismissively as he made a show of staring down the noisy Celts. As the two camps engaged in their pre-bout battle of wills, officials began watering down the bare earthen ring, while several drummers settled into ringside positions. From the nearby boxing ring, a huge roar split the air, signaling that the bout was over and a victor had emerged. Glancing back, Pelops could see the Elean official raise the hand of one of the fighters, while the other lay unconscious on the ground. The victor unceremoniously left the ring as attendants dragged the fallen boxer across the sandy pit.

Mildly curious, Askari shot a question at Pelops, 'Foreigner or Greek?'

Pelops replied, 'The Greek.'

'Right. Then, either way, it's my turn', Askari said and nodded towards his Celtic opponent. 'He may be big, but if he raises that surrender finger, I'll snap it off.'

Pelops laughed and slapped Askari on his oiled back.

At the edge of the ring, Askari's assistant stepped forward and, as a final encouragement, urged, 'Don't play around with him, chief. The men expect to win their bets.'

Askari nodded assertively and called out, cryptically, to Pelops, 'Just wait for the camel ride. It's for Goliath and Saul!'

Accustomed to expecting anything from the big nomad, Pelops nodded back, knowing it would be an exciting clash whatever the outcome.

The crowd eagerly congregated as the official stepped into the ring. 'Pankration fighters, step into the ring. Now engage!'

The crowd roared forth its excitement as the drummers began a rapid beat. Askari and the Celt circled the ring, each man attempting to take the other's measure. Again and again, Askari feinted an attack, watching intently to see if his opponent would telegraph his punches. Frustrated with these showy tactics, the Celt resorted to brute power and threw a wild haymaker. Seizing the opportunity, Askari dived forward and kicked hard into his opponent's thigh. The Celt staggered backward as Askari launched a flurry of chopping blows and kicks. Over-confident that the Celt's defenses were crumbling, Askari spun to deliver a side kick but was, in turn, outfoxed when his foe lunged forward, caught the raised leg, and flipped the nomad over. Landing heavily, Askari lay winded as the Celt leaped onto his back and began to smother Askari's face into the sand. As they struggled, Askari managed to strike the Celt in the face with his elbow and break the hold he was locked in.

Both men rolled to one side with surprising agility, jumped to their feet and began warily circling one another. Launching a series of jabs aimed at Askari's eyepatch, the big Celt succeeded in momentarily stunning the nomad before resorting to a snap-kick to the hip; this knocked Askari to the ground once again. An exultant roar burst forth from the band of Celtic spectators in anticipation of their champion's victory.

Sensing the momentum shift, Askari's camp, Pelops included, fell into a stunned silence. Dreading the prospect of such a defeat for their proud friend, they watched through hands over faces as the Celt, a machine of muscle and fury, power-lifted Askari into the air to finish him off with a piledriver into the ground. The act would not only end the bout but could well prove fatal — if not for Askari's next move. As the Celt raised him into the air, Askari's hands shot out, fingers extended, and clawed the Celt in both eyes. Blinded and in pain, the Celt dropped his burden. Landing cat-like on all fours, Askari was on his feet in an instant, as the Celt still staggered blindly around the ring, rubbing his eyes and bellowing his rage at being incapacitated in such a manner.

Working his way behind the Celt, Askari chose his moment carefully before leaping onto his opponent's back and, from there, levered himself further up to lock his legs in a scissorhold around the Celt's throat. From his perch upon the bigger man's shoulders, he began to rain chopping blows down upon the Celt's head. Desperately trying to wrench the nomad's legs away from his windpipe, the Celt staggered about the ring. However, his struggles soon weakened as his body was starved of oxygen. It was all he could do to remain standing with Askari's weight on his shoulders and the world swimming in his vision.

Like a deranged jockey riding an enraged mount, Askari clung on tightly, exerting the full strength of his legs to choke the man below. Now enjoying himself, he ululated a war cry, feared in the deserts of his homeland but known in Olympia only to his followers. Askari's tribesmen joined in their chief's cries, a chorus as wild as the lands they stemmed from. The absurdity of the scene struck the crowd, and many began to howl with laughter, cheering on with glee as Askari rode the Celt like a camel driver steering an unruly beast. Contrariwise, the Celtic tribesmen howled with rage that their champion had been so shamed.

Askari delivered a final indignity to the Celt as, falling to his knees through lack of oxygen, he flailed his arms wildly before falling sideways into the sand. Askari fell with him, legs still locked in place, and refused at any point to break the chokehold on his opponent's throat. Holding up one finger in surrender before blacking out completely, the Celt did the almost unthinkable, and ca-pitulated. The officiating Elean referee glanced at the Celt's trainer and, receiv-ing confirmation from that man, also with his finger raised, called the bout in Askari's favor.

Askari jumped to his feet and bowed ostentatiously, first to the Elean of-ficial, then to his unconscious opponent, and finally to the crowd, turning in a tight circle, flinging himself up and down like a performer receiving an encore.

So entertaining was this sight that even some of the Celts joined in and laughed freely. Stepping from the ring, Askari was greeted with slaps on the back and words of praise by his amused supporters. Although winded from his exertions and the very enthusiastic backslapping, Askari turned to Pelops and stated, 'That, my boy, is how you turn a Celt into a camel!'

Pelops enjoyed a peripeteian laugh, one ripped from his belly just when he thought he would be comforting his friend over an ignominious defeat.

Observing all intently from nearby, Melqart turned to his Carthaginian strongman and said, with just an edge of admiration in his voice, 'He's tough.'

'That desert rat?' replied the Carthaginian colossus. 'I'll crush him,' he said with booming confidence.

Melqart's grin was the kind that scared children in the middle of the night.

ΨΨΨ

Prince Lycurgus strode through the grounds of the statue park, away from the competition areas but not beyond the echoes of the crowd roaring for one competitor or another. As he passed a large pavilion, he noticed King Kleosthenes and King Iphitos seated at a gaming table, playing a form of draughts known locally as *petteia*. Contemplating these two previously fierce rivals, Lycurgus stood for many a moment before them. 'A new way to resolve disputes?' he finally asked.

Both kings glanced up and chuckled. 'Only if he loses,' qualified Iphitos with a wry smile.

The prince nodded, and an approving smile flickered across his face as he walked on. His path led him to the large red pavilion that temporarily housed the dyarchy of Sparta. Upon entering, he saw King Arcelaus seated on a divan while his father, King Prytanis, sharpened his sword. 'You sent for me?' asked the prince.

Without looking up, his father asked, 'The competition has begun, by the sound of it?' Lycurgus nodded affirmatively.

King Prytanis now locked onto his son's gaze, 'No more mistakes, then. I... we... Sparta cannot afford them.'

'Mistakes?' Lycurgus snorted. 'And this from a man holding a sword at Olympia?'

Prytanis snapped, 'We are surrounded by enemies. It would be madness not to be prepared if we are attacked.'

Incensed by his father's attitude and his refusal to see anything but evil, weakness, or betrayal in his fellow Greeks, Lycurgus's temper gave way, 'Attacked? That has never happened at Olympia. Why would you threaten the truce — and our prospects — with that weapon?'

Arcelaus joined the conversation, 'Your father already felt so threatened that he used a priest as that sword's scabbard.'

Prytanis slammed his sword down on the table. He glared at Arcelaus, a contemptuous manner he often deployed to disregard his fellow King. Arcelaus looked away.

'It was you!' the prince blurted out, louder than he had intended.

Prytanis scowled at Lycurgus and spat out, 'He is no priest. He was bought and sold like a cheap harlot.'

'As we are by the Carthaginians! When you are gone, I will no longer betray my fellow Greeks,' he raged at his father.

About to pivot away and storm off, he froze at the prickle of cold steel at his throat. In one swift motion, Prytanis, with all the grace of a man schooled to battle over a lifetime, had thrust the tip of the sword under his son's chin. Without flinching, Lycurgus gazed into his father's eyes and saw the cold, calculating madness within.

The sword-wielding king growled menacingly, 'No. You will do exactly as you are told. Fellow Greeks? We are Spartans, Eleans, Pisatans — not Greeks. Your Greeks are a fantasy that will never come into being.'

Lycurgus turned his head slowly towards the door, deliberately slicing his neck on the sword. 'I used to believe that. Now, with these games, I can no longer. Things must change for all of our people,' he said evenly.

Still glaring at his son, yet taken aback by the composed bravery Lycurgus had just displayed, Prytanis let his sword fall. He reached out to staunch the trickle of blood that flowed from the superficial neck wound his son now bore.

Lycurgus said wearily, 'Leave it. It will remind me of what you hold sacred.' Holding his head high, he strode from the tent.

Outside the tent, Lycurgus passed Kleosthenes and Iphitos once again, both kings still engaged in their peaceful battle over the board game. They glanced up at him expectantly, ready to welcome Lycurgus to join them. He moved quickly beyond them, oblivious to the unspoken offer. Seeing the melancholy look on his face, they could only wonder at the blood which now stained his tunic.

ΨΨΨΨ

The following day, under a blazing morning sun, Pelops stood upright in a marble-lined pool located near one of the streams that watered the sanctuary of Olympia. Attentively, Iphicles scrubbed his left shoulder with oil and water, drawing the occasional wince of pain from the young man. Other athletes also cleansed and washed themselves in the pool. Among these, Simonides, Agathon, and the Elean runners were gathered near Pelops and Iphicles.

Approaching them, Hippodamia sat gracefully on the pool edge and, dangling her legs in the water, smiled at her friends. Seeing the attention Iphicles was paying to his shoulder, she asked Pelops, 'Still in pain?'

Without waiting for his charge to speak, Iphicles reported, 'There is damage to the shoulder.'

Finding his voice, Pelops added, 'Iphicles has promised to brace it. It will heal. You know how grateful I am.'

Holding his gaze, Hippodamia's look became wistful, 'Yes. Your father, for all of his faults, he... he did help to heal you.'

'Let us not speak of that. Ever.' Pelops blurted, clearly reluctant to examine his wounded feelings. His friends all glanced away from his pained face.

Not to be dissuaded, Hippodamia begged, 'He won't be with us much longer. Could you not forgive him this final time?'

Pausing long and hard, with tension crackling around him from his friend's concerned looks, Pelops finally responded, 'I will think on it. That is the best I can do.'

Koroibos broke the uncomfortable tension by leaping noisily into the pool, oblivious to the tense exchange that had preceded his arrival. 'Where is your victory wreath?' he asked of Hippodamia.

'I gave it to the Spartan runner, Cynisca,' she replied nonchalantly.

Disbelief registered on the Elean cook's face, 'You gave it away? That's very generous of you.' He paused, then abandoning his usual cheer, added, 'Unfortunately, we can't afford to be that noble. My friends here depend on our trading two of the finest olive leaf crowns ever made for their lives. And so do you.'

The bathers all fell silent as the cook's words again reminded them of the gravity of the situation. As the moment stretched into an awkward silence, Pelops quietly interjected, 'He is right. For once.' A couple of the Eleans attempted a smile at Pelops's wit; it was less than convincing.

Hippodamia felt compelled to change the subject. Looking to Koroibos, she asked of him, 'Are you confident of your chances?'

'I don't hold out much hope for the cripple here,' he said, nodding at Pelops, 'but my own chances are better than good.'

His Elean friends actually managed a chuckle at this. Pelops responded by splashing an armful of water at Koroibos. Koroibos retaliated by splashing Pelops, then Iphicles and Hippodamia for good measure. As their Elean friends also joined in the water sports, their shared tension briefly dissolved, with the pool erupting into cavorting bodies and laughter.

A drenched Hippodamia rolled out of the pool, giggling helplessly. Regaining her self-control, she told Koroibos, 'I look forward to your race today, Elean cook.'

'You'll be there? I thought only virgins could attend?' he replied, grinning from ear to ear, greatly enjoying the opportunity to tease his friend.

Hippodamia looked briefly shocked before once again bursting into laughter at Koroibos's temerity. Pelops grinned at both his friends, glad that the levity had lifted all their moods before the stakes were once again raised by the games.

ΨΨΨΨ

Still a little damp, Hippodamia sliced her way through the jostling crowds at Olympia, passing several sporting events that were already in motion. Down one side of Zeus's temple, athletes were lining up on a running track to compete while closer to the field adjoining Hera's temple, discus throwers were making practice casts with their carved stone equipment. All around them, spectators pulsed with excitement.

Reaching the front stairs of the temple of Zeus, Hippodamia approached an award ceremony that was being conducted. A swarthy athlete from the far-flung Isle of Tin stood on the temple steps. An Elean official placed a wreath on his head while King Iphitos stood alongside, nodding in approval. As she merged with the ceremony audience, the official announced, 'This is the first victory wreath awarded to a foreigner at Olympia. Sego, son of Tasciovanus, from Bretannic, the Isle of Tin. We congratulate you!' As the Bretannic victor raised his arms in triumph, the audience received him warmly.

Standing alongside Hippodamia, an old man turned to his wife and whispered hoarsely, 'This is disgraceful. Bad enough even having these barbarians here, but now we actually let them win.'

Before she could respond to the bitter local, the glowering face of Melqart interposed itself. He barked, 'Watch your mouth, old goat. That dwarf made a mockery of Greek manhood. And keep watching — there is much more of that to come.'

Frightened by the aggressive foreigner who spoke their tongue, the old man and his wife blanched and fought their way through the crowd to find safety.

Melqart laughed at their reaction, then reached over to grab Hippodamia by the arm, 'Ah, the runaway slave. I see now that you are fond of us barbarians. You will join me after I beat that boy of yours.'

Hippodamia wrenched her arm free, 'He has beaten you before. He will do it again.' Melqart's face twisted with rage at Hippodamia, but before he could give it voice, their ears were assaulted by a roar from the pankration ring. Staring in that direction through a gap in the crowd, they both spotted a bloodied Askari, down on his knees and holding a hand over his one good eye as gore pulsed from its socket. The Carthaginian strongman stood over him, arms thrown up in victory.

Melqart crowed, 'Your boy is next.'

XIII

I n the temple of Hera, King Kleosthenes, King Iphitos, Homer, and Europa stood before the statue of Hestia. The goddess's eternal flame burned brightly as Europa poured a pitcher of cleansing water over her arms. While the men watched solemnly, Europa threw up her arms, 'Virgin Hestia, elder sister of Zeus, mother of the eternal flame, we call upon your aid. Speak to your brother, have Zeus smile upon our Games. Ask him, O flame of our lives, to lift the drought and send us rains. Ask him to alleviate the suffering of his people. We, the supplicants of the first Olympiad, ask this.' With this, she dropped her arms, exhausted.

The two kings stepped forward and supported her, one on each side. Homer then moved forward, the light of the flames flickering over his face. 'Hestia, in the highest dwelling of all, above both deathless gods and the men who walk on this Earth. You have gained an everlasting abode and the greatest honor. Glorious is your portion and your right, for, without you, mortals hold no banquet where one does not duly pour sweet wine in offering to Hestia both first and last.' Iphitos then placed a pitcher in Homer's right hand while Kleosthenes put another in his left. Homer upended both vessels, a stream of water and red wine mixed on the floor before the eternal flame. They all bowed their heads and, after a moment in solemn prayer, turned and walked once again into the light of day beyond the chamber.

King Iphitos asked of Homer, 'Will it be enough?'

'Zeus is always capricious. I fear his anger as much as his indifference. We can only hope she helps him find pleasure in these games,' Homer replied.

As the two kings assisted Homer down the temple stairs, Europa stopped and stared. A flock of white doves flew across the temple entrance, bringing forth a smile from her. Hestia had heard! Zeus had heard!

Ψ

Pelops wove through the throng of spectators towards a large, white pavilion. He appeared deeply troubled. Reaching the tent, he nodded grimly to the nomad guards stationed at its entrance before striding through to its interior. Askari lay on a pallet bed, his head completely bandaged. Rameses sat nearby with concern deeply etched into his usually calm features. Around the two men, Askari's tribesmen sat — some picking desultorily over a meal, some sipping half-heartedly from their cups — and all looked glum.

Pelops acknowledged the Egyptian prince before lowering himself down next to the nomad. Identifying himself to his heavily bandaged friend, he said, 'Askari, it is me, Pelops.'

'Young hero of Carthage. It is good to... hear your voice again', he gasped out.

Not wasting time with small talk, Pelops cut to the heart of the matter, 'How bad?' he asked the nomad.

'The eye can be saved. Thankfully I'll not have to join your Homer. Or take up poetry for a profession', he replied.

Rameses attempted a chuckle, 'Thank Osiris for that! Imagine the havoc he would wreak upon art?'

Turning his head towards the young priest's voice, Askari whispered, 'Pelops, you must be... very careful. They are more dangerous than I thought. That Carthaginian bested me in a fair fight, though he should have fallen many times. They burn with hatred.'

'Yes,' added Rameses, 'they are out for blood, it seems. All of our blood.'

'I know,' replied Pelops, 'I saw what Melqart did to Saul. But there is no other way.' Rameses turned his gaze towards the young priest who, not able to hold it, glanced down at Askari before turning his head away.

ΨΨ

With the afternoon sun upon them, Pelops walked with Koroibos towards the running track. Many other runners were on the sidelines, limbering up and being oiled by trainers. A huge crowd encircled them, waiting impatiently for the upcoming event. Among the competitors, Prince Lycurgus stood with his Spartans, each man having their long hair braided by slaves, a battle custom they preserved even before sporting competitions. Nearby, Melqart warmed himself up with short weaving sprints near the rest of the Carthaginian contingent. Ruthlessly competitive, he tried to stare down Pelops and Koroibos as they passed him. Koroibos glared back, while Pelops tried with all of his strength to turn his thoughts inward before this most important of races.

Seeing his friend bristle at the sight of Melqart, Pelops asked, 'Are you ready?'

'I've waited most of my life for a chance like this,' the cook replied.

Pelops smiled, proud of his friend's courage, 'You are running against royalty, lords, and captains; men who have had much time to train. I can run this now if you want me to?'

Silently acknowledging that Pelops had offered him an honorable escape, 'No. If I win, our friends will be closer to freedom. Besides, the Carthaginian noble will fear being beaten by a peasant. He will be focused on his fear of a shameful defeat rather than the glory of victory.'

Pelops nodded earnestly, grabbed Koroibos by the forearms, and gazed into his eyes, 'For our friends, then.'

Koroibos echoed the refrain, 'Our friends.'

Pelops patted him on the back and walked over to the sidelines, where Iphicles, Hippodamia, and the other Elean athletes awaited. They smiled, but the tension on each of their faces showed plainly.

Pelops sought to calm their nerves, 'He is well prepared.'

On the track, Koroibos took his place at the start of the half-stade marker. As he did so, he glanced across the line at the other runners. From amongst their number, Melqart stepped forward and taunted, 'Ready to lose this race, Greek? Ready to lose your friends?'

Koroibos stared through him without offering a reply. He would not be drawn into the Carthaginian's games of psyche. Amusing, he thought, that he is not as confident as I once thought him to be.

Melqart swaggered back into place on the line. A silent witness to this display of braggadocio, Prince Lycurgus shook his head with disgust before seeing to his own starting preparations.

Two Elean officials stepped up to the starter position. One raised the starter sash. Taking their cue from the officials, the trumpeters assumed their places. From under a well-shaded trackside awning, a figure leaned forward in her seat — it was Queen Dido. She stared at the runners with great intensity. The honor of her city rested upon the mercurial shoulders of Melqart.

The second official boomed out above the sibilant noise of the crowd, 'Take your starting places!'

Like a stunned beast, the crowd fell mute as the runners assumed their standing-start postures.

The presiding official raised his forked switch and continued, 'Be ready. Be set. Go!' The crowd immediately roared into life as the men flung themselves forward.

Melqart and Lycurgus cleared the pack with an initial burst of speed. His nerves showing, Koroibos lost his footing and slipped awkwardly at the start. As the trumpets continued to blare, he knew he had much ground to make up if he was to have a chance at the victory wreath.

From the stands, Pelops, Hippodamia, and the other Elean athletes looked on with their hearts in their mouths, shocked at the initial stumble of their friend.

Rapidly finding his stride, Koroibos regained traction and, with his mind now clear of the panic that the god Phobos threatened him with, shot past the tail runners. Far from being overawed by the moment, as he had at first feared, Koroibos discovered a fierce joy in his heart as the crowd, seeing his recovery, began to now to chant his name. He reached into some reservoir deep within and began to hurtle through the pack, his feet pounding furiously as his legs accelerated him to a speed he had never before known. At the head of the field, Melqart and Lycurgus still raced neck-and-neck. Moving with honed athleticism, the two noblemen were only body-lengths away from the finish line when the seemingly impossible occurred. Lycurgus and Melqart watched in disbelief as the Elean cook slipped first between, and then past, them. Trying to pick up their own pace, breath bursting in their lungs, they kept pace with Koroibos but failed to close with him or collapse the lead that he had almost miraculously generated. Koroibos crossed the finish line half a body-length in front of his nearest rivals, to the wild adulation of the crowd. Chanting his name, Pelops, Hippodamia and the Eleans bounded up and down in rapture.

At the finish line, a third Elean official pointed his switch at a now-decelerating Koroibos and cried out, 'The victor!' His friends and Elean countrymen flooded onto the running track to congratulate this unlikeliest of champions.

Watching with a wry sense of chagrin, Lycurgus was doubled over, sucking air in deeply. He winced at the stitch he felt deep within his lungs. Glancing around, he spotted Melqart stalking away from the track. The Carthaginian walked towards his queen, who now delivered his greatest humiliation. As he sought to enter her pavilion, she nodded her head, and her bodyguards physically blocked his path. Almost apoplectic with rage, he spat on the ground before storming away to his own tent.

Cognizant of the high stakes, Lycurgus realized why the trounced Carthaginian had lost control of himself in front of his queen; he also knew that there would be consequences as a result of this insult to the Mediterranean world's most powerful regent. He knew, too, that he would face repercussions when he saw how his own rulers observed him — King Arcelaus looked on, as expressionless as a statue, eyeing him coldly, while King Prytanis closed his eyes and shook his head angrily. And everywhere Lycurgus turned, he could hear only the boundless salutes of the audience, as the new running champion was hoisted into the air by his friends.

ΨΨΨ

With a smile reaching from ear to ear, Koroibos rubbed himself down with oil outside the Elean tents at the Olympia sanctuary. He remained exultant, still wearing his victory wreath and ribbons. Other Elean competitors lounged around on the grass, chatting excitedly. He glanced up to see King Iphitos standing before him, holding up two wine goblets, one of which he offered to Koroibos.

The king proclaimed, 'You have made Elis proud, my cook. Let us drink to your health.'

The Elean team found their voices yet again and cheered as the two men drank deeply. Simonides rose up, stepped forward, nodded respectfully to the king, and turned to his friend, 'By the gods, that was a race to remember, Koroibos. You have brought Elis glory and have, at the same time, taken us closer to freedom. We salute Elis's fastest ever cook!'

Approaching the celebrating Eleans, Pelops and Hippodamia hailed them. 'A great victory!' announced the young priestess.

'Yes, it was a stunning victory,' agreed Pelops. He added, worriedly, 'But is it enough?'

The grin fading from his lips, Koroibos asked, 'What do you mean?'

Pelops paused, looked hard at the Elean king for verification, then said, 'Well, if I don't beat him tomorrow, will he demand our friends still return to Carthage?'

Agathon rose up from the grass and cried out, 'No, he can't!'

King Iphitos countered, 'He may well. The horse race is the last event of the games, and great prestige is attached to it. Melqart may claim that race has priority in this matter'.

A shocked Koroibos interjected, 'More prestigious than the foot race?'

'You have made your name immortal, Koroibos, but horses belong to gods, aristocrats, and heroes. Pelops is right. Our countrymen and the priestess Hippodamia are still in danger,' he added, gravely.

Absorbing his king's counsel, Koroibos turned to Pelops, 'Then, my friend, it falls to you.'

'We know you can do it,' encouraged Hippodamia. The Eleans all nodded affirmatively.

Although he tried to smile reassuringly, Pelops had never felt less certain of anything in his life.

ΨΨΨΨ

On the stone step before a neglected shrine in Olympia's statue park, Homer sat playing a lyre. Lost in his music, he chanted softly, 'Sing, O goddess, of the anger of Achilles, son of Peleus, that brought countless ills upon the Greeks. Many a brave soul did it send hurrying down to Hades, and many a hero did it yield as prey to dogs and vultures. For so were the counsels of Zeus fulfilled...' Stopping mid-verse, he raised his head and asked, 'Who is there?'

Moving hesitantly forward, a young slave of some fourteen summers addressed the poet, 'My apologies, Master. Are you the one known as Homer?'

'Yes, replied Homer, 'it is I whom you seek.'

'Queen Dido has sent me to you as part of a gift. I am to pass it into your hands and your hands alone. My name is Cadmus,' said the youth.

Homer smiled, 'A Greek name? Thank your queen, although I do not partake of slavery. You must return to her.'

'I cannot, Master,' replied Cadmus, 'Queen Dido has now left Olympia to return to Carthage.'

Homer's face registered his surprise.

Cadmus continued, 'I do not fully know why, Master. It is rumored that she has lost faith in Lord Melqart. Some say he will not be welcome if he tries to return to Carthage.'

'Then that is a message of great value,' said Homer. 'I will have you pass that onto a young friend for me.'

Nodding, Cadmus added, 'I have another gift for you from the queen. Payment for offenses done to your gods by Lord Melqart.' Cadmus reached into a leather bag and extracted a scroll of parchment. He unrolled it, stepped forward, and placed Homer's hand upon the sheet. 'Can you feel the tiny bumps and grooves?' he asked of the poet.

'Yes,' replied a puzzled Homer, as he lightly ran his sensitive fingers across the engraved sheet.

Cadmus smiled and said, 'Good. It is a thing that the Carthaginians call writing. It is a lasting memory of things done and said. It is known by my queen that the Greeks do not have this thing.'

Wonderstruck, Homer asked, 'You know this thing?'

'I am trained in it as a scribe. I am here to teach it, if I may,' replied Cadmus.

'Such an incredible gift!' exclaimed the poet, still incredulous as he continued running a hand over the parchment to feel out its tiny corrugations.

ΨΨΨΨΨ

At the gates of Olympia, the Spartan kings and their retinue had assembled into a marching formation, clearly preparing to depart. Nowhere evident were any of the Spartan athletes of this first Olympiad.

Alerted by his own bodyguard, Lycurgus strode over to the kings, 'You are leaving? These games have yet to run their course.'

King Arcelaus spat out, accusingly, 'These games do Sparta no honor. Olympia has not been kind to us.'

'Sparta is shamed! And now, with that Carthaginian witch gone, the alliance between our cities has collapsed. What do you have to say for yourself?' King Prytanis fumed at his son.

Lycurgus bit down on his mounting temper, 'Olympia is not here for our gain. It is a symbol of hope for many. I have never seen Greece so united. My men and I will remain. We honor Sparta just by competing.'

His face flushed, Prytanis barked out, 'Honor? The Spartan code, the code your whole life is built upon, is victory or death. What victory have you brought us?'

Lycurgus said flatly, 'That code is for war. We honor no god by fighting here. At least some of us understand that, Father.' He turned on his heel and walked away before either of the kings could retort.

Enraged by the exchange, Prytanis moved to follow his son.

Arcelaus grabbed him by the shoulder, 'Leave him. Each generation brings change. He believes what he does is right. There is nothing you can say or do to alter that.'

'And that is Sparta's future!' bemoaned Prytanis before striding angrily through the gates. With a deep sigh, Arcelaus could only signal the Spartan retinue to shoulder their marching kits and begin the long journey home.

ΨΨΨΨΨ

Pelops groomed Pegasus vigorously as Iphicles held up a bucket of water for the stallion to drink. Clearly enjoying the attention, Pegasus snorted gently, now and again lifting his snout to nuzzle the old manservant, who chuckled indulgently. Hippodamia leant against the stable wall, watching with pleasure. In the adjacent stall, Prince Rameses worked on his steed, having rejected the ministrations of his team in order to build a stronger bond between animal and human. All around them the stables swarmed with activity as jockeys, trainers, and feeders administered to their mounts, while everyone from charlatans to animal doctors provided husbandry advice to eke out any performance advantages to be found.

It was here that Cadmus, the boy-slave from Carthage, found them. Approaching Hippodamia, he enquired, 'I seek the one called Pelops. I bear a message from the poet Homer for him.'

Hippodamia tilted her head towards her lover; Cadmus smiled gratefully. 'I am he,' said Pelops, emerging from beside Pegasus.

Cadmus stepped in close to Pelops and whispered, 'I am sent to warn you about Lord Melqart. He faces exile from Carthage if he should lose the horse race today. Homer fears for your safety.'

Pelops slowly digested the warning then stared down the length of the horse stalls to where Melqart and his trainers worked on a magnificent steed. He noted their intensity. Nodding his head in acknowledgment of the danger he might face, he turned back to Cadmus, 'Thank the poet for me. I understand.'

Cadmus urged, 'I have seen him treat men much worse than animals. And now he is desperate. Please beware, Master Pelops.'

Pelops smiled lightly and patted his steed between its shoulder blades, 'Pegasus has never let me down before. He will not start now.'

'We all hope so, Master. Greece is with you today,' the expatriate added. Cadmus nodded respectfully at Iphicles and Hippodamia and walked back to join Homer.

As Pelops watched Cadmus depart, he was surprised to see Lycurgus directly approaching after walking past Melqart with no acknowledgment.

The Spartan prince looked approvingly over Pegasus and declared, 'Sparta has withdrawn from this last race. To even the field. We wish you well, young Greek.'

Perplexed, Pelops did not even get a chance to reply before Lycurgus turned away and walked out of the stable doors.

Prince Rameses broke the stunned silence, 'Most gracious, for a Spartan. We Egyptians are still here to win, though, so you'll not be out there alone with the Carthaginian. I will keep a close eye on him.'

Still shocked, Pelops acknowledged this show of support with a warm smile, 'Thank you, my friend.' Glancing back to where Melqart worked feverishly on his horse, the two men locked gazes, their hostility now open and mutual. Hippodamia stepped protectively in front of Pelops, blocking the Carthaginian's line of sight. She smiled as Iphicles placed a reassuring hand on Pelops's shoulder. Pelops nodded gratefully at his friends and returned to tending Pegasus, his mind awhirl with racing stratagems.

XIV

Leaping to their feet, the massive crowd at Olympia burst into applause as the equestrians trotted their horses across from stalls and pavilions to the hippodrome. They had assembled from every quarter of the Mediterranean world for this most prestigious of events. Many jockeys rode for their masters or aristocratic horse owners, although a few competitors like Pelops, Melqart, and Prince Rameses rode for their own glory. The hippodrome was a simple, though vast construction dug across one of the empty fields near the River Alpheous; it measured some three stades long and one stade across. The earth scraped from its innards was banked up along the sides to form natural viewing ramps and piled high through its center to ensure that horse and rider had to obey the course. Olive and cypress trees fringed its perimeter, forming a natural enclosure for the event. Mounted upon the central spine of the hippodrome were the flags and banners of all the competing peoples, along with towering wooden statues of Zeus and Poseidon at either end, the latter deity being the especially revered Greek god of horses. An elaborate mechanism — consisting of a large bronze dolphin that, when dropped by an official, triggered the lifting of an equally large bronze eagle that, in turn, raised the starting rope — would regulate the discharge of the riders and drew many an admiring look from the spectators for its ingenuity and beauty.

Pelops rode Pegasus across from the permanent stables at Olympia, accompanied by Rameses on an exquisite desert charger. Both riders waved energetically at the crowd. Pelops's arm movements were a little restricted by the shoulder brace he wore, constructed from stitched-together ivory pieces that normally adorned the statuary which dotted the grounds and temples of Olympia. It was a makeshift solution, but an exceedingly clever one that the healer who had dragged him back from the portal of Hades had insisted upon. The ivory glinted in the bright sunlight, giving Pelops's all-white riding costume an unmistakable cast.

Within the royal boxes placed in positions of prominence around the course, King Iphitos of Elis, King Kleosthenes of Pisa, Kings Arcelaus and Prytanis of Sparta, Queen Dido of Carthage, and countless other monarchs and aristocrats from Greece and beyond began settling into their seats. Their retinues filled the seats behind them under the purpose-built structures, while lesser entities, like Homer, Cadmus, Europa, and her fellow priestesses, filled out the back rows. King Iphitos had invited the entire Elean team to join him within his box, with the Olympian Koroibos having pride of place alongside his monarch. Prince Lycurgus had yet to join his father, seemingly reluctant to leave his vantage point near the Carthaginian team, having remained vigilant for any sign of further foul tactics by Melqart's underlings. Hippodamia was nowhere to be seen.

With no Elean competing in the horse race, King Iphitos was content to support the young priest who had accomplished so much for these Olympics. Turning to Koroibos, he asked, 'He has fully recovered, has he not?'

Still fiddling with the victor's wreath on his head, Koroibos leaned towards the king and replied, 'Almost, my lord. The shoulder still troubles him, but he is a very fine rider.'

The king signified his understanding with a grunt and gave a satisfied nod, although the rest of the closely-packed Elean athletes — Simonides and Agathon among them — appeared more concerned, exchanging apprehensive glances. They knew that Pelops had only just been rescued from the gates of Hades from the poisoning, and now there was this lingering shoulder injury; he needed to be at his very peak to defeat their nemesis, the Carthaginian Melqart, to ensure their freedom. They quietly worried that so much rested upon his shoulders with this race.

At the start line, the equestrians began maneuvering their horses into place. Trainers and coaches assisted with the more fiery steeds. Most of these highly-strung animals were skittish at the close proximity of so many others of their breed, while the cacophony of spectator roars only spooked them further. As they were jostled and coaxed into place on the start line, Elean race officials moved carefully amongst them, flicking their switches impatiently and ever-alert for unfair stratagems being employed; fairness and rigorous compliance with the Olympian code was their primary objective. And they were relentless in their pursuit of that goal, as the reputation of their kingdom and the games rested upon this adherence. With an admonishing cry, a senior official lashed out brutally at one trainer with his switch, striking him multiple times across the face and hands — the miscreant had been caught leaning under another rider's mount to either loosen the saddle blanket strap or squeeze the stallion's testicles, both of which were well-known ploys to unseat a jockey. The rider of that horse added insult to injury by then lashing out with a bare foot and kicking the guilty trainer in the head. Many of the other riders and officials laughed aloud at the treatment — the rules of the games were well understood and often severe in their enforcement.

Rameses was backing his horse into position, assisted by two of his Egyptian rebels. He glanced over at the commotion, grateful that the rules were so strictly prescribed, and then looked towards Pelops. Although a well-trained mount, Pegasus was flighty amidst so many strange sights and sounds, and Pelops was struggling with him. Rameses called out to him, 'You need help! Where is Iphicles?'

Pelops cried back, surprise in his voice, 'You're right. I haven't seen him.' He craned his neck around, trying to see past the riders to either side of him, but failed to detect the elderly manservant.

Some distance away from the track, Iphicles was moving with as much pace as he could muster. He was not alone. He was supporting a grievously wounded Tantalus as they emerged through the front entrance of the temple of Zeus. Ashen-faced and wincing with every small step he took, a heavily bandaged Tantalus leaned upon his priestly staff, while Iphicles did the best he could to support his other side. Iphicles eased him against one of the temple's prostyle columns and said, 'You should be able to see the results from here. I must get to your son now.'

Tantalus slowly slid down to the base of the column. With drawn features, he extended a clenched hand to Iphicles and mumbled, 'Take this to him... it belonged to... his mother.' Tantalus was wracked with coughing by the effort, a trickle of blood emerging from the corner of his mouth.

Though greatly torn, Iphicles stared into the bloodshot eyes and accepted the offering from the proffered hand. It was a necklace of some sort. He nodded and moved down the steps of the temple towards the start line of the horse race, hoping that Pelops would not be disappointed by his delay. He finally reached the hippodrome just as an official was accosting Pelops.

'What is wrong with that horse? Get it in line! This race waits for no-one,' the Elean cried out officiously.

As Pelops continued to struggle, Iphicles slid between the Elean and Pegasus and grabbed the horse's reins.

Delighted, Pelops called down to him, 'There you are! I was starting to think you must have changed teams!'

Iphicles grinned and gently pressed Pegasus towards his designated starting position. Familiar with both rider and trainer, Pegasus calmed and submitted, neighing with pleasure that he was in loving hands. Once horse and rider were aligned with the competition, Iphicles took advantage of the delay while the starting sash was raised and spoke to Pelops, 'I had to help your father. He watches from up there.' He pointed to the top steps of Zeus's temple.

A shocked Pelops followed the line of Iphicles's arm and could just make out the silhouette of his father, seated at the base of a temple column. He peered more closely to try and establish how the mortally-wounded man was faring. Before he could enquire of Iphicles how he had managed to be pried from his death bed, the Elean official barked at the elderly manservant, 'Move man! This race begins.'

Iphicles turned first to the official, 'We're ready.' Then he turned to Pelops, 'We are ready, aren't we?'

Pelops nodded tensely and continued to pat Pegasus to keep him calm; the horse was as on-edge as his rider.

All along the line of horses, trainers and coaches were now moving away from their charges. As Iphicles raised his section of starting sash to move under it, he paused and spun back to Pelops, 'Remember — keep that Carthaginian in sight at all times. He is your biggest threat. Let Pegasus do the rest. He runs like you do... Oh, and your father wanted you to have this for luck. It was a possession of your mother.'

Pelops reached down and took the necklace. He glanced at it quizzically. After a quick glance at the dove intaglio, he placed it around his neck. He glanced up a final time at his father's vantage point, then leaned forward over the neck of Pegasus, the necklace brushing against the horse's mane.

Iphicles slapped him excitedly on the leg and moved off with the departing rider assistants. He stood trackside with the team supports and looked on expectantly.

The head race official stared intently down the race line, the mechanically-activated horizontal sash holding the horses in check, and then stepped up to the release mechanism. Following his every movement with rapt attention, the crowd renewed its fevered applause, with the women as fulsome in their cries as the men.

Pelops stole an opportunity to flash a smile at Rameses. The prince returned his *esprit* with a grin. Glancing too, towards Melqart, he caught only a fixed, stony stare by way of return; the Carthaginian must have been studying me for some time, Pelops mused.

The head race official broke into Pelops's thoughts. He proclaimed in a booming voice, 'In this, the final event of the games, the Olympians will race three times past the finish post. Before you are men from every corner of the known world. The first past the post gains the victory wreath. The rest of you will be forgotten by history!'

Despite the language barrier among the non-Greek contingents, the head official's next gesture very clearly signaled his intent to the audience; he placed one hand upon the dolphin-shaped start mechanism and raised the other, the switch held aloft for all to see. Now on their tiptoes with excitement, the crowd screamed encouragement to their favorites. While the afternoon sky was already peppered with ominous-looking cumulonimbus clouds, pregnant with moisture, the reaction of the heavens stunned many an onlooker as they stared expectantly at the official's raised switch. The anvil of one thunderstorm cloud generated a mighty bolt of lightning, striking downwards towards the near horizon with a brilliant flash. Several ear-splitting re-strikes followed it, frightening even the least superstitious among the onlookers and spooking the horses once again.

Shocked into silence, the crowd looked to one another in consternation. Some even made gestures to ward off evil.

Fortunately, the head official broke the impasse when he beamed with joy and cried out at the top of his lungs, 'A sign from the gods! This race is blessed!'

The crowd settled, took heart, and began whispering prayers; the riders calmed their horses once again, and the tension of Olympia's ultimate race crackled anew. Sensing imminent release, Pegasus whinnied with pleasure while Pelops remained transfixed by the official's starter hand and mouth.

After what seemed like an eternity, the Elean official filled his lungs with air and bellowed, 'Make ready... release!' He dropped the dolphin starter-device, which elevated the giant bronze eagle at its other end, and raised the holding sash, as well as the switch he held in his other hand. It was a perfect start; the riders broke clean over the line and hurtled towards the first course marker.

As the crowd erupted afresh, Melqart led the field. He laid heavily into his horse with a riding crop, relentlessly pushing the animal from the outset. The other competitors fanned out, following him closely; Pelops and Rameses barely a horse length behind. As the first turn post approached, Rameses leaned heavily into the corner and drew alongside Melqart. Catching sight of him, the Carthaginian grinned savagely and lashed out with his riding crop, repeatedly striking the prince on his hands, shoulder, and face. Bleeding and disoriented, with his horse now running amok, Rameses tried to pull away from the field while Melqart kept raining blows upon him.

Pelops drove Pegasus between the two riders in a desperate attempt to shield his friend from any more abuse. Rameses took the opportunity to break away. He wiped the blood from his eyes and tried to rein in his horse. Melqart laughed maniacally at the easy target Pelops represented and swung his crop even more viciously. Pelops ducked and wove, but a flurry of blows struck him on the upper body. He reached across and tore the crop from Melqart's hand, hurling it from him in disgust. Melqart laughed again and took the opportunity of the lapse in Pelops's concentration to streak ahead. So confident was Melqart at having now stemmed his two chief rivals that he twisted on his horse blanket and cried out, 'Weaklings!'

The rest of the field caught up to Pelops as he took another moment to flash a look rearward at Rameses; the Egyptian had fallen to the back of the pack, and his face bled freely. His race looked over. Enraged, Pelops spurred on Pegasus like never before. The prize equine of Olympia responded heroically, sensing the urgent need in his beloved keeper. They caught up with Melqart at the second turn post, having now completed a full circuit of the hippodrome. Before Pelops could close the gap any further, the heavens split asunder, and a deluge descended upon the sanctuary; horse and rider alike were almost immediately drenched, and the field quickly became sodden.

Within the royal stands and upon the seating ramps of the hippodrome, aristocrat and commoner alike looked up at the heavens in astonishment. The warm rain ran liberally over the bodies of those exposed while, within the box of the Elean king, Cadmus leaned across to Homer and asked wondrously, 'Is this normal? Does Greece often experience rains like this in midsummer? And during a drought?'

Europa watched intently for Homer's reaction and was rewarded when he finally smiled and replied, 'No, my young friend. This is not natural.'

For Melqart's desert-bred horse, the deluge was a cruel shock. Unaccustomed to the sensation while lathered in sweat and racing, the horse started to fight its rider. Despite lacking his riding crop, Melqart responded true to form and began laying into the charger with the palms of his hands and by kicking the animal in its stomach. The sight was ugly, but the tactic effective. He regained control of his mount before sacrificing too much of the lead. For Pelops and Pegasus, the rain and the result it generated for the race leader was fruitful; they gained significantly upon Melqart. Less than three horse lengths away from Melqart, Pelops was startled to see that two of his fellow competitors had responded even better on the damp terrain. A Thracian horseman and a Bedouin mounted on a local animal both passed him on the inside of the track. As they neared the halfway mark of the race, with the second turn post presenting itself again, Melqart twisted on his horse blanket to turn and mockingly egg on the competition behind with waving motions. Pelops gritted his teeth in anger, lowered himself right across Pegasus's neck, and crooned words of encouragement into the steed's ears. The Thracian and Bedouin riders reached Melqart at the turn post, and all three riders leaned into the corner in unison. Melqart took the opportunity, mid-turn, to fling a booted heel at the belly of the Thracian's horse. Stunned and winded, it broke its rider's control of the reins and careered off the track. Running wildly, and beyond the Thracian's ability to rein it in, the horse ran straight under an imposing tree and, with a sickening crunch, unseated its rider across several branches. Distracted by the Thracian's fate, the Bedouin's horse felt its rider ease up on the reins, and it pulled up sharply, almost tossing the jockey over its head. Melqart's horse spooked at the mayhem and fought its rider, shaving away the narrow lead that the Carthaginian held. An Iberian, Nubian and Scythian rider all bypassed the struggling race leader and hurtled towards the end of the second course lap, with the finish line turn post less than a third of a stade away.

Despite the constant rain, Pegasus had regained his rhythm, and Pelops was gaining on the new lead trinity. Swerving past Melqart, who cursed wildly at both his rival and his own horse, Pelops closed the gap on the rear of the threesome and drew abreast with the Scythian and Iberian, then passed them both to match pace with the Nubian. Pelops and the Nubian rider thundered down the back straight for the final lap of the hippodrome; they increased their shared lead as the huge clods of damp ground their horses threw up unsettled the mounts of the two riders directly behind them. Pelops stole the opportunity to glance rearwards to confirm his lead. Melqart was gaining, but, to his surprise, Rameses was emerging through the sheets of rain just behind him.

As the crowd continued screaming for their favorites and the Carthaginian team wailed in despair from the stands at Melqart's fate, Pelops leaned into Pegasus and whispered soothing words to will him on. Pegasus responded valiantly, drawing upon all of his equine reserves to stretch half a horse length in front of the Nubian rider. This proved to be gods-sent providence. As the Nubian strove to make up the shortfall while steering his mount around the final guidepost turn of the race, the horse completely losirectly behind him, the Scythian rider's mount barreled into the obstacle they presented, flinging both horse and rider sideways. An Etruscan and Germanic rider collided with the stack of bodies, only being saved from substantial harm by the saturated ground they sprawled across.

The crowd somehow managed to increase its volubility — now this was what they had assembled at Olympia for, many of the more sanguinary cried. Re-energized, the Carthaginian team flipped from despair to delight that the field had cleared for their champion. Boasting heartily that the gods of their land still cherished them, they screamed anew at Melqart to prove the dominance of Carthage. If anything, the Egyptian rebels were even louder, having sighted their prince's miracle recovery and his closeness to his damnable rival, the Carthaginian. Within the box of the Elean king, Hippodamia had finally found the courage to join her friends after nervously praying at the temple of Hera and Hestia for Pelops, and was quickly swept up in the anxiety-tinged jubilation that Pelops remained mounted, and at the tip of the spear that was charging around the hippodrome. They chanted at the top of their lungs, much to the amusement of the king and his courtly retinue, who dispensed with any sense of impartiality and joined their cries for Pelops's success. On the steps of Zeus's temple, Tantalus cursed wearily as his eyesight started to fail him; he could just make out his son's progress through dimming vision and the rain, but he felt his life-force ebbing away: if only he could survive long enough to see Pelops prevail, he wished. As another stream of blood leaked from his mouth, he struggled with his clothing and pulled out the bravery wreath that Pelops had won from Elis. He clutched it as only a dying man can.

As Pelops and the Iberian jostled for position on the home straight, Melqart and Rameses caught them on the inside line. Melqart immediately reached across and grabbed Pegasus's halter, trying to tear the reins out of Pelops's hands. Pinned on the outside by the Iberian rider and under attack by the Carthaginian, Pelops found it impossible to maneuver his way out of the trap; only by lessening his pace and dropping back could he survive the encounter — a prospect that was unthinkable to his deeply-competitive mind. As he struggled to wrest Melqart's grip away from the halter of Pegasus, the poor horse increasingly pained by the wrenching at his mouth, Rameses catapulted his horse forward. With blood in his eyes and burning with rage, he leaned precariously across the gap separating himself from Melqart and began wrenching at the Carthaginian's left arm, fighting to drag him away from Pegasus. Melqart swung toward Rameses in shock, and, struggling to break the Egyptian's grip, loosened his hold on Pegasus. It was enough. With a toss of his powerful neck, Pegasus broke clear of his grasp and surged away. Melqart spun and pounded blows upon the prince, but Rameses had abandoned reason and the desire for victory and rained bruising punches in return. Both were at grave risk of toppling from their mounts.

Pelops summonsed his voice and yelled desperately at his friend, 'Save your-self. Let him go!'

Unable to respond, the Egyptian continued exchanging vicious blows with Melqart. Their terrified horses had not failed to keep pace though, yearning with all their might for the race's final turn post, which they could now see ahead. Pelops could spare Rameses no further thought as the Ibe-rian rider on the track's outer running line had pressed his horse inwards to better close out the finish. Neck-and-neck with the Iberian and con-tinually jammed between the horse of Melqart, with Rameses fighting alongside him, Pelops urged Pegasus towards the final goal. And victory.

With warm summer rain still streaming down their bodies, the crowd chant-ed delirious appeals for their favorites — riders from four differing peoples, only one of whom was Greek, hurtled towards the final turn post. In the royal boxes, the enthusiasm was no less; heightened in the Elean king's stand by the anxiety shared by Hippodamia and her friends for their freedom or the prospect of in-dentured slavery should Pelops be defeated by Melqart.

On the track, the finish line was but a few horse-lengths away. Pelops could now see Iphicles, alongside the many other trainers and coaches, cheering madly for him through the rain. Pegasus inched forward of his rivals; the horses of the Iberian and the Carthaginian caught him, even Rameses was still in the hunt for the victory wreath. Pelops whispered in his ear one last time, and the courageous stallion pressed ahead by just under half a horse-head as the line loomed…

ΣPILΟᏩUΣ

The German archaeological team worked industriously under an iridescent Greek sky, the sort that El Greco had made famous through his paintings centuries earlier. Inspired by the work of great artists, antiquarians, and explorers, this new breed of archaeologists had forged a scholarly discipline armed with the logic of scientific inquiry. Their mission was to rigorously uncover the secrets of past glories held deeply within the arms of Mother Earth. Hidden through all of these long years from the ravages of time, the treasures they brought to light would change humanity's understanding of self, identity, and purpose. A strange hybrid of science and earth-scraping drudgery, this fresh approach to the past fired the imagination of the contemporary world while breathing new life into the myths and legends of antiquity.

On this day, over two and a half thousand years after the dramatic conclusion of the first Olympic games, Baron De Coubertin listened intently as his Greek tour guide concluded the saga of Pelops while the archaeologists labored around them. It was a near-perfect blend of the romantic story-telling art that Greeks were famous for and the new breed of scientific romantics who sought to corroborate the past. Exhilarated by the tale and his majestic surroundings, the baron turned a delighted face towards his English companion to share his joy. Where the English educator hunted inspiration to re-introduce the gymnasium and Grecian sports into the schooling system of his homeland, the baron's vision was grander; he was fired by excitement at the heights which could be achieved if he could turn the human spirit again towards its natural nobility in these days of endless conflict and bloody colonialism. He caught a glimpse of the English newspaper his companion still carried and shook his head with concern at its blaring headline: "WAR! BOERS ATTACK BRITISH IN SOUTH AFRICA. DUTCH AND SULTANATE OF ACEH EXCHANGE FIRE."

Snapping back to the present, the baron enquired of the animated guide, 'So he won? Did Pelops triumph?'

The tour guide said with a flush of pride, 'Of course he won, sir. That is why we call this part of Greece the Peloponnese. I am a son of Pelops — a Peloponnesian.'

'And the drought that afflicted Greece — it broke? The wars ended?' asked the Frenchman.

The elderly Greek nodded, pleased at the retention of his educated audience, 'Yes, Baron, the old gods smiled on my ancestors, and they flourished. Carthage retreated from their world, and my country moved closer to its famous Golden Age. Even though warring did not end, Greece found her identity again, and her achievements spread across the planet.'

The Frenchman pressed further, 'And the story, my good man, is it true? Did he claim victory and save his friends the way you say he did?'

The Greek composed his thoughts and then replied, 'What is myth and what is history, Baron? My ancestors had no writing at the time, and even history had not yet been invented, but that is one version of the story of Pelops. In any case, we remember him as the founder of the very first Olympiad. And we revere Pelops because he was a very different sort of hero from a Heracles or Achilles; he brought peace and sporting rivalry where there was only war and chaos before him.'

The Frenchman nodded soberly, 'And this is his shrine?' He swept an arm around to indicate the site where the German archaeologists toiled.

The tour guide smiled wryly, 'These Germans think so. I am not so sure. So much time has passed.'

The baron was about to question further when a cry arose from the head archaeologist, 'You must see this — another one!'

Intrigued, the baron nodded his thanks to the tour guide and walked over to the dig pit; the German archaeologist held a large shard of painted pottery beneath the direct sunlight in order to inspect it more closely.

As the baron leaned into the pit to gain a better look, the Greek tour guide turned to the Englishman and asked, 'Why is he so interested? He is no archaeologist. Not even an historian, I believe.'

The Englishman grinned, 'Baron Pierre de Coubertin is an unusual man with a very unusual ambition. He wants to bring the Olympics back to life. Another Pelops, old chap!'

The guide stared at him in disbelief, then slowly beamed with pleasure. As he continued nodding his approval, the two men walked over to join the baron and the archaeologist as they discussed the implications of the newest find. As they merged with the entire archaeological team, now as excited as their team leader, they leant against the reputed shrine of Pelops, made distinctive by a heavily weathered rendering of an olive-leaf victory wreath with a dove flying through its center.

The baron pointed to the geometric black figure rendering, visible on the pottery fragment, which depicted horses and riders racing around a hippodrome, and enquired, 'Could that be Pelops there? The one leading with his horse?'

The leader of the German excavation team grinned, 'Ja, it is possible. Anything is possible, Herr Baron.'

HISTRIA
BOOKS

Addison & Highsmith

Other fine works of fiction available from Addison & Highsmith Publishers:

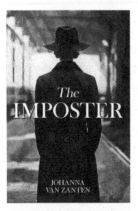

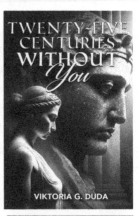

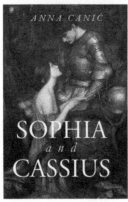

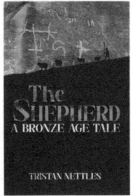

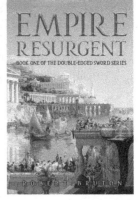

For these and many other great books visit
HistriaBooks.com